Deadly Overtures

Also by Sarah Fox

Deadly Overtures

A Music Lover's Mystery

SARAH FOX

WITNESS
IMPULSE
An Imprint of HarperCollinsPublishers

EPub Edition JUNE 2016 ISBN: 9780062413055

Print Edition ISBN: 9780062413062

RRD 10 9 8 7 6 5 4 3 2 1

For Helen Lee

Chapter One

When I entered the Abrams Center for the Performing Arts, a buzz of activity greeted me. As the stage door shut behind me, I stood still for a moment, taking in the sights and sounds. Two men emerged from a room farther along the corridor and disappeared around a corner. A woman paced the hall as she spoke on a cell phone, chattering away in French to whoever was on the other end of the line. Voices rumbled in the distance, and somewhere not too far off, something hit a hard surface with a bump and a clang.

My violin in hand, I set off along the corridor, barely managing to dodge the French-speaking woman when she gestured wildly, the tempo and volume of her chatter increasing. As I continued onward, a woman in a pantsuit and heels exited a room to my right and set off briskly along the hallway ahead of me, a clipboard in hand. A young man in a sweater vest and hipster glasses hurried along behind her, clutching two take-out coffee cups.

While they rushed along, I followed in their wake at a more sedate pace, my destination the musicians' lounge farther along the hallway. Voices from the theater's back rooms floated down the corridor toward me and a hum of energy tickled my skin. Although it was the evening of the dress rehearsal for the Point Grey Philharmonic's latest concert, the theater was more of a hub of activity than was usual on such an occasion. That was because the concert taking place the following night was no ordinary concert.

The Point Grey Philharmonic, or PGP, was hosting a young composers' competition, and the entrants—all under the age of thirty—had been whittled down to four finalists. The upcoming concert would feature the pieces composed by two of the finalists, while the other two qualifying compositions would be performed in a second concert one week later. So instead of just the usual musicians and conductor present for the dress rehearsal, there were also the competition organizers, the finalists, a recording engineer, and a few extra sets of hands.

As I made my way toward the musicians' lounge, I kept my eyes open for my best friend, JT. He wasn't a member of the orchestra—although he was a musician—but he worked as a recording engineer, and the PGP had hired him to record the concerts and turn them into an album. I didn't see any sign of JT before I reached the lounge, however, and I figured he was probably out in the theater proper, setting up his equipment and preparing for the upcoming sound check.

The door to the lounge stood open and half a dozen people were already present when I walked in. As I headed for my locker, I waved to Katie Urbina, a fellow second violinist. Since I'd arrived quite early, I stashed my instrument in my locker for the time being and shrugged out of my coat. As I hung it up, Katie came across the room to join me.

"It's chilly out there today, isn't it?"

I pulled off my gloves and wiggled my cold fingers, almost numb from the frosty November weather. "You can say that again."

Once I'd tossed my gloves onto the shelf in my locker, I swept my gaze across the room, checking to see who else was already present. My stand partner, Mikayla Deinhardt, wasn't in the room, but the woman who qualified as my least favorite person was seated on one of the couches, her attention focused on her phone.

Elena Vasilyeva was the PGP's concertmaster and an extremely talented violinist. She had glamorous looks to go with her musical brilliance, her cascading blond hair always perfect, her figure like that of a lingerie model. Her personality, however, wasn't at the same level as her looks and talent.

Perhaps my opinion of her was somewhat biased. I had, after all, discovered the previous spring that Elena was in a relationship with Maestro Hans Clausen at the same time as I was. But there was more to my opinion than that. Elena seemed to think she was superior to everyone, and in my mind she qualified as a first-class snob. I did my best to limit my dealings with her, and as I stood there in the musicians' lounge, I quickly shifted my attention away from her.

"What's Pavlina's last name again?" I asked Katie, nodding at the twenty-something finalist who was across the room, talking with Leanne, the PGP's assistant conductor. "She looks familiar, but I can't think why."

"Nicolova," Katie replied. "Most people are expecting her to win the competition. She probably looks familiar because she was on the cover of the last issue of *Classical Spotlight*."

A memory surfaced. "Right. That's it."

Katie lowered her voice to a whisper. "I heard a rumor about that."

"Oh?" I said, my curiosity piqued. "What kind of rumor?"

Katie cast a quick glance in Elena's direction before dishing out the gossip. "Did you notice there was an article about Elena in that issue of the magazine too?"

"Yes." I'd noticed, but I'd quickly flipped past that article.

"Well, I heard that Elena was supposed to be featured on the cover, but they ended up burying her article in the middle of the magazine and put Pavlina on the cover instead."

I raised my eyebrows. "I bet Elena wasn't thrilled."

My eyes wandered back to the subject of our conversation. As Pavlina let out a burst of laughter in response to something Leanne said, Elena shot a cold, venomous glance in her direction.

"That's putting it mildly," Katie whispered.

As the concertmaster tossed her hair over her shoulder and fixed her eyes back on her phone, Katie and I turned away from her.

"I'm going to grab something to eat from the vending machine," Katie said. "I'll see you in a bit."

Her wallet in hand, she left the lounge. Still standing by my locker, I surreptitiously studied Pavlina as she continued to chat with Leanne. As in the photo that had graced the cover of the latest issue of *Classical Spotlight*, Pavlina wore several necklaces and rings. At least half a dozen bangles encircled her left wrist, while a single charm bracelet dangled from her right one. Like Elena, Pavlina had long, fair hair, but she had a stylishly rumpled look going on, whereas every lock of Elena's hair was glossy and smooth.

If Pavlina was aware of Elena's presence, she gave no indication of it. I doubted she'd be the type to let Elena get to her anyway.

From what I'd read about Pavlina in the magazine, she was a rising star with plenty of confidence and moxie. She was being touted as one of the most innovative and inventive young composers in North America, and I wasn't the least bit surprised that she was considered the frontrunner in the competition.

I had to admit, at least to myself, that knowing Pavlina had been featured on the cover of the magazine instead of Elena brought me a sense of glee. Nevertheless, I decided not to dwell on my delight and instead dug through my quilted tote bag until I came up with a granola bar.

Although I earned some money from playing in the Point Grey Philharmonic, my main income came from teaching private violin lessons. I'd taught lessons all afternoon and had only munched my way through an apple before heading for the theater. At the time, a piece of fruit had seemed like a good enough supper, but now my stomach was complaining of insufficient fuel and I didn't want it grumbling all the way through the dress rehearsal.

As I tore open the wrapper and took a bite of the granola bar, the clipboard-wielding woman I'd spotted upon my arrival strode briskly into the lounge, still followed by the guy in the sweater vest and hipster glasses. Two others entered the lounge in their wake, one a scrawny, fair-haired young man who I didn't recognize. The other was Dongmei, the younger sister of one of my friends from university. Dongmei was one of the finalists, and I was secretly hoping she'd win the top prize, despite the stiff competition.

"Finalists, gather around, please," the woman with the clipboard called out.

I figured she must be Olivia Hutchcraft, the competition's coordinator.

"Dongmei," she said as she checked something off on her clipboard. She nodded at the scrawny young man and checked off another item. "Sherwin." As Pavlina and a guy with dark hair joined the group, Olivia made two more checkmarks. "Pavlina and Ethan. Good."

The coordinator went on to rattle off instructions to the finalists before ensuring that none of them had any unanswered questions.

"We've got the program for tomorrow night, if you'd like to keep one as a souvenir, Pavlina and Sherwin." She flicked her hand at Mr. Sweater Vest. "Sasha, hand those out, would you?"

He did as asked, and after a few more words for the finalists, Olivia headed out of the lounge as briskly as she'd arrived, Sasha once again hurrying after her.

Ethan, the dark-haired finalist, snatched Sherwin's copy of the program away from him and opened it. As he ran his eyes over the print inside, he gave a derisive snort. "'Edgy and innovative,'" he read from the program, "'Nicolova's music straddles the line between classical and contemporary, with hauntingly beautiful results.'" He snorted again. "With cacophonous results, more like."

"Jealousy doesn't become you, Ethan," Pavlina said with equal scorn.

He flicked the program back at Sherwin while addressing Pavlina. "I'm not jealous of anyone, least of all you."

"Could've fooled me."

"Amateurs," Ethan muttered as he turned for the door.

Pavlina shook her head once he was gone. Dongmei and Sherwin looked uncomfortable and I didn't blame them. I wasn't enjoying the situation myself, and I was more removed from it than they were.

Deciding to escape the tense and awkward atmosphere, I tossed my empty granola bar wrapper in the trash and left the lounge to go in search of JT. As I made my way along the red-carpeted hallway, I passed a few people I recognized and a few I didn't. I exchanged hellos and smiles, but didn't stop to chat with anyone.

When I slipped through the door that led to the wings of the stage, I paused for a moment to allow my eyes to adjust to the change in lighting. Although the stage was currently lit from above, the wings were filled mostly with shadows. Once I could see well enough to avoid any mishaps, I descended a short staircase and passed through the door that would take me into the theater. The rows and rows of red seats were currently empty, as was the balcony, but movement near the stage drew my attention.

JT was there with Cameron Rask, the newest member of his band, cables and equipment on the floor around them. As I turned in their direction, Cameron said something to JT and headed my way.

"Hey, Midori," he said as he passed me without stopping.

"Hi, Cameron," I returned.

At the sound of my voice, JT glanced up from the jumble of equipment.

"Hey," he said with a grin.

"Hey yourself. Everything going all right?"

"Yep. Just getting the mics set up."

"Cameron's helping you out?"

"Yes." JT glanced past me, but Cameron had disappeared from sight a moment earlier. "He lost his job last week so I asked him if he wanted to earn a bit of cash."

I perched on the arm of one of the front-row seats. "That's too bad about his job, but nice of you to help him out like that."

"Just doing what I can." JT attached a microphone to a stand before lifting the entire contraption and setting it on the stage above him.

As he wound up what appeared to be a spare cable, I watched him work, marveling not for the first time at what a great guy he was. Not only was he always there for his friends—including me—he had a long list of talents. He worked as a recording engineer, he composed music for a locally filmed sci-fi TV show, and he played several instruments, including the guitar and piano. When I added his good looks to all those qualities, it was no wonder I'd fallen in love with him.

"Everything okay?" he asked when he caught me watching him.

"Perfect."

"You looked deep in thought there."

"I was just admiring you."

He grinned at me. "Because of my rugged good looks and impressive physique?"

I rolled my eyes, even though he was partly right. "I meant I was admiring the fact that you're so good at so many things."

"So are you."

I wasn't sure about that, but it was nice he thought that was the case.

"How are things backstage?" he asked.

"Tense. Unpleasant, even. There's enough animosity in the musicians' lounge to fill the entire building." I explained about the distinct lack of admiration between Pavlina and Ethan. "And Elena doesn't seem too fond of Pavlina either."

"I guess there's bound to be some bad blood when artistic egos are involved."

"True enough."

Movement up on the stage drew my eye. A couple of musicians were heading for their seats and Maestro Hans Clausen had emerged from the wings, deep in conversation with his assistant, Leanne.

"I need to have a chat with Clausen," JT said when he noticed the maestro.

"A professional one, right?" I asked, knowing JT wasn't Hans's biggest fan by a long shot.

"Keeping things professional with someone I don't much like is one of my talents," he replied with a grin.

"Good," I said with relief. "Because the last thing we need is spilled blood."

JT AND I parted ways at the top of the staircase leading to the wings of the stage. As he set off to chat with Hans about the equipment setup, I headed in the direction of the musicians' lounge. Hopefully the atmosphere in the room wouldn't be quite as tense as when I'd left, but I wasn't about to hold my breath. Hell would probably freeze over before Pavlina and Ethan became friends.

On my way down the red-carpeted hall, I spotted Cameron leaning against the wall, tapping out a message on his phone. When he glanced up and saw me approaching, he quickly shoved his phone in the pocket of his jeans and gave me an uneasy smile before hurrying off toward the stage. I paused, watching him go, puzzled by his skittishness.

Shaking my head, I continued on, returning to the lounge, where I retrieved my violin from my locker. Fortunately, the four finalists had dispersed to different corners of the room and Elena had disappeared entirely, so I didn't have to dodge any murderous looks or scornful remarks when I entered the room. By the time I had my instrument and folder of music out of my locker, my stand partner, Mikayla, had arrived. Together we made our way to the stage and tuned our instruments while more musicians filled in around us.

JT had disappeared from sight and I figured he was probably in the control booth or wherever he'd set up his laptop and recorder. Hans was near the conductor's podium, chatting with two percussionists. He didn't look any worse for wear, his thick blond hair still in place, his tie straight, so I knew JT hadn't given in to any urge to throttle him.

Not that I really thought he would have, but I was pretty sure that a few months ago JT wouldn't have minded giving the maestro a knuckle sandwich he wouldn't forget. But I'd moved on from the fact that Hans had two-timed me, and hopefully JT had too.

As the time for the dress rehearsal to begin drew closer, more musicians arrived on stage, tuning their instruments and warming up, sounds clashing all around me. Soon Hans signaled for quiet and the preparation for the next night's concert began in earnest. I took comfort in the familiarity of the rehearsal process, in the act of creating music. Whatever animosity lurked backstage, out here in the theater I could easily forget about it. I lost myself in the music, and by the end of the evening the finalists' petty differences had slipped away to the back of my mind.

Chapter Two

THE FOLLOWING EVENING found me back at the Abrams Center, dressed in my black concert clothes. I was looking forward to the night's concert, even more than usual. While I always loved performing music for an audience, this time there was an added degree of excitement. Knowing that the Point Grey Philharmonic was helping young composers get their work heard was gratifying for me and my fellow musicians. Classical composition wasn't an easy profession to navigate and make a mark in, so it was nice to know we were doing something to help young composers.

As usual, I entered the building through the stage door and headed straight for the musicians' lounge. Unlike the day before, I was the only one present in the corridor, although I did hear indistinct voices floating toward me from somewhere in the distance. As I passed the stairway leading to the second floor, the voices became more audible. There were two people speaking somewhere up above, and whoever they were, they didn't sound too happy.

I probably should have kept walking, but my inexhaustible

curiosity brought me to a halt and I stood at the foot of the stairs, listening.

"What do you think people will say when they find out about your . . . *liaison* with Pavlina?" a woman asked, spitting out the word "liaison" as if it repulsed her.

"When they find out?" a man's voice echoed in an unconcerned drawl.

I recognized the voice right away as belonging to Jeb Hartson, one of the competition's judges. He always dressed like a cowboy and spoke with a drawl, even though he was born and raised in Halifax, Nova Scotia, the son of two lawyers.

"You going to tell on us, Liv?" he asked, still sounding unconcerned.

Liv. So the woman with him was Olivia Hutchcraft, the competition's coordinator. Interesting.

"This could get her disqualified from the competition," Olivia said without answering Jeb's question. "She *should* be disqualified."

"And why's that? You really think a little hanky-panky's gonna influence my decision?"

"Of course I do! And so will everyone else once they know." Olivia let out a sound of disgust. "And you strutting around like some ridiculous, self-absorbed peacock. You do know she's only sleeping with you to ensure she wins the competition, don't you?"

Jeb laughed. "You think that's the only reason? You should know better than that, honey buns."

"Don't call me that." Her words almost sizzled with hot anger.

"Aw, don't be jealous, darlin'."

"Jealous?" Olivia seethed. "Hardly."

"Really? Don't you miss what we had back in the day?"

"Not in the least," Olivia said, her voice full of scorn. "This isn't over, Jeb."

Her voice was closer when she spoke those last words and I jerked myself into motion. I dashed away from the foot of the stairs, only slowing my pace when I was within a stone's throw of the open door to the musicians' lounge. Before passing through the doorway, I cast a look over my shoulder in time to catch sight of Olivia reaching the bottom of the stairway, one hand clutching her clipboard in a death grip, her nostrils flared.

Not wanting to give any indication that I'd overheard the argument, I slipped into the lounge and made my way over to my locker. All four finalists and a handful of musicians were already in the room, but I barely registered their presence. Jeb and Olivia's conversation occupied too much of my attention.

So Pavlina was sleeping with one of the competition's judges. That was potentially scandalous, and Olivia was right—it was more than enough to get Pavlina disqualified from the competition. Would Olivia reveal what she knew and take Pavlina out of contention for the top prize? She'd certainly sounded angry enough to do so. It wasn't any of my business, however, so I tried to forget about the matter.

As I hung my coat up in my locker, Elena flounced into the room and sat down on one of the couches with a toss of her blond hair. She didn't so much as glance in Pavlina's direction, and the finalist took no notice of her either. That was probably for the best, and I hoped they'd continue to ignore each other, for the sake of everyone else in the room.

Janine, one of the PGP's first violinists, approached Pavlina with two other female members of the orchestra. They gathered around the finalist, exchanging a few words before Janine asked, "What was it like being on the cover of *Classical Spotlight*?"

"It's been great," Pavlina replied. "Everyone's been really excited for me. And, of course, the exposure is good for my career."

Elena let out a short, disdainful laugh. Everyone's attention focused on her, and I could sense the tension in the room rising.

Pavlina raised her voice. "Do you have a problem?"

Elena stood up, flipping her hair over her shoulder. "A problem, no," she said, her accented words scathing and condescending. "I simply find it amusing that one bit of media attention has inflated your head to the size of a beach ball."

My eyebrows shot up and I had to slap a hand over my mouth to stifle the burst of incredulous laughter that tried to escape. If anyone in the room had an overly inflated head, it was most definitely Elena.

She shot a glare in my direction but spared me no more attention than that.

"At least I'm not a sore loser," Pavlina retorted.

"Sore loser? I haven't lost anything. I'm in the midst of a successful career."

"You lost the cover of *Classical Spotlight*. Everyone knows your story got buried in the middle of the magazine when they put me on the cover instead."

Yikes. I had no desire to get caught in the crossfire of Elena's reaction to Pavlina bringing up that subject, but at the same time I was transfixed by the exchange, unable to tear myself away. The same seemed to be true for everyone else. Every set of eyes was focused on the two blondes facing off in the middle of the room.

Elena's perfectly plucked eyebrows drew together and a flush of color touched her cheeks. "For your information, I *chose* to give up the cover. I'm already so successful that I thought it was only kind to give the publicity to someone much less fortunate than myself."

I didn't believe that for a second. There was no way Elena would have given up the spotlight for anyone or any reason.

Pavlina obviously didn't believe her either. She let out a harsh laugh. "Nice try. I'm sure the magazine's editor would dash that claim to pieces in a matter of seconds."

The color in Elena's cheeks deepened and I wouldn't have been the least bit surprised if white-hot sparks of anger had flown from her narrowed blue eyes. "You might think you're something special. But you'll see—*everyone* will see—that your time in the spotlight will be fleeting."

With that, Elena strode from the room, her chin up, ignoring everyone she passed.

Pavlina shook her head, smirking. "Can you believe her?"

She directed the question at Janine and the others gathered around her, but none of them would meet her eyes now. Janine in particular kept her gaze toward the floor as she led the others in drifting away from Pavlina.

I wasn't surprised. Janine practically worshipped Elena—why, I never could quite fathom—and although she'd momentarily become enthralled by Pavlina, no doubt she still didn't like seeing her idol cut down to size. Heck, I hadn't enjoyed the scene and I didn't even like Elena.

An awkward silence had fallen over the room and I had a sudden urge to run from the theater to escape all the tension and animosity. But of course I couldn't. The concert would start before long and I needed to get ready.

Pavlina stared at everyone for a moment before dropping into a chair and focusing all her attention on her cell phone. I turned my back on the room and busied myself with removing my instrument from its case and tightening my bow. If the past two evenings were a good indication of what the atmosphere would be like at the theater until the competition was over—and I figured that it was—the next week couldn't go by fast enough for me. Playing in the orchestra was normally something I thoroughly enjoyed, but putting up with all this backstage drama was anything but fun.

As I rubbed some rosin on my bow, Olivia Hutchcraft strode into the room, all signs of her earlier anger gone, her face a mask of bland professionalism. Her gaze flitted ever so briefly in Pavlina's direction, but aside from that there was no sign that the young woman was on her mind to a greater degree than any of the other finalists. When she called them over to gather around her, I held my breath, wondering if she would announce then and there that Pavlina was disqualified and why. But instead she simply went over some final instructions before shooing the finalists out the door so they could go take their seats in the front row of the theater.

Strange, I thought.

Why hadn't she disqualified Pavlina? As far as I knew, Olivia was the person in charge so surely she had the authority to do so, based on the information she had. But maybe I was wrong. Maybe there was someone else not present at the theater who was ultimately in charge of such decisions. If that were the case, it might take some time before a disqualification could be made official.

I didn't bother to mull the matter over any further. Mikayla had arrived, and minutes later we left the lounge together, our violins in hand. On our way to the stage, I spotted Elena speaking with a scowling young man. She didn't appear much happier than he did, but since they were conversing in Russian, I couldn't tell what they were so displeased about. As Mikayla and I drew closer, Elena spat out one last word and stalked off toward the lounge.

Mikayla and I exchanged a look, but then we both shrugged and continued on to the stage, forgetting about the concertmaster within seconds. We took our places on the stage, our fellow musicians joining us over the next few minutes. Once we'd all tuned our instruments and the audience members were settled in their seats, Maestro Hans Clausen stepped up to a microphone set near the edge of the stage. A hush fell over the theater, broken only by a man's cough. When that too subsided, Hans addressed the full house.

"Ladies and gentlemen, thank you for coming tonight. The Point Grey Philharmonic is proud to have the honor of hosting the bi-annual young composers' competition, a contest which showcases the incredible talent of composers in our country. While the competition was stiff this year, with many worthy entrants, the judges have narrowed the field to four rising stars among today's classical composers."

After a brief moment of applause, Hans continued. "Before moving on to the music, I would first like to introduce the three esteemed classical music experts who are serving as judges for this year's competition." He outstretched his left hand toward the wings where the judges waited. "Please join me in welcoming Jeb Hartson, Yvonne Charbonneau, and Harold Dempsey."

As the audience applauded, Jeb Hartson led the judges' procession across the stage, wearing a bolo tie and cowboy boots with his gray suit. He waved and winked at the audience, a big smile on his face as he strode across the stage, enjoying every second of his time in the spotlight. Behind him came Yvonne Charbonneau, gray-haired and in her early sixties. As reserved as Jeb Hartson was outgoing, she held herself primly as she walked toward Hans, only the barest hint of a smile on her face.

Bringing up the tail end of the procession was Harold Dempsey, a professor of music at the University of British Columbia here in Vancouver. I'd taken one of his classes when I was a student there, and he hadn't changed much in the intervening years, except perhaps for the addition of little more gray in his wavy dark brown hair. He raised a hand to the audience, giving them a nod and a smile on his way across the stage. When all three judges had shaken hands with Hans, they descended a short flight of stairs and took the seats reserved for them near the front of the theater.

When the applause for the judges had died down, Hans introduced the first piece of music we were going to play, Pavlina's *Storm of Sorrows*. He provided a snippet of information about Pavlina herself, including an outline of her musical education. Then he moved on to speak about her composition, describing it as innovative and beautifully eerie. After he added a few more words about the piece, it was time to begin.

Hans took his place on the conductor's podium and I raised my violin to my shoulder as my fellow musicians readied their own instruments. A short stretch of silence hung over the theater. Then, with a signal from Hans, we were off, bringing Pavlina's composition to life.

Storm of Sorrows had a distinctly modern flair, with the occasional dissonant, jarring phrase. Those parts weren't quite to my personal musical taste, but overall, I couldn't deny that the piece was beautiful, that it was uniquely Pavlina's. The mournful and at times turbulent sounds created by each section of the orchestra blended together to create a haunting and memorable piece that I knew would leave a lasting impression on many members of the audience.

When we reached the last note and drew it out until Hans signaled the end of the piece, barely a second of silence held the theater in a captivated hush before a roar of applause erupted from the audience. The bright lights hid Pavlina from view where she sat in the front row of the theater, but I knew she had to be pleased. We'd given life to her musical vision, and the audience had accepted it with appreciation and gratitude.

Eventually, the applause died down and Hans approached the microphone once more. This time he spoke about Sherwin Banes and his composition, *A Winter Symphony*. While Sherwin hadn't had the same media attention as Pavlina, he was still exceptionally talented. *A Winter Symphony* adhered more closely to the classical music of old than Pavlina's did. In his music I could detect influences from Vivaldi, one of my favorite composers of all time. Although Pavlina's *Storm of Sorrows* was arguably the most innovative of all the entries, Sherwin's was more to my personal taste and I thoroughly enjoyed every movement of the symphony.

After we played the last bar of music and applause once again filled the theater, my eyes strayed to the wings of the stage where Sherwin stood with Olivia Hutchcraft. Olivia was speaking to him quietly but urgently, and when Sherwin shook his head in response, she hurried off backstage, her ever-present clipboard in hand. Sherwin glanced around, uncertainty plain on his face.

I turned my attention back to Hans as he spoke to the audience.

"Please join me in welcoming to the stage tonight's featured finalists, Pavlina Nicolova and Sherwin Banes."

The audience clapped and my eyes returned to the wings where Sherwin still stood, more uncertain than ever. He glanced behind him, but he was alone. My eyebrows drew together as I watched him. I was as puzzled as Sherwin apparently was. Where the heck was Pavlina?

After receiving an encouraging nod from Hans, Sherwin took a hesitant step onto the stage. As he emerged into the bright light, he blinked, but then focused on Hans and crossed the stage with more confidence. Hans leaned toward him and whispered something in his ear, but when Sherwin shrugged and shook his head, Hans returned his attention to the audience.

"I'm afraid Pavlina is unable to join us at this moment, but I'm pleased to present to you the composer of *A Winter Symphony* and one of our four finalists, Sherwin Banes."

If the people in the audience were thrown off by Pavlina's absence, they didn't let it affect their enthusiasm. They clapped warmly for Sherwin and he bowed twice before shaking hands with Hans. Then Sherwin retreated to the wings and I rose with the other members of the orchestra as Hans gestured to us. The audience applauded for us as well, and moments later the concert was officially over.

Chatter filled the musicians' lounge when I returned to the room with my fellow members of the orchestra. Everyone was in a good mood after the successful concert and I spotted Sherwin across the room with Dongmei, a big smile on his face. He had reason to be happy, but what about Pavlina? She should have been basking in the attention and success as well.

I swept my eyes over everyone present, but there was no sign of Pavlina.

Strange. I would have thought she'd want to enjoy every minute of her well-deserved attention. Whatever had kept her from her moment on stage at the end of the concert must have been significant.

Forgetting about the finalists, I loosened my bow and tucked it into my instrument case along with my violin. Leaving my belongings in my locker, I snapped the combination lock shut and headed for the door.

"Washroom?" Mikayla asked as she fell into step with me. When I nodded, she added, "Me too."

"The concert went well," I commented as we made our way down the hallway and around a corner.

"It did," Mikayla agreed. "But it's weird that Pavlina is missing."

"It's definitely weird," I said as we arrived at the washroom. I turned the knob and pushed the door open. "Maybe she's sick or . . ."

The rest of my sentence died out on my tongue and I came to an abrupt halt.

Mikayla bumped into me from behind. "Oh my God," she said as she looked over my shoulder at what had brought me to a standstill.

Pavlina lay sprawled on the washroom floor, her eyes closed. Her head had lolled to one side and her hair was fanned out around her. Dark blood matted the hair at the back of her head and pooled beneath her on the tile floor.

Still shocked, I took a tentative step toward her. "Pavlina?"

She didn't stir.

A shrill scream cut through the small room, assaulting my eardrums. Mikayla and I both turned sharply. Janine Ko stood behind us, holding the washroom door open. Her eyes wide and horrified, she drew in a breath and let out another scream.

The piercing shriek jolted me and Mikayla into action. I took another step toward Pavlina as Mikayla grabbed Janine's arm and tugged her out of the washroom.

"I'll call an ambulance," Mikayla said to me over her shoulder before the door shut behind her.

Careful to avoid the pool of blood, I crouched down next to Pavlina and touched my fingers to her throat. I said her name again, but her eyelids didn't so much as flutter and I felt no pulse against my fingers. A flare of panic set my heart beating faster. I moved my fingers to her wrist, trying once again to detect a pulse. I still couldn't find one.

Swallowing the lump of unease and distress forming in my throat, I straightened up and took a step back. I couldn't tear my eyes away from Pavlina and found that I was watching for the tiniest movement, the slightest sign that she was breathing, that she was alive. At the same time I already knew there would be nothing of the sort.

Pavlina would never draw another breath.

Chapter Three

I DIDN'T KNOW how long I stood there, staring down at Pavlina's unmoving form, at the blood on the tiled floor, before the door cracked open behind me. When I glanced over my shoulder, Mikayla was peering tentatively into the room.

"The ambulance is on its way," she said.

The apprehension in her brown eyes told me she feared what I already knew.

"She's dead," I said in a hollow voice.

Somehow saying the words out loud made the situation more real. I took a step back as Mikayla came into the washroom, letting the door fall shut behind her. She tucked her arm around mine and I was grateful for her comforting presence.

"Are you sure?" she asked, her eyes fixed on Pavlina's pale face.

"I'm sure."

We remained there in silence. I didn't know what to do next. Part of me wanted to retreat from the washroom, to hide away from the sight of Pavlina's body, but another part of me couldn't leave her alone, abandoned on the floor, even if she wouldn't know whether anyone was with her or not.

I should have realized the silence that had settled over us was only temporary, that a flurry of alarmed activity was imminent. It began mere seconds later when the washroom door opened and Olivia Hutchcraft stepped over the threshold, Hans right behind her.

"Dear Lord!" Olivia exclaimed when Mikayla and I stepped aside so she could see Pavlina. She pressed her clipboard to her chest and stared at the body on the floor.

His forehead furrowed with concern, Hans stepped around Olivia.

"Is she breathing?" he asked me.

I shook my head, a fresh lump of emotion blocking my voice.

"Does anyone know what happened?"

I shook my head again. "This is how we found her."

My eyes finally strayed from Pavlina's body, taking in the rest of the washroom in a quick study.

I pointed to the edge of the marble countertop that ran along one wall. "Look, there's blood on the counter. Maybe she slipped and hit her head."

Hans nodded as he too studied the scene.

Mikayla gave my arm a squeeze. "I need to step outside."

She released her hold on me and slipped out the door.

"I think we should all wait outside," Hans said.

Olivia didn't move, her eyes still fixed on the body, her face almost as pale as Pavlina's. Hans put an arm around her shoulders and turned her gently toward the door.

I took one last look at Pavlina, at the bloody, matted hair on the back of her head, at the streak of blood running down her right arm to her wrist, which suddenly seemed terribly pale, thin, and fragile.

"Midori?" Hans called to me as he guided Olivia out of the washroom.

I wrenched my gaze from Pavlina and followed him out the door, my body moving numbly, as if on autopilot.

Out in the corridor, several musicians had gathered along with judges Jeb Hartson and Harold Dempsey; Olivia's assistant, Sasha; and finalist Ethan Rogerson. Hans handed Olivia off to Sasha. The young man seemed uncertain about what to do with his boss, but after a slight hesitation, he led her off down the hallway.

"I think it would be best if we kept this corridor clear," Hans said to everyone present. "The paramedics will be here soon."

He didn't add that their attendance would be futile, but I guessed from the expressions on all the faces around me that everyone already knew that. After casting uneasy glances at the closed washroom door, everyone except me, Mikayla, Hans, Harold Dempsey, and Jeb Hartson drifted away from the scene.

"Is she really dead?" Harold asked once the others had left.

"I'm afraid so," Hans replied.

Jeb ran a hand over his hair. "What a damn shame."

With a shake of his head, he walked slowly off down the corridor, Harold following. As they disappeared around a corner, I wondered why Jeb didn't seem more distressed by Pavlina's death. He wasn't devoid of emotion, but his level of sadness seemed appropriate for someone who'd barely known her. If not for the conversation I'd overheard earlier that evening, his reaction would have seemed fitting. But knowing as I did that there was far more to his relationship with Pavlina, it struck me as odd that he wasn't more broken up.

Maybe he was though, deep down. It was possible that he was hiding his real feelings because he knew his relationship with Pavlina was inappropriate. Maybe later, once he was on his own and away from the eyes of anyone else involved in the competition, his true grief would surface.

Hans addressed Mikayla. "I'll stay here by the door to make sure no one goes inside, but would you please head to the lobby and direct the paramedics this way when they arrive?"

"Of course," Mikayla said. She gave my arm a brief squeeze and set off to do as requested.

Hans slid his cell phone from his pocket. "I'd better call the police."

That took me by surprise. "The police? For a slip and fall accident?"

"We don't know exactly what happened," Hans pointed out. "It'll be for the police or the coroner to rule it accidental."

I nodded, realizing he was right.

As Hans pressed numbers on his phone, I turned away from the washroom door where he stood guard and wandered back toward the lounge, his last words echoing in my head. I'd assumed that Pavlina's death was purely an accident, but was it really?

I shook my head. I had no reason to believe otherwise. The most likely scenario was that she'd slipped on a damp tile and hit her head on the counter on the way down, sustaining a fatal head injury. It was a tragic and unfortunate accident, but there was nothing sinister about it. That at least provided me with a small measure of comfort.

BACK IN THE musicians' lounge, approximately half of the orchestra was still present, along with the three remaining competition finalists. Nobody seemed eager to leave and I didn't doubt that all the hushed conversations going on revolved around Pavlina's untimely demise. I stood by my locker, at a loss, not knowing what to do with myself. Somehow it didn't seem right to go home, not with Pavlina still lying there on the washroom floor. There was nothing I could do for her now, and I knew that, but I still couldn't bring myself to put on my coat and leave the theater.

After a minute or two of indecision, I left my belongings secured in my locker and set out to find JT. There was a chance he'd already left the theater, but I hoped he hadn't. As unsettled as I was, I really wanted the company of my best friend.

I passed no one as I walked along the corridor and it wasn't until I reached the wings of the stage that I spotted another soul. Fred, one of the theater's maintenance workers, was moving chairs and music stands on the stage, clearing the floor so he could clean it. I raised a hand in greeting when he glanced my way and he nodded in return, but I didn't pause to strike up a conversation. Continuing on my way, I descended the short flight of stairs leading down from the wings and pushed open the door at the bottom.

Peering into the theater, I searched for any sign of movement. The audience had long ago cleared out and the only sounds I heard were the occasional scrapes and bumps coming from the stage where Fred was working. I almost turned around and retraced my steps, accepting the fact that JT wasn't around, when I heard a hushed, urgent voice speaking words I couldn't make out.

Pushing the door open farther, I stepped into the theater and looked around. I spotted Cameron off to the side, in a shadowy corner, his back to me as he talked on his cell phone. The door shut behind me with a soft click, but in the quiet of the theater the sound was enough to alert him to my presence. He swung around, startled, and brought his phone call to an abrupt end.

"Hi, Cameron," I said. "Is JT around?"

He hesitated for half a second, but then slipped his phone into his pocket and replied, "Somewhere."

"Right here."

I turned at the sound of JT's voice and spotted him crossing in front of the stage, a laptop tucked under one arm, his recorder held in the other. When JT was close enough, Cameron relieved him of the recorder.

"I thought maybe you'd already gone home," I said.

"I was just about to head out. I didn't think you'd still be here."

"Normally I wouldn't be. But tonight has turned out to be anything but normal."

"How do you mean?"

"Pavlina, one of the finalists in the competition, fell and hit her head in the washroom." I remembered what Hans had said about the fact that we didn't know for sure what had happened. "At least, it looks like that's what happened. Mikayla and I found her."

"Ouch," Cameron said.

"Will she be okay?" JT asked with concern.

"No." I swallowed. "She's dead."

Cameron's eyes widened, but he said nothing.

JT put his free hand on my back. "I'm sorry, Dori. That's terrible. I guess that's why she didn't turn up on stage at the end of the concert."

I nodded.

"Are you all right?"

"Just a bit unsettled. I'll be fine."

"You seriously saw a dead body?" Cameron asked, looking both fascinated and slightly sick at the thought.

"Yes." I didn't add that it wasn't the first dead body I'd seen.

JT gave my shoulder a gentle squeeze. "Why don't you grab your things and I'll walk you to your car?"

"All right. Thanks." I was more than ready to head home by then.

I made my way back up to the wings of the stage, JT and Cameron falling in behind me. I waved once more to Fred and continued on to the musicians' lounge. Mikayla had returned from the lobby and was deep in conversation with fellow violinists Katie and Bronwyn. When she saw me, she excused herself from the others and came to meet me at my locker.

"The paramedics arrived?" I asked as I twirled the dial on my combination lock.

"Yes," she replied. "And a couple of police officers." She shivered. "I can hardly believe she's dead. Imagine having your whole life and career ahead of you and then dying because you happened to slip in a washroom." She shook her head. "It's awful."

"It is," I agreed as I opened my locker.

I reached for my coat but my hand fell to my side as Hans's voice filled the lounge.

"Everyone, could I have your attention, please?"

Along with everyone else, I turned to face Hans. He stood just inside the lounge door, a uniformed police officer at his side. JT and Cameron had come in from the corridor and waited off to one side, their eyes on Hans and the police officer. I wondered briefly if they'd come into the lounge of their own accord, or if the officer had requested that they do so. My attention quickly shifted to Hans, however, as he resumed speaking.

"The police would like for everyone to remain at the theater for the time being so they can speak to each one of you about the unfortunate event that occurred this evening. I know some people have already left, but the police would appreciate it if those of you still here would take the time to provide a statement." Hans gestured to the uniformed man standing next to him. "This is Constable Ryan. I'll let him take over from here."

"Thank you, Mr. Clausen," Constable Ryan said.

Hans nodded and left the lounge.

The constable addressed the rest of us. "As Mr. Clausen said, my colleagues and I would like to speak with each one of you. We're attempting to piece together what happened to Ms. Nicolova and even the smallest piece of information could help us greatly with that endeavor. If you'd please remain in this room, I'll return shortly with my colleagues and we'll begin taking statements."

As he turned to leave, clarinet player Hettie Vallance spoke up. "It was an accident, wasn't it? I mean, didn't she slip and fall?"

Everyone, including myself, directed our full attention at the constable, waiting for his response.

"At this time, it does look as though that could be the case. However, I understand there were no witnesses to Ms. Nicolova's death, and because of that we're not prepared to make any assumptions. I assure you that what we're doing is routine in such circumstances, and my colleagues and I will do our best to speak with you all as quickly as possible so you can get on home."

With that, the constable stepped out of the room, shutting the door behind him. My fellow musicians and I all looked at each other in silence for a moment, but then several conversations sparked up around the room, all related in some way to Pavlina.

JT and Cameron came over to join me and Mikayla by my locker.

"Do the police want to talk to you guys too?" I asked.

JT nodded. "Since we were in the theater when the woman died."

"Not this part of the theater, though," Cameron said. "I don't know what they expect to get out of us when we weren't anywhere near the washroom when she died. Not to mention the fact that we wouldn't have used that washroom anyway."

"I guess they're just trying to be thorough," Mikayla said.

I nodded in agreement with her, thinking over the issue of the timing of Pavlina's death. She'd been alive before the concert started, and she was dead by the time Mikayla and I reached the washroom shortly after the concert ended. And she'd likely died before that, since she hadn't appeared on stage with Sherwin. That narrowed the time of death down to approximately two hours.

Something else occurred to me. Pavlina should have been sitting in the audience with the other finalists until the performance of Sherwin's composition ended. At that point—as I knew from the dress rehearsal—Olivia would have ushered Sherwin and Pavlina out of the audience and up to the wings to await their moment in the spotlight. If Pavlina was in her seat when Olivia went to fetch her and Sherwin, the window for the timing of her death narrowed significantly. There would only have been a couple of minutes for her to slip off to the washroom before she was meant to appear on stage.

Since all of us musicians were present on the stage at that time, I didn't see what we could add to the investigation. Those who had remained backstage during the concert would be far more likely sources of valuable information. Still, I knew Mikayla was right.

Since the police didn't know for certain what had occurred, they needed to be thorough. Even so, I hoped the taking of statements wouldn't eat up too much time. It was already getting late and I had to stifle a yawn as we stood around waiting for Constable Ryan to return. At least it was Friday, so I didn't have to teach violin lessons the next day, but I still didn't fancy staying at the theater until the wee hours of the morning.

Cameron seemed even more anxious to leave. While Mikayla, JT, and I settled on one of the lounge's couches, he paced around, checking his cell phone every minute or two. His edginess was getting on my nerves when, thankfully, the door opened and Constable Ryan reappeared with three other uniformed officers.

All the conversations going on died off and everyone's attention fixed on the police officers.

"We'll start talking with each one of you now," Constable Ryan announced. "We'd like to start with those of you who were first on the scene."

Mikayla and I stood up and a teary-eyed Janine stepped away from the group of musicians she'd been huddled with in one corner. I exchanged a quick glance with JT and headed toward the officers with Mikayla. One officer remained in the lounge, gesturing to the musician standing closest to him, and the other three led me, Mikayla, and Janine out into the corridor. Once out of the lounge we split up, with one officer each.

Constable Ryan stayed with me, and led me a short distance down the hallway where he paused, a notebook and pen in hand. Once I'd given him my name and told him about my connection to the orchestra, he asked me to fill out a witness statement form, relating everything I could remember about finding Pavlina's body. That wasn't a whole lot, and it didn't take long to write down all the information I had. As I signed the form, Fred came around the corner and hovered a few feet away from us.

"Officer?" he said, his tone hesitant.

Constable Ryan looked up. "Yes?"

Fred stepped forward and offered his hand. "I'm Fred Marsh, a maintenance worker here at the theater. Is it possible that the young woman's death wasn't an accident?"

Constable Ryan's eyebrows drew together. "We haven't ruled out anything yet. Why?"

Fred swallowed, his age-creased face tinted a sickly shade of green. "Because if there's a chance foul play could be involved, I think there's something you need to know."

The constable's attention sharpened. "What's that?"

Fred swallowed again and seemed to brace himself to speak his next words. "A few minutes ago I went to fetch my tools to fix a loose screw in the backstage area and I noticed . . ." He cleared his throat and tried again. "I noticed that there was blood on my hammer."

Chapter Four

"BLOOD?" I ECHOED, my voice faint.

Constable Ryan took charge before I had a chance to say anything further. "I'd like you to show me those tools, if you would, Mr. Marsh."

Fred nodded. "Of course. This way."

He started to head back the way he'd come. I moved to follow him, but Constable Ryan put out a hand to stop me.

"Thank you, Ms. Bishop. You can head home now, if you'd like."

The message behind his words was clear. I was to mind my own business.

"Also, if you'd please keep this development to yourself, I'd appreciate it. There's no need to start a panic when we don't yet know the facts."

I nodded numbly. I'd heard his words but I was still focused on Fred's discovery. If the blood was Pavlina's, then that could only mean one thing—she'd been murdered. But I knew the constable was right—all the facts weren't known yet and there was no point in jumping to conclusions. Perhaps the blood had been on the hammer for some time, a result of some minor accident, like a cut finger. It could have nothing to do with Pavlina. I certainly hoped that was the case. As tragic as Pavlina's death was, an unfortunate accident was far less alarming than a violent death at the hands of a killer. A killer who might still be in the theater.

Suppressing a shudder, I vowed to do as Constable Ryan had requested and keep Fred's discovery to myself for the time being. As the two men disappeared from sight, I turned around and saw that Janine had already finished giving her statement and was returning to the lounge. Mikayla too had finished speaking with the other police officer, and she joined me as I left the corridor for the musicians' lounge.

"Everything all right?" she asked.

"Yes," I replied, trying to rein in my thoughts. I didn't want to let on that I'd heard some potentially unsettling information.

"At least we can head home now."

I hesitated by my locker, my eyes going to JT where he still sat on the couch, chatting with one of the orchestra's bass players. "I think I'll wait for JT."

"Okay," Mikayla said as she headed for her own locker. "I'll see you on Tuesday."

"See you," I echoed.

I was about to join JT on the couch when one of the police officers gestured to him to go and provide his statement. So instead of sitting down I changed my route and approached Dongmei where she stood across the room, on her own, her eyes red-rimmed.

She tried to smile when she saw me approaching, but she was only partly successful. "Hey, Midori."

"Hi. How are you doing?" I asked.

She shrugged and blinked back tears. "Okay. It's just upsetting, you know?"

"It is," I agreed. "Is your family here tonight?"

"No, I'm on my own. But my parents and sister will be here for the next concert." She drew in a deep breath. "How are *you* doing? Didn't you find Pavlina in the washroom?"

"Yes, my stand partner and I did." The first seconds after finding Pavlina's body replayed in my memory. "It was disconcerting, but I'm all right." I once again noted Dongmei's red-rimmed eyes. "Did you know Pavlina well?"

"Not really," she replied. "But we've been acquaintances for a few years. We were at a music and composition retreat together in Banff three years ago. That's when I first met her. Even then it was obvious she'd be a successful composer." She blinked against a welling of tears. "Except now she won't be, will she?" A single tear escaped and rolled down her cheek.

"No," I said with a heavy heart. "She won't." I thought of Pavlina's loved ones, and the loss they would now have to endure. "Do you know anything about her family?"

Dongmei wiped a tear off her cheek. "She mentioned that her parents still live in Toronto where she grew up. They weren't able to come out here for the concerts. But other than that, no, I don't know anything. This will be terrible for them."

I nodded, a sharp pang of sympathy cutting through me.

Catching sight of JT returning to the lounge, I gave Dongmei a hug. "I'll see you next week."

Again she tried to smile, but it was weighed down by sadness.

Leaving Dongmei, I met up with JT in the middle of the lounge. "All done?" I asked him.

"Yep. There really wasn't anything I could tell them."

"That's probably true of most people who were here," I said.

I was about to tell him about the blood on Fred's hammer, but then remembered that Constable Ryan had asked me to keep quiet about that news. It would be tough to keep the information from JT, but I'd do my best. At any rate, even if I did end up telling him, the musicians' lounge wasn't the place to do so. The crowd had thinned out significantly over the past half hour or so, but there were still several people lingering in the room, either because they were waiting to give their statements to the police or because they were talking over the terrible events of the evening with their friends.

"Ready to go?" JT asked.

"Yes." I turned in the direction of my locker. "I'll just grab my things."

Once I'd donned my coat and gloves and had gathered up my instrument case and tote bag, I waved goodbye to a couple of my friends who were still in the lounge and headed for the door with JT. Cameron fell into step with us and I realized that I'd temporarily forgotten about him. He'd spent much of the past half hour in a corner of the room with his phone, but if he was leaving with us he must have spoken to the police at some point.

"Did you already pack up all the rest of your equipment?" I asked JT, eyeing his laptop and the recorder in Cameron's charge.

"Yep. It's all in the truck."

JT pushed open the stage door and held it while Cameron and I passed through. The three of us walked down the short side alley to the parking lot at the back of the theater, our breaths forming little clouds in the cold night air. Although my coat and gloves warded off the worst of the chill, I still shivered as I walked, and I looked forward to getting home so I could snuggle up beneath some warm blankets.

When we reached the parking lot Cameron veered off to the left, in the direction of JT's truck, while JT and I continued on straight ahead to my blue MINI Cooper. After years of riding the bus everywhere I was still getting used to the fact that I owned a car. But after a scare a couple of months earlier when a man grabbed and threatened me while I was walking alone at night, I no longer felt comfortable making my way to and from bus stops after dark.

With some encouragement from JT, I'd looked into getting a secondhand car. Fortunately, I didn't have to look far. My cousin— who went through vehicles at what I considered a ridiculous rate—had wanted to offload her five-year-old MINI Cooper so she could get something new. She'd offered me the car for a somewhat decent price and I'd taken her up on it. It certainly made my life easier to have a car, and I knew JT was less anxious about my safety now. He still watched out for me, though, like he was at the moment, walking me to my car.

I was grateful for that, and his concern for me always made me happy. Not for the first time, I wished I could express my true feelings for him, wished I could let him know how much I appreciated everything he did for me, how much I loved him. But as always, a terrible fear of ruining our friendship—the most important thing in the world to me—held me back.

Letting out a quiet sigh, I unlocked my car. I was about to say some parting words to JT when Cameron swore loudly, his voice slicing through the cold night air.

"What's wrong?" JT called to him.

Instead of responding, Cameron swore again, stepping away from the back of JT's truck, one hand running through his hair, his every move agitated.

JT jogged across the parking lot toward him. Still holding my violin, I locked the car door before following after him. The tailgate of JT's truck was down, but I assumed Cameron had lowered it, until JT took one look in the back of the truck and echoed Cameron's cursing.

"What's going on?" I asked as I stepped closer so I could see into the covered bed of the truck.

"Everything's gone." JT was more bewildered than I'd seen him in a long time.

I took in the sight of the empty truck bed. He was right. Whatever equipment he and Cameron had stored there was gone, not even a single cable left behind.

"But how?" I asked, my stomach sinking.

"Did you lock it the last time you were out here?" JT directed the question at Cameron.

"I thought I did but . . . I must not have." Cameron looked as though he might be sick.

JT checked the tailgate. "There's no sign that the lock was jimmied."

Cameron swore again. "I'm so sorry, man."

JT didn't respond, and I knew he had no idea what to say. I could tell from his expression that he was still shocked by the theft. He'd not only lost hundreds—maybe even thousands—of dollars' worth of equipment, he needed that equipment to finish the job at the theater.

I put a hand on his back. "We should tell the police."

Still dazed, JT nodded.

I took his arm and led him back down the alley to the stage door. Cameron followed several feet behind us, not saying a word. By the time we'd reentered the theater, JT had recovered enough to shake himself out of his daze. He approached Constable Ryan and told him what had happened.

While JT spoke with the police officer, my gaze drifted past them, down the hall to where two men in suits were speaking with Olivia Hutchcraft. As I watched, the two men showed her their identification and Olivia put one hand to her throat, clearly upset. Even though I couldn't see the men's identification from my vantage point, I didn't doubt for a second that they were police detectives.

Would they have arrived on the scene even if Fred hadn't found blood on his hammer? Or had the focus of the investigation shifted from a routine review of what was believed to be an accident to a possible homicide case?

I knew it would take time for the police to find out if the blood on the hammer belonged to Pavlina, but I wondered if the investigators had found any other signs that pointed toward murder. As that thought wandered through my head, a man and a woman dressed in crime scene coveralls appeared from the direction of the women's washroom and caught the detectives' attention.

The two men in suits excused themselves from their conversation with Olivia and moved farther down the corridor to join their colleagues. I wished I could overhear what they were saying, to know what they'd discovered by examining Pavlina's body and the scene of her death, but I couldn't hear a single word.

Disappointed, I returned my attention to JT and his predicament. Sympathy for my best friend and anger at the unknown thieves battled for dominance inside of me. A flicker of annoyance at Cameron also made an appearance, but I did my best to extinguish it when I saw how upset he was. He'd made a dumb mistake by forgetting to lock the truck, but it was a mistake anyone could have made.

Still, I worried about the effect the theft would have on JT, especially while he waited for his insurance claim to be processed. He needed his equipment to finish the job at the theater and to take on any similar jobs in the future. He could use his studio to record his own music and for sessions with other musicians, and luckily he hadn't lost that night's recordings since he had his laptop and recorder, but the loss of his expensive equipment was still inconvenient.

As JT stepped away from the police officer, I moved to his side.

"What did Constable Ryan say?" I asked.

"He and the others are tied up with Pavlina's death, but he's going to call in another officer to deal with my problem."

I glanced Constable Ryan's way, and sure enough, he was speaking into his radio.

"Hopefully we won't have to wait long," I said.

"You don't have to stick around," JT told me. "You should head home and get some sleep."

"I can't leave you here after what happened," I protested.

JT smiled, the first relaxed expression on his face since he'd found out about the theft. "I'll be fine, Dori."

I still didn't want to leave, even though he'd have Cameron there for company while he waited for the police.

JT noticed my reluctance and rested a hand on my shoulder. "You really don't need to stay. I'll walk you to your car, okay?"

I relented, only because I was suddenly aware of how late it was and how tired I'd become. "All right." I let him guide me toward the stage door. "But call me tomorrow and let me know what happens?"

"I will."

With that assurance, I climbed into my car and drove off, waving to JT as I turned out of the parking lot. On my way home I marveled at the unexpected turns the evening had taken. In the space of only an hour or two there'd been a death and a theft. At the moment only one of those was considered criminal, but I had a funny feeling that would soon change. The more time that passed since Mikayla and I had found Pavlina's body, the more I suspected that her death was the result of something far more sinister than an unfortunate accident.

Chapter Five

ALTHOUGH THE NEXT day was Saturday, I didn't get to enjoy the luxury of lounging around in bed. Once I woke up, my brain was far too alert for that. Thoughts of Pavlina and the theft of JT's equipment kept swirling around in my head, leaving me restless and unsettled. Within minutes of waking, I threw back my covers and left their warmth behind, heading straight for the bathroom. As soon as I'd showered and dressed for the day, I checked my phone, hoping I might have heard from JT. I hadn't.

I fixed myself a simple breakfast of toast and honey but could barely sit still long enough to eat it. As I washed my dishes and put them away, I considered using some of my restless energy to give my apartment a good clean. Before I had a chance to dig out my cleaning supplies, my phone chimed with the arrival of a text message. It was from JT, asking if I wanted to join him for a walk in the forest with his dog, Finnegan.

Smiling, I sent an affirmative reply, telling him I'd be at his place in ten minutes. Fresh air and time with my best friend and favorite dog sounded far more appealing than spending the day cooped up indoors cleaning. Although I wanted to ask JT what had happened at the theater after my departure the night before, I decided to wait. It would be easier to go through all that in person than via text messages.

Peering out my living room window, I noted the presence of frost on the grass, trees, and parked cars, wintry white crystals that winked and gleamed. It would be another chilly day, at least for the next few hours, though the sun was doing its best to break through the gray clouds overhead.

Slipping into a pair of flats, I pulled on a warm jacket, a pair of gloves, and a knitted, slouchy hat that would keep the worst of the cold away from my ears. Then I left my apartment and set off for JT's house, located a short distance away from my Kerrisdale apartment.

Never a long trip, even by bus, the journey to JT's place only took me about five minutes now that I had a car, and I arrived within the ten minutes I'd predicted. As I parked my MINI Cooper in front of JT's white two-story house, he came out the front door with Finnegan, a leash attached to the collie-malamute's collar.

"Morning," JT called out as he and Finnegan came down the front steps to meet me.

"Morning," I returned.

I crouched down so I could give Finnegan a big hug, his fluffy tail wagging enthusiastically. Once I'd ruffled his fur and he'd given me a wet kiss on the cheek, I straightened up and we set off in the direction of the forest that began at the edge of JT's neighborhood and extended out to the campus of the University of British Columbia.

"Did you get much sleep last night?" JT asked as we walked.

"Surprisingly, I did all right," I said. "Although I think I had a nightmare that I can't quite remember." Only flashes of fear and looming shadows remained from the dream, and I was glad of that. It wasn't something I had any desire to recall in more detail. "How about you?" I checked his face for signs of stress or unhappiness, but while he wasn't at his most relaxed, he seemed all right.

"It took me a while to fall asleep," he replied. "But then I got a few solid hours in."

I tucked my arm through his as we crossed the street and entered the forest, following a wide, well-used path. "What did the police have to say about your equipment?"

JT grimaced. "Not much. They made a report and told me to keep an eye out on Craigslist and other online classified sites. Most of the equipment was inscribed with my driver's license number, but that only helps to identify it as mine if the police find it."

"And you don't think they will?" I guessed.

"The police didn't seem too hopeful so I'm not going to hold my breath."

"I don't suppose the thief or thieves were caught on security camera."

"No," JT confirmed. "There's a camera in the alley pointed at the stage door and another one that covers part of the lot, but not where my truck was parked. And whoever the thief was, they were aware of the cameras and stayed out of their range."

"That's so . . . argh," I said, frustrated. "Are you mad at Cameron?"

JT paused to unhook Finnegan's leash so he could bound about freely and sniff all the interesting smells along the path. "A little. I wish he'd been more careful, but I know he feels bad about it, and it's not like I've never forgotten to lock my truck before. Just never with lots of expensive equipment in the back."

A middle-aged couple with a toy poodle approached us from up ahead. JT and I exchanged pleasantries with them while the two dogs gave each other a thorough sniffing before moving on.

"I'm a bit mad at Cameron too, on your behalf," I admitted once we were on our own again. "But you're right—it was an unintentional slip-up on his part and he did seem to feel really bad about it."

At least, I hoped it was unintentional. Suspicions crept into my thoughts, but I ignored them for the moment.

"And it's only equipment that was lost. Ultimately, it can all be replaced and nobody was hurt. That's what's most important."

I couldn't argue with that, especially after what had happened to Pavlina—whatever that was, exactly. The theft was inconvenient for JT, but not disastrous. At least it wouldn't be disastrous if he could still complete the job at the theater.

"What are you going to do about recording the concert next week?" I asked.

"I talked to a buddy of mine this morning, one I met in a sound engineering course a few years back. He's got some equipment he can loan me for a couple of days. Together with some of the spare stuff I've got lying around, that should get me through this job, at least."

"That's good," I said with relief, glad he'd found a solution to the most pressing problem. "Did anything else happen at the theater after I left?"

"Like what?"

"I don't know. Maybe something to do with Pavlina?"

JT shot me a glance full of what I thought was unwarranted suspicion. "Her body was taken away by the coroner."

"But nothing else happened? You didn't overhear the police saying anything about her death?"

"No," JT said, the suspicion now leaking into his voice. "I didn't go back inside after you left. I talked to the police out in the parking lot. Why?"

"No reason," I said, trying to sound casual.

"Yeah, right." The suspicion in his voice had transformed into outright disbelief. "What's going on, Dori? What are you up to?"

"I'm not up to anything."

"Why do I find that hard to believe?"

"I have no idea," I said innocently.

JT watched me out of the corner of his eye as we continued to walk through the forest.

"Seriously, JT, I'm not up to anything. I've just been thinking."

"Uh-oh."

I released his arm so I could give it a swat. "Very funny." I became more serious as I remembered the events of the night before in detail. "It's just that I can't help but wonder if Pavlina's death was really an accident."

"Why?" JT asked, surprised. "Was there something about her body that makes you suspect foul play?"

"Not her body, no." I reached up to tug my left earlobe, wanting to share what I knew with JT but remembering that I was supposed to keep quiet.

"Something else then?" When I still hesitated, JT nudged me with his arm. "Come on, spill it."

"Okay," I relented, "but I'm not really supposed to say anything so don't spread this around." I glanced over my shoulder to make sure no one was within earshot, but we were alone on the forest path. "Fred, one of the maintenance guys at the theater, found blood on his hammer."

We paused in the middle of the path as Finnegan stopped to sniff the base of a tree.

"And was the hammer found anywhere near the scene of Pavlina's death?" JT asked once Finnegan moved on and we'd resumed walking.

"No, I don't think so. It was in Fred's toolbox, although I don't know exactly where that was."

"So maybe the blood has nothing to do with Pavlina's death. Maybe Fred or another maintenance worker cut themselves while working sometime recently and didn't notice that they got some blood on the hammer."

"It could have happened like that," I conceded.

"You find trouble easily enough as it is," JT pointed out. "You don't need to go looking for it."

"I'm not," I assured him.

"Good."

I hooked my arm through his again and did my best to push all thoughts of Pavlina's death from my head, at least for a while, focusing instead on the fresh air and JT's company.

THE REMAINDER OF my weekend was uneventful and I spent Monday in the usual way, teaching several of my violin students. Each day JT had checked the online classifieds, but so far he hadn't had any luck finding his stolen equipment. With every day that passed I knew he became less hopeful of recovering the stolen items, and as his hope diminished so did mine. I tried to remind myself that it wasn't the end of the world, however, and JT had taken the same attitude. Still, whenever I thought of the missing equipment, a flicker of anger at the person or people responsible made itself known for a second or two.

On top of that, the suspicions that had crept into my thoughts the other day hadn't disappeared. Cameron easily could have been involved in the theft, but I didn't want that to be the case. His involvement would only make the situation worse for JT. I tried my best to silence my suspicions, but they continued to whisper at me, regardless of my efforts.

When Tuesday evening rolled around I wrapped up my last violin lesson for the day, ate a quick dinner, and set off for the theater. That night we'd be rehearsing the compositions by Dongmei and Ethan, preparing for the performance scheduled for Friday. I was looking forward to spending the next couple of hours at the theater. I loved rehearsing with the orchestra and I knew from practicing on my own that I liked both pieces of music we'd be working on that night.

It was more than the music that I was looking forward to, though. I wanted to know if anyone knew more about Pavlina's death, if it had been officially ruled an accident or if the investigation was still ongoing. Although my gut told me there would be no official ruling of accidental death, I still hoped that would be the case. It would bring closure and peace of mind to everyone involved, whereas the alternative was unsettling to think about.

When I arrived at the theater and made my way to the musicians' lounge, I knew right away that I wasn't the only one whose mind was on Pavlina's death. There didn't seem to be any other topic of conversation in the lounge, but although I spoke to Dongmei and some of my fellow members of the orchestra, no one seemed to know anything more than they had on Friday night. In fact, it seemed as though I was the one among us with the most information. Nobody else seemed aware of the blood found on Fred's hammer and I kept that information to myself. Sharing it with JT was one thing, but I wasn't going to feed that potentially frightening tidbit into the orchestra's rumor mill.

With people still chatting all around me, I left the lounge to take my place on the stage. I spent the next several minutes tuning my violin and warming up by running through a few passages of music. Shortly after Mikayla settled into the seat next to me, Hans approached the conductor's podium at the front of the orchestra. The last straggling musicians took their seats and bit by bit everyone fell silent, all our gazes resting on Hans. He had creases of worry across his forehead, and his face was set in a grim expression.

He cleared his throat before addressing the orchestra. "In light of the tragedy that occurred last Friday night, there has been much discussion over the past few days regarding how to proceed with the competition. However, the judges, the organizing committee, and our board of directors have decided to continue as planned. The remaining finalists have worked hard to get to this point and we don't wish to deprive them of the opportunity to advance their careers through this route."

He paused, and a few quiet murmurs ran through the orchestra. However, the buzz of voices broke off again when Hans resumed speaking.

"We do wish, of course, to honor Pavlina's memory, and we've decided that we'll observe a moment of silence at the beginning of the finale concert next Tuesday."

He paused again and glanced toward the wings of the stage. When I followed his line of sight I spotted the two detectives I'd seen after Pavlina's death. Again, they were both wearing suits. One stood well over six feet tall and had broad shoulders. The other was smaller and more compact, but still imposing with his steady dark gaze.

"Now," Hans said, recapturing my attention, "before we get started tonight, the detectives in charge of the investigation into Pavlina's death would like to have a few words with you." He nodded at the approaching detectives and stepped away to allow them to take his place in front of the orchestra.

"Thank you, Maestro Clausen," the taller of the two detectives said. He then addressed us musicians. "Good evening. I'm Detective Van den Broek." He gestured to the other detective. "And this is Detective Chowdhury. I'm sure you're all aware of the unfortunate death that occurred here in the theater on Friday night. While the incident first appeared to be a tragic accident, we are now conducting a murder investigation."

A couple of people gasped, and Mikayla and I looked at each other with wide eyes.

"Murder?" she whispered.

Others around us were voicing similar exclamations of surprise and dismay.

As the rumble of voices reached a crescendo, Detective Van den Broek raised a hand and called out, "If I could have your attention again, please."

Slowly, the conversations faded away, although the shocked expressions remained on the faces around me. When the last of the noise had dwindled away, Detective Van den Broek spoke again.

"This is, of course, a very serious matter, and I can assure you that we're working hard to solve this case. But in order to do so, we need the help of any witnesses who might have seen or heard anything that could move our investigation forward. If anyone knows anything or saw anything remotely suspicious on the night of Ms. Nicolova's death, we ask that you please let us know. Even if you're not sure of the significance of your information, please share it with us. Detective Chowdhury and I will remain here at the theater throughout the evening. If there's anything you would like to speak to us about, please approach us after the rehearsal."

Van den Broek removed a notebook from the pocket of his suit jacket and flipped it open. "I understand that two of Ms. Nicolova's fellow finalists are present this evening. He consulted his notebook. "Ms. Pan and Mr. Rogerson, is that correct?"

Hans stepped forward. "That's right." He gestured toward the theater seats where Dongmei and Ethan sat in the third row, waiting to hear the rehearsal of their compositions.

"We want to disrupt the rehearsal as little as possible, so whoever you don't need here right at the moment . . ." Detective Van den Broek said.

Hans nodded. "We'll be rehearsing Mr. Rogerson's composition first."

Van den Broek nodded, looking out into the theater. "Ms. Pan, will you please come with us?"

Dongmei stood up slowly, her eyes wide and terrified. She moved as if on autopilot, heading for the stairs that would take her to the wings of the stage.

"Thank you, Maestro Clausen," Detective Van den Broek said. "We'll let you get on with it now."

Hans thanked the detectives and returned to his place at the conductor's podium. Although he made some preliminary remarks about the piece we were about to rehearse, my attention was on Dongmei. The detectives had joined her in the wings and now headed backstage. As Dongmei turned to follow them, she looked as terrified as if she were being led off to the gallows.

Chapter Six

MIDWAY THROUGH THE rehearsal we wrapped up our work on Ethan's composition and moved on to *The Crimson Night*, Dongmei's piece. By then she'd returned from her time with the detectives and Ethan had gone off with them in her place. She conferred with Hans during the rehearsal process, and seemed able to focus, but she still appeared shaken and upset. I wondered if she was unsettled because someone she knew had been killed or if there was something more going on.

The possibility that she could be a suspect passed through my head, but I highly doubted she was the guilty party. Although I knew her sister better, I'd spent time with Dongmei now and then over the years. I didn't think she'd hurt a fly, let alone cosh someone over the head, as I suspected the killer had done to Pavlina.

But whatever might have been going on with the murder investigation, I didn't have much time to mull it over during the rehearsal. My thoughts attempted to stray a few times but I forced myself to focus on the music so I wouldn't get lost or mess up my part. As soon as the rehearsal was over, however, my gaze zeroed in on Dongmei. After exchanging a few more words with Hans, she left the stage, and I hurried after her. She returned to the lounge and I kept an eye on her as I tucked my violin and bow safely away in my instrument case. Once the case was stored in my locker, I approached Dongmei as she shrugged into her coat.

"Hey," I said as I put a hand on her arm to draw her attention. "How are you doing?"

Her eyes still held a touch of fear but she managed a hint of a smile before it faded away. "I'm all right, thanks." Her lower lip trembled and she bit down on it to stop the tremor.

I put an arm around her and led her to a quiet corner of the room. "Are you sure?"

She drew in a long, shuddering breath, and that seemed to steady her. "I'm okay—just a little shaken up by everything that's happened. I've never known anyone who was murdered and I've never been interrogated by the police before."

"Is that what they did? Interrogated you? Or did they just want to know if you'd seen anything suspicious the other night?"

"It felt like a bit of both," she said. "They started out by asking me what I knew about Pavlina and what I'd seen on Friday, but then they asked me about my movements during the concert, and if I'd had any conflicts with Pavlina, if I saw her as my toughest competition." She took in another deep breath and let it out in a rush. "I think they suspect me of killing Pavlina, Midori. But I didn't. I wouldn't kill anyone." Tears welled in her eyes.

"I know that," I said. "And the police will figure it out too, if they haven't already. It's their job to look at every angle and they don't know anything about you, so they have to ask their questions. I'm sure that's all it is."

"I hope so. They did back off a bit when I told them I was in the audience during the concert, from start to finish. If someone else can confirm that for them, I should be okay."

"Then they've probably eliminated you as a suspect already, since they've spoken to Ethan too."

A shadow of unease passed across Dongmei's face. "Except Ethan wasn't in the audience the entire time."

My thoughts upped their tempo, each one scurrying over the next. I did my best to sort them out. "Do you know why Ethan left his seat?"

Dongmei shrugged. "I assumed he went to the washroom, but he was gone quite a while."

"How long?"

She considered the question as she buttoned up her coat. "Maybe fifteen minutes. Probably not more than twenty."

That was plenty enough time to follow Pavlina into the women's washroom and bash her over the head. Of course, that scenario depended on another factor.

"What about Pavlina? Was she in her seat until Olivia fetched her and Sherwin near the end of the concert?"

"No," Dongmei replied. "She left after her piece was performed and I never saw her again."

That left a window of approximately one hour between the time when Pavlina left her seat and the moment when Mikayla and I found her body in the washroom.

"Did she leave before or after Ethan?" I asked.

"A few minutes before." Dongmei glanced around and lowered her voice. "Do you think Ethan killed her?"

"I don't know, but it sounds like he had the opportunity, if nothing else." I remembered the unease I'd seen on her face moments earlier. "Do *you* think he killed her?"

Dongmei bit down on her lower lip. "I don't know either. They didn't like each other—I know that for sure—but that's not enough reason for him to kill her."

Perhaps not, but there was more to his possible motive than his dislike of Pavlina. She was also his competition. His toughest competition, if the rumors about Pavlina being the frontrunner were true. Even if the rumors weren't true and the playing field was relatively level, Ethan might still have believed that Pavlina was more likely than him to capture the top prize. Of course, that could be said of all the other finalists. But, unlike Dongmei, Ethan didn't have an alibi for the time of Pavlina's death, unless someone was with him the entire time he was away from his seat and could vouch for him.

"What about Sherwin?" I asked, wondering if his whereabouts could be pinned down.

"He was in the audience the entire time, right up until Olivia came to get him at the end."

So unless he had someone do the deed for him, Sherwin was innocent.

"Did you see anyone else from the audience head backstage during the concert?"

"Only Mr. Hartson. He disappeared between pieces, but only for a minute or two."

I absorbed that information before asking, "What about the other judges?"

"They didn't leave the audience until the concert was over. Anyway, why would a judge want to hurt Pavlina?"

That was a good question. Although it seemed Jeb Hartson was the only judge with an opportunity to commit the crime, and that window was a narrow one, according to Dongmei.

"I hope it wasn't Ethan," she whispered as two clarinet players passed us on their way out of the lounge. "It's terrible to think of one of my fellow finalists doing something so awful."

"It is terrible," I agreed.

I didn't add that it was disturbing to think that anyone connected to the competition or the orchestra could be a killer. My eyes swept over the room, conducting a quick scrutiny of everyone present. At least I knew my fellow musicians weren't responsible for Pavlina's death, not directly anyway. We'd all been on stage together when she was killed. That didn't rule out the possibility of someone having an accomplice, but I didn't know of any reason why someone in the orchestra would want to conspire with another person to kill Pavlina. That didn't mean there wasn't a reason, of course, but I figured it was best to focus on what I did know. And what I did know was that I needed to speak to Detectives Van den Broek and Chowdhury before I left the theater.

After saying good night to Dongmei, I wound my way around those still hanging out in the lounge, heading for the door. Once out in the hallway I went in search of the detectives, knowing I had some information to share with them. What I had to tell them might not be important, but as Detective Van den Broek had said, that was for them to decide, and I didn't want to hold anything back in case it did turn out to be significant.

It didn't take me long to track down the detectives. I found them standing on the stage, conferring with one another. They were the only ones present, all the chairs now empty, the music stands holding nothing save for the occasional forgotten pencil used for marking up music.

My footsteps caught the attention of the detectives and they broke off their conversation as they looked my way.

"My name's Midori Bishop," I said when I reached the two men. "My stand partner and I were the ones who found Pavlina's body the other night."

"Right," Detective Chowdhury said, consulting his notebook. "We've read your statement."

"Did you have something to add to it?" Detective Van den Broek asked.

"Not exactly," I replied. "I don't have any more information about finding Pavlina's body, but there are some other things I thought you should know, since her death is no longer being considered an accident."

Detective Van den Broek gestured to the nearest chair. I sat down as he pulled up another chair and produced his own notebook and pen from the pocket of his suit jacket. Detective Chowdhury also reached for another chair, but when his cell phone rang he abandoned the piece of furniture. As he answered the call, he nodded at his partner and headed off the stage, speaking in a low voice to whoever was on the other end of the line.

"Did you know Ms. Nicolova well?" Detective Van den Broek asked as he flipped his notebook to a blank page.

"No," I said. "I didn't know her personally at all. I'd heard about her before, but I'd never actually seen her in person until the dress rehearsal the night before she was killed."

Van den Broek made a short note. "So what was it you wanted to tell me?"

I did my best to order my thoughts. "You might have already heard this from someone else, but Pavlina and Ethan Rogerson didn't like each other much."

"What gave you that impression?" Neither his voice nor his expression indicated any particular interest in what I'd said.

"The way they spoke to each other backstage. They didn't respect each other's music, that's for sure."

"I suppose that's not surprising," the detective said. "They were each other's competition, and big egos aren't exactly a rarity among you musician types, are they?"

I bristled at his words, though they had some merit. "We aren't all egotistical and self-centered, but no, such people aren't a rarity in this profession, especially among the exceptionally talented ones."

"Like the finalists in the competition."

I nodded.

Detective Van den Broek flipped his notebook shut, his attention already drifting away from me. "Is that all?"

"No." I tried not to grit my teeth together. The detective's disinterest irked me, but I still felt obligated to share with him what I'd overheard the previous week. "It's my understanding that Pavlina was involved with one of the competition's judges, Jeb Hartson."

"Involved?"

I fought the urge to roll my eyes. "Romantically."

"I see," the detective said, his voice still neutral. "And how did you find out about this?"

"I overheard a conversation between Jeb Hartson and Olivia Hutchcraft, the competition's coordinator. Accidentally," I hastened to add. "I gathered that Olivia had been involved with Jeb as well, at some point, and Jeb thought she was jealous. But she insisted that her concern was for the integrity of the competition."

Van den Broek regarded me impassively for a moment. "If Mr. Hartson and Ms. Nicolova were indeed involved and Ms. Hutchcraft knew about it, wouldn't Ms. Nicolova have been disqualified from the competition?"

"You'd think so," I said. "But I was under the impression that Olivia had only recently come by that information. Maybe Pavlina would have been disqualified if she'd lived long enough."

As I spoke, I had to quell a sense of growing frustration. All I was doing was attempting to help the police with their investigation, yet the detective seemed completely uninterested. Maybe the information I'd shared wasn't relevant, but could he really be so sure of that already?

"Anything else?" Van den Broek flipped open his notebook and made a brief notation before shutting it again.

I battled the glower that wanted to take over my face, somehow managing to keep my expression neutral. "No. That's all. I just wanted to make sure you knew what was going on behind the scenes, whether it turns out to be of importance or not."

The detective stood up. "I appreciate that."

He didn't sound particularly appreciative.

"If you have any more information to share, please get in touch." He handed me a business card, although he didn't sound like he was at all eager to hear from me again.

"I'll do that," I said, a hint of a chill to my voice. I stood up and pocketed the card. "Good night, Detective."

He didn't offer any parting words in return.

As I left him on the stage and made my way back toward the musicians' lounge, I silently cursed the circumstances that had led to Detectives Van den Broek and Chowdhury taking charge of Pavlina's murder case. Detective Salnikova, who'd investigated two previous murders connected to the orchestra, was much more pleasant to deal with. Sure, she had an annoying habit of not answering my questions and she tended to get exasperated with me at times, but at least I never doubted her interest in the cases she was working. With Detective Van den Broek, I couldn't tell if he cared at all about solving the crime or if he was simply going through the motions so he could get paid.

If it was the latter, would the murderer ever get caught or would he or she be free to roam among us indefinitely? I shuddered at the thought of possibly passing the killer in the hall, not knowing their dark secret. Perhaps the killer had followed Pavlina to the theater and had no connection to the competition or the Point Grey Philharmonic, but for some reason I found that hard to believe. After all, there must have been less populated places to do away with Pavlina than the theater. If the murder had been premeditated, then why carry it out here? And if it wasn't premeditated, then how would anyone without a connection to the theater have ended up in the women's washroom with Pavlina?

No, it was more likely than not that there was a connection.

As I passed by the closed door of a maintenance cupboard, my thoughts turned to Fred and his toolbox. If the blood on his hammer belonged to Pavlina, did that narrow the list of suspects at all?

I wondered how many people would have had access to Fred's tools. Pausing in the hallway, I decided there was only one way to find out. Giving up on my plan to gather up my belongings and head home, I instead set off in search of Fred.

Considering the time of night, I didn't know for sure if he would still be at the theater. I'd often spotted him working after rehearsals, but I'd remained at the theater longer than usual and didn't know if he worked the same hours each day or not. I remembered hearing something about a judges' meeting being held in one of the upstairs conference rooms, so I knew I wasn't alone in the theater, but it felt like I was. Heavy silence hung over the corridor, broken only by the soft sound of my footfalls on the red carpeting.

I couldn't hear any voices and wondered if the detectives had gone home. That was entirely possible since the stage was empty of life when I returned to the wings and peeked out at the unoccupied chairs and music stands. I stood still and listened for a moment, but could hear no telltale sounds of maintenance work going on. Crossing the stage, I passed through the wings on the opposite side and followed a corridor lined with dressing rooms, all of the doors currently shut tight.

At the end of the hallway I pushed through a door and stepped into the theater's lobby. Still lit up, the lobby featured more red carpeting, ticket windows, a shuttered concession stand, washrooms, four cushioned benches, and two elegant, curving stairways that led up to the balcony and private boxes. The silence was as heavy in the lobby as it had been in the corridor and I decided to give up on my search. But as I turned to make my way back through the door, a clanking sound drew my attention. The door to the men's washroom opened and Fred emerged, his toolbox in hand.

"Evening, Midori," Fred said when he caught sight of me.

"Hi, Fred."

The maintenance man had worked at the theater for many years and we'd been on a first-name basis for a long time.

"You're here late tonight," he commented.

"I am," I agreed, as I left the door to approach him. "I was looking for you, actually."

"Something need to be fixed?"

"No. I wanted to ask you about your tools." Both our gazes shifted to the toolbox in his hand. "Did the police ever tell you if the blood on your hammer was Pavlina's?"

"The dead woman?" He shook his head. "That was a real shame, losing her life so young. But no, the police haven't told me anything. And I'm not sure I want to know. If my hammer was used to kill that poor young woman . . . Well, that makes me feel responsible for her death."

"Even if it was the murder weapon, her death wasn't your fault," I tried to assure him. "If the killer didn't use your hammer, he or she would have found something else to use."

"I suppose that's true." Fred sighed heavily. "Still, it's a terrible thing. Does everyone know that blood was found on my hammer?"

"No. I only know because I overheard you telling the police the other night. It doesn't seem to be general knowledge."

A hint of relief registered on Fred's creased face. "That's something, at least. I wouldn't want people thinking I'd killed her."

"I'm sure no one would think that."

He didn't seem entirely convinced. "Of course, people might still find out, and I'm just grateful the police haven't hauled me off to jail."

"Surely they don't think you're a suspect?" The idea seemed preposterous to me, but I'd known Fred for years whereas the police knew nothing about him.

"They sure asked me a lot of questions the other night. It's their job to, of course, but I'm not sure my old ticker could handle time in the slammer."

"I'm sure it won't come to that," I said quickly, hoping fervently that was the truth. "Maybe the blood wasn't Pavlina's. Even if it was, you weren't the only one with access to your tools that night, were you?"

"No, I sure wasn't." Fred scratched his head, thinking back. "The police asked me this as well. I'd left my toolbox out in the hall while I went to my maintenance cupboard to fetch a mop. I'd fixed a leaky pipe in one of the men's rooms, but there was water all over the floor. When I got back, I didn't notice whether my hammer was there or not. It wasn't until I went to put my tools away that I noticed the blood, but the toolbox was still out in the hall while I was mopping up the water. If someone was quiet about it, they could have taken my hammer and returned it without me being any the wiser."

"Hopefully the killer left fingerprints behind," I said. "That would help the investigation. If your hammer really was the murder weapon."

"I sure hope it wasn't, but my gut tells me it was. And there aren't many times when my gut is wrong."

I gave him what I hoped was a reassuring smile. "Everything will turn out all right in the end."

"I hope so." He nodded at me. "I'd better get on. You have yourself a good night, Midori."

"You too, Fred."

He passed through the door leading to the corridor I'd followed to the lobby. I almost took the same route as him, but then decided to cross the lobby to get to the other side of the theater where the musicians' lounge was located. I passed by the shuttered concession stand and reached a recessed door on the far side of the lobby. As I was about to push through it, a man's voice caught my attention.

"It's all taken care of," the man said. "They don't suspect a thing."

An eerie chill ran up my spine and I remained frozen to the spot. Glancing over my shoulder toward the nearest curving staircase, I spotted Jeb Hartson in a suit and bolo tie, descending the stairs, lowering a cell phone from his ear.

With a sudden stab of fear cutting through me, I opened the door as silently and as quickly as I could. Then I slipped through it and fled down the hall toward the musicians' lounge, hoping with all my might that Jeb had no clue I'd overheard him.

Chapter Seven

By the time I returned to the musicians' lounge, the door was locked, all other members of the orchestra now gone. Fortunately, I had my key in my pocket and was able to retrieve my belongings from my locker. While quickly shrugging into my coat and pulling on my gloves, I kept glancing toward the door. My nerves were worn thin like a well-used violin string, ready to snap under the smallest amount of pressure.

As soon as possible, I hitched my tote bag over my shoulder, grabbed my instrument case, and shut and locked my locker. I flipped off the lights as I left the room and locked the door behind me. Pausing outside the lounge, I glanced up and down the corridor. It was empty, thick silence ringing in my ears.

Not wanting to hang about any longer, I hurried to the stage door and left the theater for the chilly, dark night, my warm breath puffing out in small clouds in front of my face. While I was relieved that I hadn't run into Jeb since I'd overheard him in the lobby, I couldn't get away from the theater fast enough. It was usually a comforting place for me, but it was nothing of the sort at the moment. I couldn't help thinking of Pavlina's killer stalking the hallways, whether that killer was Jeb or someone else.

As I made my way down the short alley, I kept glancing this way and that, jumpier than a hyper kangaroo. When I reached the parking lot, my footsteps slowed. Voices danced through the cold night air, jumbled words I couldn't decipher sounding at two different pitches. As I continued toward my MINI Cooper—one of only four cars left in the lot—I spotted Elena near her silver Mercedes-Benz, speaking with the same man I'd seen her with before the concert on the night of Pavlina's death.

I strained my ears but still couldn't make out their words, and I soon realized they were once again speaking Russian. But while I couldn't understand their words, Elena's body language required no translation. As I watched, she threw her hands up in the air and spat out several exasperated words. The man said something in return and she shook her head, cutting him off with a rapid stream of Russian.

Arriving at my car, I fumbled with my keys as I kept an eye on Elena and the mystery man. I managed to get the door unlocked and when I opened it, the movement caught Elena's eye. Her head snapped in my direction and she glared at me from across the parking lot. Feigning disinterest, I stashed my violin behind the driver's seat, tossed my tote bag over to the passenger's side, and climbed in.

When I pulled the door shut my eyes went back to Elena, but she too had climbed into her car. The mystery man climbed in next to her and the engine roared to life, the headlights slicing through the night. Elena wasted no time reversing out of her parking spot and careening out of the lot. I followed in my MINI Cooper at a safer pace, and by the time I reached the main road, Elena's vehicle had disappeared from sight.

I would have been lying if I said I had no interest in knowing who the man with Elena was. I was far too curious by nature not to wonder. But as I paused at a red light a minute later, other memories of the evening crept to the forefront of my mind, crowding out any lingering thoughts of Elena and the man who'd left with her.

Clanging the loudest for my attention was my memory of Jeb Hartson's recent words. What was it that was all taken care of? What did nobody suspect? That he'd killed Pavlina?

If that was the case, who was he talking to? And why would he have wanted Pavlina dead?

If Pavlina had threatened to make their relationship public, it was entirely possible that such news could have negatively affected his reputation and career. It was unlikely that he'd ever be asked to judge another contest once it was widely known that he'd had an inappropriate relationship with one of the finalists in the young composers' competition. Maybe his colleagues would have looked down on him as well, causing more damage to his career by reducing other future opportunities.

The problem with that scenario was that—as far as I could see—Pavlina herself had stood to lose plenty by making their relationship public. Revealing such information during the competition would likely have led to her disqualification, as I suspected would have happened if she'd lived long enough for Olivia to set that ball rolling. Even if she'd won the competition and had already made off with the prize money before revealing her relationship with Jeb, she likely would have been disgraced in the media, and people would have surmised that she'd won because she was sleeping with Jeb, rather than because of her talent. Whether or not that would have been true or fair, the perception could have darkened the prospects for her otherwise bright future.

It was entirely possible that there were facts still unknown to me that would paint a clearer picture of why Jeb would want Pavlina dead, but based on what I knew at the moment, it seemed far more likely that he would have wanted Olivia out of the way. She knew Jeb and Pavlina's secret and whether or not she herself could have made the decision to disqualify Pavlina and boot Jeb from the judging panel, she certainly could have taken the first step toward that outcome by telling what she knew to those in charge.

Since Olivia had that power, I would have been convinced of Jeb's guilt if she'd been the victim rather than Pavlina. As it was, a note of uncertainty jingled at the back of my head, making me wonder if the words I'd overheard held any real significance after all. If his statements were indicative of his guilt, the police needed to know what I'd overheard. But I could already imagine how completely disinterested Detective Van den Broek would be when he heard the brief tale of that moment in the lobby.

Still, even if the detective didn't seem to appreciate anything I'd already told him, I wouldn't feel right holding back what I'd overheard. Maybe it meant nothing, but maybe it was the vital clue that would put the police on the track of Pavlina's killer.

With a heavy sigh, I decided to make a trip to the police station the next morning. Once again I wished Detective Salnikova was in charge of the murder investigation. Even if I had a tendency to exasperate her with what she probably viewed as nosiness, I knew she would at least listen to me. I wasn't sure if I'd get the same consideration from Van den Broek. Nevertheless, I would pay the detective a visit in the morning and tell him what I'd heard.

I TOSSED AND turned that night, jumbled thoughts bouncing around in my head, thumping out an irregular beat against my skull. Even when I did manage to sleep, a confused muddle of dreams kept me from truly restful slumber. I awoke in the morning with a groan, pulling the blankets up over my head, wishing I could turn back the clock and give the night another try. Since that, unfortunately, wasn't an option, I soon forced myself to push back the covers and leave the warmth of my bed.

Yawning, I stumbled my way to the bathroom and took a quick shower. By the time I'd toweled off and dressed I was as awake as I could be after the night I'd had. I made myself a quick breakfast of toast and strawberry jam and washed it down with a cup of green tea. Although I would have liked to lounge about reading a good book while enjoying another cup of tea, I remembered my decision from the night before and got bundled up in my coat, slouchy knitted hat, and gloves. Then I rode the elevator down to my building's underground parking lot and set off in my car for the police station.

I had to circle the block before I could find a parking spot and when I finally did get my MINI Cooper tucked up next to the curb, I remained in the driver's seat, reluctant to get out. While I couldn't be completely sure of the reception I'd receive from Detective Van den Broek, I figured the odds were pretty good that he wouldn't be enthralled by what I had to tell him. Then again, maybe I didn't have to talk to Van den Broek. Maybe I could ask to speak with Detective Chowdhury instead. Whether he'd be any more interested in the information I had to share than his partner had been with my insights the other night, I didn't know, but speaking with Chowdhury appealed to me more than another round with Van den Broek.

Finally leaving the warmth of my little car, I hurried along the street to the police station, the cold air stinging my cheeks. Inside the reception area, warmer air greeted me and I pulled my hat from my head. I immediately regretted the action, realizing that my hair was probably all staticky and sticking up in every direction. Feeling self-conscious, I ran my hand over my hair, trying to smooth it down as best I could as I approached the reception desk.

I asked the middle-aged woman behind the desk if I could speak with Detective Chowdhury and she requested that I wait a moment. As I did so, I wandered over to the posters adorning one of the walls, but barely noticed any of them except one. A missing person's poster showing a teenage girl with hair the same length and color as Pavlina's caught my attention, shifting my focus back in time to the terrible scene Mikayla and I had stumbled upon in the theater's washroom.

For the briefest of moments it was as if a flag were waving at me from the back of my mind. But as soon as I tried to grasp on to what my brain was trying to tell me, the thought slipped away. Staring at the posters without really seeing them, I sifted through my memories, trying to find what it was that I'd almost remembered. I had a feeling it related in some way to Pavlina's body, or the scene of the crime.

Had I seen something significant without realizing it at the time? But what?

I tugged on my left earlobe, picturing all the details I could recall from the moments following the discovery of Pavlina's body. But the harder I tried to figure out what was nagging at me, the farther away it seemed to slither.

When the woman behind the reception desk called for my attention, I turned away from the posters, annoyed with myself, but deciding to forget about the matter for the time being. Whatever it was that I was missing, maybe it would come back to me later.

"Detective Chowdhury will be out in a moment," the woman told me when I returned to the reception desk.

I thanked her and wandered over to the nearest chair. I'd barely had a chance to sit down before the door next to the reception desk opened and Detective Chowdhury stepped through it.

"Ms. Bishop?" His eyes settled on me, the only person in the waiting area.

I jumped up and hurried over to meet him. He offered his hand and I shook it. Then he ushered me through the doorway and into a hallway I'd been down several times before.

"I presume you're here about the investigation into Ms. Nicolova's death," Chowdhury said as he led me to an open area at the end of the hall where several detectives worked away at their desks.

My eyes quickly scanned the room, but I saw no sign of Detective Salnikova's familiar face. "Yes," I said as Chowdhury offered me a seat by his desk.

"You've remembered something since you spoke to Detective Van den Broek the other night?"

I settled into the offered seat, resting my purse, hat, and gloves on my lap. "No, but I overheard something after I spoke to him. It might not be important, but it sounded suspicious to me and I thought you should know about it."

Detective Chowdhury dug around in one of his desk drawers and produced a pen seconds later. As he flipped through the pages of his notebook, a shadow fell over me. Chowdhury and I both looked up at the same time. Detective Van den Broek loomed over us, appearing even taller than his six and a half feet from my low vantage point.

"Ms. Bishop, isn't it?" he said, peering down at me from his great height.

"That's right," I confirmed.

He pulled out the chair that was tucked under the neighboring desk and sat down. It seemed I'd be talking to both detectives.

"Ms. Bishop has something to tell us regarding the murder investigation," Chowdhury said, bringing his partner up to speed.

Van den Broek fixed his eyes on me.

Determined not to shrink beneath his gaze, I sat up straight and focused on Detective Chowdhury, clearing my throat before speaking. "As I said, I'm not sure if it's significant, but last night after the rehearsal I overheard Jeb Hartson talking on his cell phone. He said something was all taken care of and nobody suspected a thing. He didn't know I'd overheard him and I'm pretty sure he thought he was alone, since most of the orchestra had already left the theater."

Even though I remained facing Detective Chowdhury, I could still feel Van den Broek's intimidating gaze boring into me. I clasped my hands in my lap to prevent myself from fidgeting and cleared my throat again. "Anyways, it sounded suspicious to me so I thought you should know."

"Did he say anything else?" Chowdhury asked.

"Not that I heard."

The detective wrote something in his notebook before flipping it shut and setting down his pen. "All right. Thank you, Ms. Bishop. We appreciate you coming in to share this with us."

"You're welcome," I said as I stood up.

"Ms. Bishop," Van den Broek said as he got to his feet. "You seem to overhear quite a few conversations."

I met his dark blue eyes straight on. "What are you implying?"

"I simply hope you aren't wasting police time."

Heat flared in my cheeks as the full implication of his words hit me. "You think I made this up?"

It was Detective Chowdhury's turn to stand up. "Nobody's saying that."

"Really?" I knew that was exactly what Van den Broek was saying. A fire of anger and indignation flared to life inside of me, heating my next words. "The community at the Abrams Center is a small one. I overhear things accidentally all the time. Most of it is of no importance, and maybe this information isn't either, but I thought it was my duty to share it with you. If you'd rather not know what goes on at the theater when you're not around, just say so and I won't bother you again."

"We do appreciate the information you shared," Chowdhury hurried to assure me, but I barely heard him.

Van den Broek's impassive expression hadn't changed and I was ready to storm out of the police station. I'd even spun around, prepared to leave without another word, when a familiar voice stopped me before I'd taken a single step.

"Midori?"

Detective Salnikova had arrived at some point during my conversation with her colleagues and now stood next to her desk, only a stone's throw from those of Detectives Chowdhury and Van den Broek.

"Detective Salnikova. It's nice to see you again." Although I managed to get the words out, my voice was still stiff with anger, my tone not matching my words. "I was just on my way out."

"I'll walk with you," she said quickly, halting Detective Chowdhury, who was about to carry out the task.

My teeth gritting together, I walked briskly across the room and turned down the hallway that would take me to the reception area. It was only once we were out of sight of the other detectives that Salnikova put a hand on my arm to stop my progress.

"Is something wrong, Midori?"

I spent a second or two fighting against the storm of angry emotions raging inside of me. As I let out a breath, I tried to expel some of my frustration with it. It helped, although only slightly.

"I came here to share some information I thought might be pertinent to a murder investigation. I was only trying to be helpful, but Van den Broek seems to think I made everything up. Maybe he thinks I want attention or that I have a couple of screws loose. But when I overhear something that could be a clue, am I supposed to keep quiet? Is that really what they want me to do?"

Despite my attempt to calm down, the storm inside of me was back to gale force. I closed my eyes briefly, trying to regain my composure.

"Why don't we sit down for a moment?" Salnikova opened a door and indicated that I should precede her through it.

Embarrassment now mingling with all my other emotions, I entered the small interview room and plunked my hat, gloves, and purse on the table before sitting down on one of the two chairs.

"I'm sorry," I said as Salnikova took the other seat. "The suggestion that I'm an attention-seeking liar got me riled up."

"I'm guessing this has to do with the Nicolova murder case."

"Yes." I told her about the conversation I'd overheard between Jeb and Olivia, as well as Jeb's suspicious telephone conversation. "Should I really have kept that to myself?"

"No," Salnikova replied. "You were right to share that information."

"For all the good it'll do," I muttered. "If Detectives Chowdhury and Van den Broek think I made it all up, they might ignore everything I told them."

"That won't happen. Detective Van den Broek might not be the most personable man on the force, but he's good at his job and he won't leave any stone unturned, despite what he might have led you to believe. And Detective Chowdhury is a sharp investigator too. Everything you told them will be checked out, I can assure you of that."

I was willing to believe what she'd said about Detective Chowdhury, but I wasn't quite as convinced about Van den Broek. Still, her reassurances had at least snuffed out the dancing flames of my anger and frustration.

"How come you're not working this case?" I asked.

"I was tied up with another investigation when the call came in."

That was unfortunate.

"How's Detective Bachman?" The last time I'd seen Salnikova's older partner, he'd been off duty, recovering from surgery.

"He's had an unfortunate health setback, but we're hoping he'll be back to work before long."

"I'm sorry to hear about the setback."

That was true, but part of me was also relieved he wasn't present because he never shied away from suggesting I had a tendency to get mixed up in police investigations. Although Salnikova had been known to do the same. In fact, I was surprised she hadn't already warned me about interfering with police business.

"I hope you'll be careful, Midori."

Maybe the thought had passed through my head too soon. "I'm always careful."

I figured it was a good thing JT wasn't there to hear me say that. Salnikova looked skeptical enough, and JT wouldn't have held back any of his disbelief. The detective didn't, however, lecture me about keeping my nose out of the official investigation, and I was grateful for that.

She might have decided I could do with a lecture if I'd told her about questioning Fred about his tools, but I didn't need to go there. Actually, I didn't think I needed to do anything more at the police station. As far as I was concerned, I'd done my duty by filling in Detectives Chowdhury and Van den Broek on what Jeb had said the other night, and—as long as Salnikova was right about their qualities as investigators—they'd likely track down the killer without any further input from me. In the meantime, I could focus on other matters, like the theft of JT's equipment. Maybe that was a hopeless cause, but I wasn't ready to give up on it yet.

Thanking Salnikova for her time, I parted ways with her and left the police station, hoping I'd be able to steer clear of Detective Van den Broek in the future.

Chapter Eight

I MADE A quick stop at home to eat an early lunch and pick up my violin. Then I set off to JT's house, where my studio was located. For several years now I'd rented one of the front rooms of his house for teaching purposes, and I enjoyed the fact that I got to hang out with my best friend far more often than if I'd worked elsewhere. Some days I didn't see JT at all if he was working long hours down in his recording studio or off at a meeting about the science fiction TV show he composed music for, but most days I got to spend at least some time with him.

Lately, however, spending time with him wasn't always as easy as it had once been. In the past I'd been so at ease in his company, but now I sometimes found myself worrying that he'd catch on to the fact that my feelings for him had evolved. I knew there was only one way to erase that anxiety, but I wasn't sure I was brave enough to do what was necessary. I was all too aware of what could go wrong.

Fortunately, I didn't have time to dwell on such thoughts right at that moment. Since my first lesson of the day was scheduled for noon, I didn't have a chance to say much more than hello to JT before I had to get ready to teach. But once my last student of the day had left, I wandered toward the kitchen at the back of the house. I didn't find JT or Finnegan there, but the door to the basement was ajar and the light above the stairway was on. After helping myself to a drink of water and putting the empty glass in the dishwasher, I made my way down the stairs. Before I'd reached the last step, Finnegan bounded my way, his fluffy tail wagging with excitement.

"Hey, boy," I greeted him, giving him a scratch on the head.

"Finished teaching for the day?" JT asked as he emerged from his recording studio.

"Yep. The rest of the day is mine. How about you?"

"I just wrapped things up. The guys are coming over soon for an extra band practice. We need to iron out a few wrinkles before our next gig on Saturday night."

"Speaking of your band," I said, "are you going to ask Cameron if he knows anything about the theft of your equipment?"

"No. Why would I? He was inside the theater when the thief was at work."

"That's what we assumed, and maybe he really was. But what if leaving the truck unlocked wasn't an accident?"

"What are you suggesting? That he was involved?"

"It's possible," I said, recalling Cameron's skittish behavior.

JT removed one of his acoustic guitars from its wall hanger. "Even if it's a possibility—and I'm not saying it is—I'm not going to accuse him of anything when I don't have any proof."

"Okay, I get that, but aren't you suspicious?"

JT strummed a random chord before hesitating.

"You are," I said. "You don't want to be, but you are."

"All right. I'm suspicious," he admitted with no shortage of re-luctance. "But I really don't want to believe he could have stolen from me."

As JT sat down and worked away at tuning the guitar, I flopped down into a beanbag chair. When Finnegan sat down next to me, I scratched his head, thinking.

"You said Cameron lost his job recently and needs money, so that gives him motive. But what about opportunity? Did he have time to shift all the equipment from your truck to another vehicle when you weren't around?"

JT frowned as he considered that. "I'm not so sure. It's pos-sible, but he would've had to work fast. But if he was working with someone else . . ."

I could tell he didn't like saying those words.

"That's probably the most likely possibility," I agreed. "There had to be another vehicle to transport the equipment. And if he was in cahoots with someone, the timing wouldn't be such an issue. His accomplice could have transferred the equipment from one vehicle to another while you and Cameron were both inside the theater. All Cameron had to do was leave the truck unlocked."

"But we don't know for sure that Cameron was involved," JT re-minded me. "And I'm giving him the benefit of the doubt. I have to."

I understood that. If JT gave his suspicions too much power, that could affect his friendship with Cameron. And if his friend-ship with Cameron was strained, that could seriously mess with the band's chemistry. I, however, didn't have to worry about that, and I wondered if there was any way I could figure out for certain if Cameron was involved in the theft.

"Still no sign of your equipment online?" I asked as my thoughts simmered.

"No. I've checked twice a day every day and there's no sign of it."

I frowned at that, but didn't pursue the topic any further. As footsteps sounded overhead, Finnegan jumped up with a bark and catapulted up the stairs. A moment later he came bounding back down with Rafael—one of JT's bandmates—following in his wake.

After greeting Rafael, I left him and JT in the basement and returned to the kitchen, hoping I could intercept Cameron when he arrived. I didn't have to wait long. Only a minute or two later he came in through the unlocked front door, shrugging out of his jacket as he arrived in the kitchen.

"Hey, Cameron," I said, giving him what I hoped was a welcoming smile. "How's it going?"

"Good," he replied. "You?"

"Not bad." I perched on one of the stools at the granite breakfast bar, my back to the counter. "But there was something I wanted to ask you."

It might have been my imagination, but I thought I detected a hint of wariness in his eyes.

"What's that?"

"The other night at the theater, did you happen to notice anyone suspicious hanging around the parking lot?"

Cameron draped his jacket over his arm. "No."

"You see, we figure whoever stole the equipment must have had a vehicle to transport it, right?"

"That makes sense." He shifted his weight uneasily. "But the police asked me all this the other night. Like I told them, there were a lot of cars in the parking lot and none of them stood out as suspicious. If someone saw me loading the last of the equipment into the truck, I didn't see them."

"The equipment's probably gone for good then. JT hasn't had any luck finding it online and there don't seem to be any leads to follow."

As I spoke, I studied Cameron carefully. He had yet to meet my eyes and I thought I detected a shimmer of perspiration along his hairline. Was he nervous or did he simply feel bad about accidentally giving the thieves an easy opportunity to take off with JT's equipment?

I couldn't be sure, and Hamish—the last member of the band to arrive—walked into the kitchen at that moment, distracting me from my study of Cameron.

"What are you two talking about?" Hamish asked with a waggle of his eyebrows.

I rolled my eyes.

"Nothing," Cameron mumbled. His eyes down, he slipped through the door and down the stairway, passing JT on his way to the basement.

Hamish's eyebrows had stopped waggling but remained raised. "You're not going to scare off another drummer, are you, Midori? If you do, we'll have to start calling you the black widow of bands or something."

I opened my mouth to retort, but JT beat me to it.

"Cut it out, Hamish."

The sharp edge to JT's voice took me by surprise. It seemed to have the same effect on Hamish. Looking more abashed than I'd ever seen him, Hamish muttered what I thought might have been an apology and escaped down the stairs to join Cameron and Rafael. Still surprised, I watched JT as he crossed the kitchen and opened the fridge with a jerk, grabbing a six-pack of cola.

"What's wrong?" I asked when I saw that he was still scowling.

JT wasn't one to get angry easily, and we were all used to Hamish's dumb comments, so his reaction puzzled me.

"Hamish," he said by way of reply.

He headed for the basement stairway with the soft drinks in hand, but I grabbed his arm to stop him.

"Hamish was just being Hamish. That's nothing new."

"No, but he crossed a line."

"With what he said about me? Forget about it. It didn't bother me."

Maybe it would have in the days following my breakup with Aaron, the band's previous drummer, but it didn't faze me now. JT, on the other hand, was clearly still displeased. The muscles in his jaw were so tense I worried they might snap.

"Seriously, JT. It's fine." I took his free hand and gave it a squeeze. "Don't be mad at Hamish, okay? Just go have fun."

He let out a breath and some of his unfamiliar sternness fell away. He almost managed a smile as he gave my hand a squeeze in return. Instead of letting go as I expected, he kept hold of it.

"Are you sticking around?" he asked.

"Actually, I think I'll head home," I said, trying not to be distracted by the warmth of his hand around mine. "But I'll see you tomorrow."

"All right." He gave my hand another squeeze before letting go. "Have a good night."

"You too," I said as he headed for the basement.

I remained seated at the breakfast bar for another moment or two, lost in thought. I wanted to read between the lines of JT's reaction to Hamish's comments, but didn't know if I should. Probably not, I decided. Maybe JT's short temper stemmed only from low blood sugar or something similarly simple. That was far more likely than him having deeper feelings for me than I knew, wasn't it?

Not wanting to answer that question, I slid off the stool and returned to my studio to grab my violin. It was time to call it a day and head home.

THE NEXT DAY passed without incident. I didn't even have time to think about crimes or suspects since a long list of errands kept me busy all morning and my students occupied my entire afternoon. It wasn't until the evening when I arrived at the theater that the subject of Pavlina's murder crept out of the shadows to once again claim center stage in my head.

On my way from the stage door to the musicians' lounge, I spotted Ethan talking with Olivia, Sasha hovering behind them. The theater was otherwise quiet, but I knew that would soon change. I'd arrived fairly early, but the rest of the orchestra wouldn't be far behind me.

When I arrived at the musicians' lounge, the only others present were Dongmei and Elena. Dongmei sat on one of the couches, picking at her fingernails, her nervousness glaringly obvious. In stark contrast, Elena sat casually in a chair on the opposite side of the room, her long legs crossed as she flipped through a magazine, all the while managing to maintain her usual haughty demeanor.

I smiled at Dongmei as I entered the room, but I ignored Elena as much as she ignored me. Stashing my instrument case in my locker for the time being, I shed all my outerwear and rubbed my chilled hands together. I was about to join Dongmei over on the couch when two more people entered the room. For the first second or two I didn't pay them much attention, assuming that more of my fellow musicians had arrived. But then I caught sight of the two men in my peripheral vision.

Detectives Van den Broek and Chowdhury.

Remaining by my locker, I watched as their glances skipped over me and Dongmei to settle on Elena. To my surprise, the two men strode over to the concertmaster and loomed over her.

"Elena Vasilyeva?" Van den Broek asked.

She raised her eyes up from the magazine, unfazed by the detectives' presence.

"Yes?" She wove the single word with threads of cool disinterest.

"We'd like you to come with us to the police station to answer some questions."

While my eyes widened with surprise, Elena's narrowed.

"Questions?" She repeated the word as if it tasted foul. "What questions?"

"About Pavlina Nicolova's death," Van den Broek replied.

"I know nothing about her death." Elena returned her attention to the magazine in her lap.

Detective Chowdhury spoke this time. "You're acquainted with one Igor Malakhov, aren't you?"

Elena raised her eyes again, and now they were like icy daggers. "He's my cousin, as I'm sure you already know."

"And your cousin had a relationship with Ms. Nicolova, did he not?"

Elena's expression closed off, like shutters slamming across a window. "They knew each other in high school. What does that have to do with anything?"

"That's exactly what we'd like to determine," Detective Van den Broek said. "Now, if you'd please come with us." He took a step back, as if expecting Elena to get to her feet.

Instead, she slapped the magazine shut and tossed it onto a neighboring chair. "Am I under arrest?" she asked without moving from her seat.

"No, ma'am," Chowdhury replied.

Now she did get to her feet. "Then if you'll excuse me, I've got a rehearsal to attend."

A muscle in Detective Van den Broek's jaw twitched. "We still need to ask you some questions."

Elena leveled her cold blue eyes at Van den Broek, somehow managing to appear just as imposing as him even though he had several inches of height on her. "I'll come by the police station in the morning, if I must. Until then, I'm otherwise occupied."

She turned for the door, her pace unhurried, her head held high.

"We'll be expecting you," Van den Broek called after her, his tone suggesting she'd better make good on her word.

The detectives exchanged a weighty glance, and then Van den Broek's eyes fell on me. A hint of a frown pulled at his mouth, but I didn't avert my gaze. Maybe he thought I was a snoop for listening in, but it wasn't my fault I'd overheard the exchange with Elena. The detectives hadn't exactly chosen a private spot for it.

After another second of attempting to stare me down, Van den Broek strode out of the room, his partner by his side. When they were gone I turned to face Dongmei, whose eyes were as wide as my own must have been.

"What do you think that was all about?" she asked.

"I'm not sure," I said.

But I wanted to find out.

Chapter Nine

SEVERAL MUSICIANS TRICKLED into the lounge over the next few minutes. I hesitated by my locker, not sure if I should stick around and chat with my friends or go off in search of Elena. While part of me wanted to make sure she was okay after her encounter with the police—in case her unflappable demeanor was an act—I mostly wanted to know what the heck was going on. As usual, my curiosity got the upper hand, and I left all my belongings behind as I headed off on my search. Although I had trouble picturing Elena crying in a bathroom stall, I decided to check the nearest women's washroom first, just in case. I wasn't surprised when I didn't find her there.

Not wanting to linger in the spot where Mikayla and I had found Pavlina's body, I quickly retreated from the washroom and set off down the hall toward the back of the building. As I reached the foot of the stairway leading to the second floor, my search came to an end. Elena descended the stairs toward me, as cool and collected as ever. Whether or not the imposing detectives had instilled any anxiety beneath her haughty façade, I didn't know, but if anyone could remain completely undaunted by them, it was Elena.

"Is everything all right?" I asked when she reached the foot of the stairs.

Her blue eyes rested on me for a second or two before she responded. "Why wouldn't it be?"

Not waiting for a response, she brushed past me and continued on toward the lounge.

I watched her go, wondering if I should follow her and see if I could get something more out of her. It only took me a fraction of a second to decide that would be a waste of time. Elena only ever shared what she wanted to share, and she wasn't about to confide in me.

That didn't put an end to my quest for information though. It wasn't hard to guess why she'd been up on the second floor.

Jogging up the stairs, I turned to the left and followed another hallway until I reached Hans's office. The door stood ajar, and the orchestra's conductor was seated at his desk, his forehead furrowed and a frown on his face. He seemed lost in thought, and didn't notice my presence until I tapped on the door frame.

"Midori." He sat up straighter. "Come in."

I stepped into the office and shut the door all but a crack behind me.

"What's going on with Elena?" I asked without preamble.

Hans let out a sigh and sat back in his chair. "Nothing to worry about."

I plunked myself down in a spare chair. "You look worried."

He regarded me in silence for a moment or two before running a hand through his blond hair. "You're right. I am worried. We can't afford to lose our concertmaster, especially not right in the middle of the season."

"Are we in danger of losing her?"

He hesitated, and I knew he was about to shut me out.

I jumped in before he had a chance to do that. "I know the police want to question her. I was there when they talked to her a few minutes ago. Does she know something about Pavlina's death?"

Hans eyed the door, as if worried we might be overheard. He lowered his voice. "She swears she doesn't."

"And you believe her?"

"I do."

"The police were asking about her cousin. Apparently he knew Pavlina."

"Yes. Elena mentioned that."

"I saw her talking to a guy here at the theater on Friday night and again on Tuesday night. Was that her cousin?"

"Probably. I never saw him, but Elena said he was here on the night of Pavlina's death."

"So do the police suspect him of killing Pavlina?"

"Perhaps. But even if they do suspect him, that doesn't mean he's the killer. It wouldn't be the first time the police set their sights on the wrong person."

I knew he was referring to the time he'd become the prime suspect in the murder of a cellist.

"If Elena does know something, if her cousin is the killer and she's protecting him, the police will figure it out," I said. "It would be better for her to come clean now. Better for her and for the orchestra."

"I told her that," Hans said, a note of weariness in his voice. "But she says she and her cousin are innocent."

I mulled that over for a second or two. "Did she give any indication of why the police might suspect her cousin?"

"Apparently he and Pavlina dated briefly when they were in high school together in Toronto. Igor—that's Elena's cousin—tried to impress Pavlina by stealing a Porsche while they were on a date. Pavlina turned him in to the police."

Ouch.

"Okay," I said as I absorbed that information. "I can see how that would make him mad, but that must have been years ago. Why wait all this time to kill her? Was he in jail for the past several years?"

"Elena said he was a first offender and didn't do much time. He's been out for a good while."

"Is this the first time they've crossed paths since high school?"

"I don't know." Hans ran a hand through his hair again. "The sooner we get this mess sorted out, the better." He picked up a pen and tapped it against the desk, his eyes on me. "You have a knack for ferreting out information."

"And?" I said, sensing where he was headed.

"Maybe you can get to the bottom of this, or at least hurry things along so we can get the police out from under our feet."

"And justice for Pavlina," I added, not wanting the most important objective to be forgotten.

"Of course," Hans said quickly. "I didn't mean to be insensitive."

"I know." After a pause, I said, "So you're saying you want me to solve the case?" I was surprised, although somewhat flattered that he thought I was capable of doing so.

"I'm saying maybe you can at least point the police in the right direction. You have an insider's view of the behind-the-scenes workings of the orchestra and the competition. Plus, you're observant."

I appreciated that descriptor. I knew a few people who would have used the word "nosy" instead, perhaps not entirely unfairly.

"Somebody must know something," Hans went on. "Maybe you can find out who that someone is."

After considering that idea for a second or two, I replied, "I guess I can try."

I'd already planned to ask a few questions anyway, and if there was potential for the orchestra to suffer as a result of a prolonged investigation, one that focused on Elena, then I wanted to do all I could to help the police wrap things up quickly.

"But if what I find out implicates Elena?" I asked, wondering how Hans would respond.

He let out a deep breath. "Then you'll have to share that with the police. But I doubt that will turn out to be the case."

I wanted to ask if he and Elena were back together after breaking things off in September, but I didn't want Hans to think I was asking because I was still interested in him. Really, I only wanted to know out of curiosity. But this time my curiosity wasn't enough to spur me on.

"I'll see what I can do," I said instead. "I'd better go get my violin."

Leaving Hans in his office, I returned to the musicians' lounge, wondering who I should set my investigative sights on first. As I unpacked my instrument from its case, I kept an eye on the room around me, noting who was present and who wasn't. Most of the orchestra had now arrived, but Elena was nowhere to be seen. Dongmei was in conversation with a clarinet player and a cellist, and Ethan Rogerson was perched on the arm of one of the couches, his attention focused on his smart phone.

Since I'd already spoken with Dongmei about the case, I decided to focus on Ethan for the moment. With my instrument case stashed back in my locker and my violin in hand, I crossed the room to stand next to him.

"Feeling nervous at all?" I asked.

"Huh?" He looked up from a game of Bejeweled Blitz.

"About tomorrow night," I clarified. "Are you nervous?"

"Oh." He exited the game. "Not really."

I had a hard time believing that, but then I remembered that his ego wasn't exactly small. Maybe he really was too confident to be nervous, or maybe he just wanted to maintain a confident veneer in front of his peers.

"I guess the competition isn't quite as intense now that Pavlina's gone," I said, hoping to draw more out of him.

He snorted. "It wasn't exactly intense to begin with."

That sent my eyebrows up an inch. "You didn't think Pavlina had a realistic chance of winning?"

"If she did, this competition is a bunch of bull. I mean, let's face it, she was popular because she was a hot chick, not because there was any real genius to her music."

My jaw almost dropped and I had to fight to keep an expression of distaste off my face. Pavlina's music might not have been everyone's cup of tea, but there was a brilliance to it, and I knew I was far from the only one who thought that her talent had exceeded Ethan's. To suggest that her success was purely a result of her physical attractiveness was both unfair and detestable.

Ethan showed no sign of knowing what I was thinking, and

maybe that was for the best. As much as I wanted to never speak to him again, I needed information from him.

"Do you have any idea who killed her?" I kept the question casual, as if it were the result of nothing but idle curiosity.

"Nope."

"You didn't see anyone backstage with her around the time she died?"

His gaze had been wandering around the room, but it now settled on me with suspicion. "How would I have done that?"

"I heard you left the audience during the concert. I thought maybe you might have seen something."

"All I did was go to the washroom. The only person I saw on my way there was Olivia, and I didn't see anyone on my way back."

"Oh," I said, feigning mild confusion. "I heard you were gone a long time."

The suspicion in his eyes intensified. "My stomach gets upset when I'm nervous. What's it to you, anyway?"

I shrugged and pretended I was losing interest in our conversation. "I was just curious, that's all."

"Yeah? Well, curiosity can lead to trouble."

With that, he shoved his phone in his pocket and walked away from me.

I watched him go, unease tickling the back of my neck. According to Dongmei, Ethan was gone from the audience for fifteen to twenty minutes. Sure, an upset stomach would explain the length of his absence, but that story didn't make sense. If he wasn't nervous now—the night before the performance of his composition—why would he have been so anxious last week during a concert that didn't involve a performance of his music?

But the inconsistency in his story wasn't the only thing that concerned me. As I returned to my locker to fetch my folder of music before heading to the stage, I noticed Ethan watching me from across the room. The weight of his gaze sent a hum of worry through my bones, and I wondered if his last words were meant as a threat.

Chapter Ten

DURING THE FIRST hour of rehearsal I had to struggle to keep my attention focused on the music. I was acutely aware of Ethan's presence in the theater and the fact that he could be a murderer. He certainly had the opportunity to kill Pavlina, but what about motive? Did he really believe he had as much or more of a chance of winning the competition as Pavlina? Or was all his egotistical bluster a cover for a lack of self-confidence?

I couldn't be sure, but if it was just a cover then maybe he had wanted to get Pavlina out of the way to improve his chances of winning. Recalling what he'd told me in the lounge, I realized that the same motive remained even if he truly did believe his composition skills were far superior to Pavlina's. He was well aware of Pavlina's popularity, after all, and maybe he believed she was likely to win regardless of what he viewed as her lack of talent. Perhaps he wanted to make way for the finalist who, in his mind, deserved to win—himself.

That was entirely possible, and it was enough to put Ethan on my list of suspects. I didn't want to focus all of my attention on him, however. I needed to find out if anyone else had the opportunity to kill Pavlina. Jeb Hartson had only left the audience for a couple of minutes, but it was still possible that he'd killed Pavlina, swiftly carrying out the deed before retaking his seat in the theater. The remaining judges had alibis since they'd never left the audience, but others had been backstage at the relevant time, and I needed to look into their whereabouts and possible motives before I could definitively zero in on a prime suspect.

When Hans stopped the rehearsal for a short break, I considered who else I should question. Olivia Hutchcraft, the competition's coordinator, had remained backstage during the concert. The same was true of her assistant, Sasha. And then there was Elena's cousin, Igor Malakhov. I'd seen him in the hallway with Elena shortly before the concert began. Had he left the theater when Elena headed for the stage, or had he remained, lurking in the back corridors for some sinister purpose?

The police wanted to question Elena about Igor, and that suggested they had reason to believe he'd remained in the theater, that he'd had an opportunity to follow Pavlina to the women's washroom and hit her over the head with Fred's hammer, or whatever the murder weapon turned out to be.

As much as Hans believed Elena had nothing to do with the murder and knew nothing of significance about it, I wasn't prepared to simply accept his belief. Both times I'd seen her talking with her cousin she'd been agitated. Maybe that agitation had nothing to do with Pavlina, but until I could rule that out, it was an avenue I intended to explore.

Not at the moment, however. I wasn't going to question Elena in front of our fellow musicians—for her sake and mine—and there were other investigative opportunities more readily available at the moment.

Knowing I didn't have much time before the rehearsal resumed, I left my seat and made my way through the wings to the back corridor. Although I was hoping to find Olivia and somehow strike up a conversation with her, I knew that might be difficult to do. She always seemed to be busy, hurrying to and fro or talking with one or more of the finalists. But as soon as I entered the corridor, I realized it would probably be far easier to talk to her assistant, Sasha, and see what he had to say. Luckily for me, he was hanging out in the hallway, leaning against the wall as he focused on the screen of his phone.

He was without a sweater vest today, but he still wore khaki pants, a button-down shirt with the sleeves rolled up to his elbows, and his black hipster glasses. I guessed his age at about twenty-three, and he was cute in a slightly nerdy way.

With my violin and bow in one hand, I approached him, trying to appear casual.

"Hey," I said when I reached him.

He glanced up from his phone for a split second. "Hey."

Although his gaze returned to the screen of his device, I didn't move and he soon looked up again.

I smiled, hoping to seem friendly. "You're Olivia Hutchcraft's assistant, right?"

"'Gofer' might be a better word, but, yeah."

His eyes strayed toward his phone again, but I wasn't about to let our conversation drop that easily.

"She keeps you busy?"

"Most of the time."

I stepped closer to the wall so two clarinet players could pass us. "Have you worked for her for long?"

"Nah." He finally gave up on his phone and tucked it into the back pocket of his pants. "Only a few weeks, and it's a temporary position, seeing as this competition only happens once every couple of years."

"Right." That made sense. "Do you like the job?"

He shrugged. "It's all right."

I decided it was time to steer the conversation down the road I wanted it to go. "It's probably been crazier than you expected, though, right?"

"Crazier?"

"Because of the murder," I said.

"Oh. Right." He glanced down the hallway, even though we were the only ones present.

With his attention threatening to stray again, I knew I couldn't waste any time. "Hey, you must have been backstage during the concert that night."

His eyes snapped back to me. "So?"

"Did you see anything suspicious?"

"No. I was upstairs during the first half of the concert. After that I went on a coffee run for Olivia. She has to have her half-fat mocha lattes."

"I wonder if she regrets that now," I said.

"Regrets what?"

"Sending you on a coffee run. If you weren't with her, did she have an alibi?"

I had his undivided attention now. "Why would she need one?"

"Maybe she doesn't. I just figured the police would be looking at everyone who was backstage as a possible suspect."

"I don't see why Olivia would want to kill Pavlina."

That wasn't clear to me either.

"How long were you gone on the coffee run?" I asked.

"Nearly half an hour, I guess. Starbucks was busy that night so I had to wait in line."

That would have given Olivia plenty of time to murder Pavlina. Tucking that information away, I asked another question.

"Did you know Pavlina?"

His eyes narrowed slightly behind the lenses of his glasses. "You think I'm a suspect?"

"No," I said quickly, although that wasn't the truth. "I was just curious if you knew of anyone who might have wanted to hurt her."

He fished his phone out of his pocket. "I never knew any of these people before I started this job a few weeks ago." He glanced at his phone and pushed off from the wall. He held up the device. "Gotta go. Duty calls."

I didn't know if he'd really received a text message summoning him to another part of the theater, but whether he'd told the truth or simply wanted to get away from me, our conversation was at an end.

"See you around," he said, and then he was off around the corner and out of sight.

I wandered back toward the stage, thinking over what I'd learned. Sasha couldn't vouch for Olivia's whereabouts during the entire concert. That meant the competition's coordinator was most likely without an alibi for at least part of the time after Pavlina left the audience.

Had Olivia purposely sent Sasha away so she'd have time to carry out a nefarious plan to murder Pavlina, or had she really just wanted some coffee?

If she had killed Pavlina, was jealousy the driving force behind the act?

I couldn't see what other motive she would have. When I'd overheard her arguing with Jeb, she'd sounded more contemptuous than jealous, but that didn't mean there was no envy lurking beneath the surface.

As for Sasha, did he have an opportunity to carry out the murder?

Possibly. He could have followed Pavlina to the women's washroom and killed her either before or after he fetched Olivia's coffee. Why he would do so wasn't so easy to figure out, though. He'd said he hadn't met any of the finalists before he started his job as Olivia's assistant. If that were true, his motive would have had to develop over the last few weeks.

It was possible that he'd set his sights on Pavlina and she'd rejected him, igniting deep rage inside of him. But that was nothing more than pure speculation, and making up stories in my head about all the possible suspects wasn't particularly constructive. If I wanted to help settle this matter and minimize any negative impact on the orchestra, I needed to work with facts and evidence. Unfortunately, I didn't have a lot of those, and that meant I needed to find a way to gather more.

For the moment, however, my only concerns needed to be of the musical variety. The rehearsal was about to resume and I didn't want to be late getting back to my seat. Setting my investigation aside for the time being, I returned to the stage and shifted my focus from murder to music.

Chapter Eleven

I DIDN'T HAVE a chance to gather more clues that night. By the time the rehearsal had ended, Olivia and Sasha had already departed from the theater, leaving me without an opportunity to attempt to question the competition's coordinator.

While driving home I thought over everything I'd learned so far, but only ended up more muddled than ever. Several people had both the opportunity and a motive to kill Pavlina, and my mental list of suspects was still too long to be of much help. Ethan was, in my view, the prime suspect at the moment, but I didn't have enough evidence to share my suspicions, nor did I have enough information to definitively rule out any of my other suspects.

I hoped that a good night's sleep would clear my mind and help me fit more puzzle pieces together, but the situation didn't seem any less jumbled when morning arrived. Breakfast and a hot shower did nothing to spark any helpful insights, so I set off for the grocery store no further ahead with my investigation.

As I pushed my cart up and down the store's aisles, I continued to mull over the circumstances of Pavlina's death, and something plucked at the strings in the far reaches of my memory, sounding a repeated note to get my attention. Try as I might, however, I couldn't figure out what my brain wanted to tell me.

Not for the first time, I had the distinct feeling that I'd forgotten or missed something, but what?

Stopping in the middle of the produce section, I tried my best to grasp at the elusive memory. Despite my efforts, it skittered away like a scrap of paper sent dancing down the street by a strong gust of wind.

Realizing that I was causing a grocery cart traffic jam, I grabbed a bunch of bananas and maneuvered my way toward the dairy products. Hopefully whatever it was that I couldn't remember wasn't lost to me forever. Even though I didn't know what it was that I'd forgotten—aside from the possibility that it might have something to do with Pavlina's body—I knew it was important, and I was frustrated with myself for failing to put my finger on it.

Frustration wasn't helpful, though. I knew that. Getting my head into even more of a muddle than it already was would only leave me less likely to pin down the fluttering, elusive memory that continued to taunt me from the depths of my mind.

Moving on from the dairy products, I added a box of granola bars and a package of green tea to my cart before making my way toward the cashier. Maybe talking things over with JT would help me see things more clearly. Or maybe he'd spot an angle to the case I'd missed entirely. If nothing else, sharing my tangled thoughts with my best friend would release some of the frustration I hadn't fully been able to quell.

There was also something else I wanted to talk to JT about. As much as he didn't want to believe that Cameron might have been involved in the theft of his equipment, I couldn't let the possibility drop. If Cameron had wronged JT, I was determined to find out about it. Whether I could convince JT to help me dig around in Cameron's life, I wasn't entirely sure, but I was going to give it a try.

Once I'd taken my groceries home and put them away, I gathered up my violin and everything else I'd need for the day before leaving my apartment again, this time setting off for JT's house.

Although the air had a cold bite to it, the sky was a brilliant shade of blue and the sun shone brightly. It only took a few minutes to drive from my apartment to the residential part of Dunbar, JT's neighborhood. Once I'd reached his street I found a place to park my car and fetched my bag and violin from behind the driver's seat. Crossing the road, I waved at Mrs. Tilley, JT's elderly next-door neighbor, as she swept off her front porch. She waved back and I headed up the concrete path to JT's house, thinking about how much I loved this part of the city.

The houses had character, the streets were lined with trees, and many of the residents kept nicely tended gardens. It wouldn't be long before the area looked great at night as well, with Christmas lights brightening up the houses and adding cheer to the cold, dark evenings. My neighborhood was nice too—and I paid the price for it with my monthly rent—but I hoped to one day live in a detached home rather than an apartment. Maybe that was a pipe dream, considering the crazy real estate prices in Vancouver, but having my own outdoor space would be nice. For now, however, it was enough that I got to spend plenty of time hanging out at JT's place, especially since he let me use his yard for gardening during the warmer months.

Climbing the steps to the porch, I fished around in my bag for my keys. I dug the keychain out of the depths of my tote, and then paused on the doorstep, listening. Piano music floated out to me from inside the house. There was nothing unusual about that, since JT often played his baby grand piano in the front living room, but this was music I'd never heard before, and it had my full attention. Unlocking the door as quietly as I could, I slipped inside the house and stopped to listen again. The beautiful melody surrounded me, leaving me barely aware of anything but the music. The notes rose and fell, the baseline adding depth and intensity to the rich and vibrant melody.

As I listened I wanted to smile and cry and float away all at the same time. But I did none of those things. Instead I remained rooted to the spot, entranced by the music, hardly breathing until the song wound down, slowing before settling on the final note. Only when the music had stopped completely did I move again.

Shutting the door, I set my violin and bag down in the foyer and stepped into the living room. Seated on the piano bench, JT turned at the sound of my footsteps. Finnegan jumped up from his spot on the floor near the piano and rushed toward me, his fluffy tail wagging.

"Morning," JT greeted with a smile.

"Morning," I returned as I crouched down to give Finnegan a hug. Once I'd straightened up again, I asked JT, "Was that one of your songs?"

"Yes. I just finished it up last night."

I crossed the room toward him and he shifted to the side to make room for me on the piano bench.

"I figured it must be new," I said as I sat down next to him. "It's not something I'd ever forget after hearing it."

"You like it?"

I caught the slightest hint of hesitation in his voice and realized that my opinion really mattered to him.

"Like it? I absolutely love it."

His shoulders lowered an inch, a sign that he'd been worried about my reaction.

"Seriously, JT." I wrapped my arms around him and gave him a quick squeeze. "It's incredible. In fact, it might be my favorite of all the songs you've ever composed, and that's saying something."

He smiled. "I'm glad."

"What's it called?"

As soon as I voiced the question, the front door opened.

"Your student?" JT guessed.

I glanced over my shoulder as Tricia, one of my adult students, stepped into the foyer.

"Yes. Hi, Tricia," I said, getting up from the bench. "I'll be there in a moment."

As Tricia disappeared into my studio, I wrapped my arms around JT's neck, giving him a hug from behind.

"I really love it, JT. I hope I'll get to hear it again."

"You will," he assured me.

I crossed the foyer to my studio while JT and Finnegan headed toward the back of the house. JT's latest composition had so thoroughly captured my attention that it wasn't until two hours and two students later that I remembered my plan to talk over the murder case with him. When I had a half-hour break between students, I wandered into the kitchen, hoping to find JT and Finnegan there. The room was empty. The door leading to the basement was open and the light in the stairwell was on, but I didn't descend the stairs. There was a good chance that JT was working in his studio, and I probably didn't have enough time to share all my thoughts with him before my next student showed up.

So instead of going in search of my best friend, I fixed myself a vanilla latte to drink with the granola bar I'd packed in my bag that morning. When my latte was ready, I perched on one of the stools at the breakfast bar, my phone on the granite countertop. Since I had a few minutes to kill, I decided to do a bit of research into Cameron's life. I wasn't sure what I was expecting to find—if anything—but I didn't want to leave any stone unturned. Maybe he had a history of committing thefts, or maybe he was known by everyone as a stand-up guy who could always be relied on. Whether the Internet would reveal any of that to me, I didn't know, but I was determined to find out.

Opening the Internet browser on my phone, I typed the name "Cameron Rask" into the search bar and scrolled through the results that popped up on the screen. Ten minutes later I'd finished the granola bar but I hadn't found anything useful online. While I'd found a couple of social media profiles belonging to the right Cameron, they provided nothing illuminating. I was about to give up when I clicked on a final search result. It took me to a short news article, and I sipped the last of my vanilla latte as I read the item.

When I reached the end of the short article, I set my cup on the countertop with a clunk, lost in thought. Apparently Cameron had been involved in a fistfight outside a bar eighteen months earlier. He'd been charged with assault as a result, although the article didn't mention whether the case had gone to trial or whether Cameron had received a conviction and sentence.

That information wasn't of great importance to me, however. I was most interested in the fact that he'd resorted to fisticuffs with another man to settle a dispute over a hockey game they'd watched at the bar. Okay, maybe he'd been influenced by alcohol at the time, but that didn't change the fact that the fight had happened. Was it an isolated incident for Cameron, or did he make a habit of settling disputes with violence?

If he did have violent tendencies, had I made a mistake by focusing on him solely in relation to the theft of JT's recording equipment? He was, after all, present at the theater on the night of Pavlina's death. Perhaps he should have had a spot on my suspect list for that crime as well.

I tugged on my left earlobe as I stared off into space, following that line of thought. I'd have to check with JT if there was any time during the second half of the concert when Cameron wasn't within his sight. If there was such a time, then Cameron could have had the opportunity to murder Pavlina.

But why the heck would he want to? As far as I knew, he'd never met Pavlina. But what if he had?

I recalled his behavior on the night in question and considered another possibility. I'd seen him in the midst of an urgent phone call, one he'd hastily ended as soon as he saw me approaching. He'd been just as jumpy about text messages he'd sent that evening too. So even if he'd never met Pavlina, could she have overheard something that made Cameron view her as a threat? Even if he'd simply thought she'd overheard something, that could have been enough to push him over the edge, if whatever it was that made him so jumpy was significant enough to drive him to murder.

If, if, if.

That was the problem. Too much supposition and not nearly enough facts.

Yes, Cameron was jumpy that night at the theater, but maybe

that was because he'd planned the theft ahead of time. Nervous behavior didn't automatically make him a murderer. Still, I couldn't completely rule out his possible involvement in the murder. Not yet, at least.

The first thing I needed to do was find out if he'd had the opportunity to kill Pavlina. If not, I could strike his name from my list of murder suspects, leaving him only on the list of suspects for the theft.

JT held the answer I needed, but seeking it out would have to wait. As I closed the browser on my phone, my next student entered the house through the front door and I got up to greet him. The next four hours would be spent teaching violin lessons, but after that I'd talk to JT and get the information I needed.

BY THE TIME I finished teaching my last lesson of the day and had eaten the sandwich I'd picked up at the grocery store that morning, JT was loading his borrowed and spare recording equipment into his truck. After washing down my dinner with a glass of water, I grabbed a couple of microphone stands from the basement and carried them outside. As JT loaded them into the back of his truck, I decided to bring up the subject of Cameron.

When I told him about the assault charge from eighteen months ago, JT gave me a suspicious, sidelong look.

"So?" he said. "Getting into a fistfight doesn't automatically make him a thief."

"I know that. But it does mean he's resorted to violence in the past."

JT shut the truck's tailgate, locking it before we headed back to the house for more equipment. "What does violence have to do with anything?"

"Murder is a violent crime."

JT halted at the base of the porch steps. "Hold on. Now you're accusing Cameron of murder?"

Finnegan barked at us from where he sat next to the front door, trying to hurry us along.

"I'm not accusing him of anything." I started up the steps, much to Finnegan's joy, and JT followed a second later. "I'm just saying that I can't yet rule him out."

"That's insane, Dori. It's bad enough to suspect him of stealing. What possible reason would he have to kill someone he didn't know?"

I stepped into the house and waited for JT to join me in the foyer. "First of all, we don't know for certain that he didn't know Pavlina."

JT opened his mouth to cut in, but I hurried on before he could stop me.

"Second of all, I can think of a possible motive, but that doesn't matter if he didn't have an opportunity to commit the crime."

JT shut the front door, and I could tell he was mulling over what I'd said. Finnegan sat down at his feet and looked up at him expectantly, his tail thumping against the hardwood floor.

"The murder happened during the second half of the concert?" JT checked.

"Yes."

Dismay flickered in his eyes and I pounced on its significance. "He wasn't with you the entire time, was he?"

Stepping around Finnegan, JT strode off down the hallway. Finn and I scurried after him.

"JT . . ."

He yanked open the basement door. "Just because I can't give him an alibi for the entire time, that doesn't mean he killed the girl."

"Of course it doesn't. But it does leave him on the suspect list."

"Your suspect list." JT descended the stairs to the basement. "The police don't view him as a suspect, do they?"

"I have no idea." As I followed him, I recalled the detectives' interest in Elena and her cousin, and their attempt to follow that line of investigation. "But if they haven't questioned him since that night, then probably not."

"Likely for good reason."

"Look," I said when we reached the bottom of the stairs, "maybe Cameron had nothing to do with the murder, but he was acting jumpy that night."

"I don't remember him acting jumpy." JT grabbed a couple of microphones and tucked his laptop under his arm.

"Is that everything?" I asked.

"Should be." He headed for the stairs again, pausing to let Finnegan dash up ahead of him.

"I remember him acting jumpy," I said as we made our way back up to the kitchen.

"Are you sure you weren't imagining things?"

"Positive."

JT stopped in the middle of the kitchen and let out a heavy sigh. "Okay, fine. But even if he was acting jumpy, that could mean anything."

"Sure it could, including the possibility that he planned the theft ahead of time—probably with someone's help—and was nervous about getting caught."

"Cameron's not a killer, Dori."

"Maybe not," I conceded. "But even you think he's a thief."

He clearly wanted to deny it, but although the muscles in his jaw moved, he said nothing.

"I don't want him to be guilty, JT. But I can't ignore the possibility that he is, especially when it comes to the theft."

"But we can't prove it. We can't prove anything."

"Not yet," I admitted.

"Then it's better left alone. My equipment's probably long gone and the police will catch the killer. We should leave it at that."

"Should, maybe," I said. "But you know me better than that."

"Yes," he said with another sigh. "Yes, I do."

Chapter Twelve

AFTER I'D CHANGED into my black concert clothes and had said goodbye to Finnegan, I set off in my car for the theater, JT right behind me in his truck. Once we'd both parked in the theater's lot, JT assured me that he didn't need help moving his equipment inside, so I headed straight for the musicians' lounge. Since I had some time to spare, I tucked my violin away in my locker and looked around for someone to chat with. I spotted Dongmei on one of the couches, her eyes darting here and there, her fingers picking at the nails on her opposite hand.

When I claimed the seat next to her, she gave me a wavering smile.

"Nervous?" I asked, even though the answer was obvious.

"Nervous. Excited. Terrified." She swallowed. "What if everyone hates my piece?"

"No one's going to hate it," I assured her.

My words seemed to bounce off of her without reaching her ears.

"What if everyone thinks I'm a terrible composer?"

"Dongmei," I said firmly, "you didn't get to be a finalist in this competition by being a terrible composer."

She drew in a deep breath and let it out slowly. "You're right. It's just . . . This is the first time such a large crowd will hear one of my works."

"And they're going to love it. You'll see."

Another tremulous smile appeared on her face for half a second. "I hope you're right." She closed her eyes briefly and took another deep breath. "I need to think about something else. Have you heard anything new about the police investigation?"

"Not much."

"Who do you think did it?"

"It could have been one of a number of people." I lowered my voice before continuing. "But I'm more than a little suspicious of Ethan."

"Me too." She glanced around before adding in a hushed voice, "You'd think he and Pavlina would have bonded over what happened in the past, but instead it only seemed to divide them."

"What did happen?" I asked, my curiosity perking up.

"Remember how I told you that the first time I met Pavlina was at a music and composition retreat in Banff a few years ago?"

I nodded.

"Ethan and another girl, Tiffany Alphonse, were also on the trip. All three of them were longtime friends. On the last morning of the retreat, Tiffany was found in a nearby lake. She'd drowned."

"That's terrible."

"It really was. But then things got even worse. Her death was ruled accidental—apparently she'd been drunk—but Pavlina, Tiffany, and Ethan had all been up for a prestigious scholarship that was going to be awarded at the end of the retreat. Tiffany wasn't much of a drinker and Ethan accused Pavlina of getting her drunk on purpose so she'd look bad to the scholarship committee. Pavlina accused him of the same thing."

"Who won the scholarship in the end?"

"Pavlina."

No doubt that had given Ethan's dislike of Pavlina a firm footing to build upon.

"So they've hated each other ever since?" I said.

"Yes. At first I thought it was just the shock of Tiffany's death that made them accuse each other of getting her drunk, and I figured maybe they'd get over it. But they never did. Of course, there was other stress after Tiffany's death, so that probably didn't help."

"Other stress?"

"I heard that Pavlina and Ethan were both harassed by Tiffany's brother, Alexander, for a while."

I absorbed that information. "He thought both of them got her drunk on purpose?"

"Maybe. He claimed that Tiffany was so terrified of water that she never would have gone in the lake voluntarily. I guess he thought someone got her drunk to make it easier to get her in the water and drown her. The rumor was that he accused both Ethan and Pavlina of murdering Tiffany because they thought she was their toughest competition for the scholarship. But for that to make sense, I guess maybe he thought one or the other was responsible, but didn't know which so he tried pointing the finger at both of them."

"And nothing came of that?" I asked, wondering if killing Pavlina wasn't the first time Ethan had committed murder, if indeed he had killed her.

"I don't think so. I'm pretty sure they both had alibis for that night. As far as I know, the police always considered Tiffany's death an accident. I don't think that ever changed. All I know for certain is that Pavlina and Ethan ended up despising each other."

That had been more than evident, and their animosity toward each other made more sense now. But did the past have anything to do with recent events? Had Ethan doubted Pavlina's alibi and the official ruling on Tiffany's death? By finding themselves in close competition again, had their acrimony boiled over, driving Ethan to seek delayed revenge for Tiffany's death while also eliminating his fiercest competition?

It was something to consider, and it strengthened his motive. He'd already been my prime suspect, but now I figured he deserved to have his name underlined and highlighted on the suspect list. While Cameron was still my number one suspect in relation to the theft, it seemed more likely now that he wasn't the killer.

"Do you think the police know about any of this?" I asked Dongmei.

"I told them about it the other night when they talked to me, but they didn't seem all that interested." She considered her words for a moment. "Well, Detective Chowdhury took notes, so at least he was paying attention, but the big one—what's his name?"

"Detective Van den Broek," I supplied.

"Right. He didn't seem all that interested in anything I said. He just wanted to know if I had a reason to want Pavlina dead." She resumed picking at her fingernails, her anxiety evident on her face again.

I rested a hand on her arm. "I wouldn't worry about that. You have an alibi, remember."

She switched to rubbing her cuticles instead of picking at them.

"And Detective Van den Broek was the same with me interestwise. I hope he's more keen on solving the case than he lets on, because he didn't seem to care one whit about anything I told him."

"I hope so too," Dongmei said. "If they don't find the killer . . . That would be horrible. I don't want it to be someone like Ethan, someone I know, but I'd rather he be arrested if he's guilty than have him in our midst. I mean, if he's killed once, what's to stop him from killing again?"

That was a valid concern.

I searched the room, wondering if Ethan was present. He wasn't, but a shiver still traveled up my spine. If he was determined to win this competition, and if he was as uncertain about the outcome as I believed him to be, were the other finalists in danger?

"Dongmei," I said in little more than a whisper, "I think you should make sure you're never alone here in the theater."

Her eyes widened. "Do you think Ethan might want to kill me?"

"If he's desperate enough to win this competition, who knows what he might do. I think you and Sherwin should both be careful."

"I'll tell Sherwin," she said. "But, Midori, I'm terrified."

That was clearly written on her face, and I realized I'd only added to her jitters, but I wanted her to be on alert.

"Just stick close to other people," I advised. "Then you'll be fine."

I hoped that was true. But the only way to truly ensure Dongmei's safety was to find definitive evidence against Ethan—or whoever the killer was—so the police could lock him away.

"I need to talk to the maestro," I said as I got up from the couch.

Dongmei grabbed my arm, fear practically radiating off of her. "Don't leave me alone."

"You're not alone." I gestured at all the musicians gathered in the lounge. "You've got all these people with you. And I'll be back soon."

She let go of my arm with reluctance and I gave her what I hoped was a confident, reassuring smile.

"Everything will be okay," I said.

As I left the lounge, I fervently hoped those words wouldn't come back to haunt me.

I DIDN'T FIND Hans out on the stage where JT had already set up the microphones, nor did I find him in the back hallways. Knowing that likely meant he was in his second-floor office, I headed up the carpeted stairway. At the top of the stairs I turned left, my destination the third door down. I didn't end up going straight to Hans's office, however, because the first room I passed drew my attention and brought me to a stop.

The door stood open, revealing a room with a long table surrounded by numerous chairs. I knew it was the room the symphony's board of directors used for meetings but, according to a sign taped to the door, it was currently being used as a lounge for the judges. A platter of fresh fruit sat in the middle of the table, with plates of other finger foods set out around it. Although I wouldn't have minded a snack, the food wasn't what caught my attention.

The only person in the room was Ethan. Since he wasn't a judge, his presence piqued my curiosity, especially since he was leaning over one corner of the table, clicking sounds emanating from his general location. When he turned his body a few degrees to the left, I realized that the clicking was coming from his phone as he snapped pictures of another cell phone lying on the tabletop. That sent my curiosity skyrocketing.

He took a step back and I hurried out of view, resuming my

journey down the hallway. Before I reached the door to Hans's office, I glanced over my shoulder. Ethan was on his way out of the judges' lounge, slipping his phone into his pocket. Pausing, he looked up and down the hallway and spotted me. I smiled at him, hoping I appeared completely natural and unsuspicious, but he only glowered in my direction before disappearing down the stairway. Once he was gone, a trickle of relief washed through me. Being in close proximity to someone I suspected of murder wasn't exactly my idea of fun, especially when no one else was in sight.

Alone in the hallway now, my eyes drifted back to the open door of the judges' lounge. Tugging on my left earlobe, I wondered if I dared to do a little snooping. It only took me a second or two to decide.

As quietly as I could, I hastened back to the judges' lounge and slipped inside. Tiny sparks of excitement ran up my spine when I saw that the phone Ethan had been snapping pictures of still sat on the table. After a quick glance over my shoulder told me I was still alone, I picked up the device and brought the screen to life.

There was no immediate indication of who owned the phone so I accessed the photos and scrolled through them. It only took a few pictures for me to conclude that the device belonged to Jeb Hartson. The selfies were a dead giveaway. Somehow it didn't surprise me that he regularly took photos of himself. It also didn't surprise me that Pavlina appeared in some of the photos, sometimes on her own and other times with Jeb, but that was only because I'd already known about their relationship.

After scrolling past a few photos of Pavlina that could only be described as suggestive, I paused, wondering if the pictures were what had grabbed Ethan's interest.

It was very possible.

But if he'd snapped pictures of these photos, why had he done so? Not for any good reason, that was for sure. Since Pavlina was already dead, he couldn't use them to get her ousted from the competition, but maybe he was hoping to use them against Jeb. Maybe he was planning to blackmail the judge to secure his vote.

That thought sent an icy chill through me. If he really was so devious, then that only made him an even better murder suspect. While being a blackmailer—if he really was one—didn't automatically make Ethan a murderer, it did say a lot about his character and the level he was willing to sink to in order to improve his chances in the competition.

The sound of approaching footsteps reached my ears and I spun around, my heartbeat upping its tempo. If Ethan was returning and he caught me snooping into what he'd been doing earlier, my life could be in danger. I hurriedly returned the cell phone to the table, but a shadow loomed in the doorway while my fingers still touched the device.

"What are you doing?"

The demanding voice didn't belong to Ethan, but that didn't calm my racing heart.

Jeb stood a foot or two inside the room, his face devoid of its usual self-assured smile. His brown eyes drilled into me and I struggled to find my voice.

"Nothing," I managed to say in response to his question. "I noticed that someone had left their cell phone behind and I was trying to figure out who it belonged to."

Jeb stepped forward and snatched the phone off the table. "It's mine. Did you mess with it?" His phony, drawling accent had disappeared completely.

"No," I lied as convincingly as I could. "I'd only picked it up when you arrived."

I held my breath, hoping he would believe me.

"That had better be the truth." He took a step closer to me and I had to force myself not to lean back. "I wouldn't advise sticking your nose where it doesn't belong."

I met his furious gaze with a steady one of my own, but a high-pitched note of alarm rang in my head and I couldn't think clearly enough to come up with a retort.

"Everything all right here?"

Some of my tension whooshed out of me as Harold Dempsey stepped into the room, his eyes going from my face to Jeb's.

Two seconds ticked by before Jeb relaxed his stance and produced his typical grin.

"Everything's just fine," he said, his drawl back in full force. "This young lady was returning my misplaced phone to me. Thank you for that," he said to me.

Although his words were courteous, a dangerous glint showed in his eyes when he focused on me.

"You're welcome," I managed to say, even though every one of my nerves was practically screaming with tension.

I edged around Jeb, and Harold stepped aside to clear my path to the door. With a nod at Harold, I left the room as calmly as I could. When I was out of sight in the hallway, my muscles went weak with relief. Getting a glimpse of Jeb's dark side had alarmed me. I didn't want to think about what might have happened if he'd caught me in the act of studying the photos on his phone. The situation had been tense enough already, and I was immensely grateful for the fact that Harold had arrived on the scene when he did. Although I'd received only harsh words and angry glares from Jeb, the encounter had left me certain that he was capable of much more.

How much more was something I had no desire to find out from personal experience, but the question played over and over again in my head like a broken record. Ethan currently occupied the top spot on my list of suspects, but Jeb's name was also on that list, and I now felt certain that he was fully capable of committing murder.

Chapter Thirteen

IT WASN'T UNTIL I was halfway down the stairs that I realized I'd forgotten to stop by Hans's office. I continued down to the first floor anyway, deciding to speak with Hans another time. My nerves were too frazzled to go anywhere near the judges' lounge, which I'd have to pass to reach the maestro's office. On top of that, my thoughts were too scattered to hold a coherent conversation. If Hans knew anything new about the police investigation, I could find out about that later. For the moment, I needed time to recover from my unsettling confrontation with Jeb, to calm down enough so I could focus on the concert.

I managed to avoid any conversations beyond brief exchanges of greetings when I returned to the musicians' lounge. Not wanting to linger, I retrieved my instrument and folder of music and made my way to the stage. Once I was seated in my usual spot, my shoulders relaxed and the whirlwind of thoughts in my head lost some of its vigor. I took comfort in the familiar surroundings, the stage like a second home to me.

With every passing minute more of my fellow musicians joined me on the stage, and their presence comforted me further. I knew I was safe here among my colleagues, safe from Jeb and Ethan and anyone else who might have a dangerous dark side. I hoped Dongmei was as safe as I was, but I hadn't seen her in the lounge when I fetched my violin from my locker. Ethan hadn't been in the lounge either, and when I realized that, a flash of panic set my heart beating at a wild tempo once again. But then Olivia appeared in the wings with both Ethan and Dongmei at her side, Sasha hovering behind her as usual.

Relief edged out my panic and I drew in a deep breath, letting it out slowly as I rid myself of more of my remaining anxiety.

"What's wrong?" Mikayla asked as she sat down in the seat next to me.

"Nothing." I tried my best to smile as I set out the sheet music for Ethan's symphony.

When I glanced Mikayla's way, she was still watching me, one eyebrow raised skeptically.

I set my bow on the music stand's ledge, realizing I'd need to provide her with some sort of explanation. "I guess I'm a bit on edge. It's hard to relax when I suspect people around me of murder."

"Who do you suspect, exactly?" she asked, her skepticism morphing into curiosity.

"Ethan and Jeb, for starters," I said quietly so no one else around us could hear.

Both of Mikayla's eyebrows shot up this time. "Ethan I can see, since Pavlina was his competition and they obviously didn't like each other, but Jeb Hartson?"

"It's a bit of a long story."

She waited expectantly, but almost the entire orchestra was

now present on the stage and we were only moments from the start of the concert.

"Later," I whispered as I picked up my bow.

She had no choice but to agree as a hush fell over the stage.

Over the next couple of hours, the last remnants of my anxiety trickled away. I became completely absorbed in the finalists' compositions, in the way the music from all the various instruments wove together to create something greater, something beautiful. Dongmei's piece in particular drew me into its depths and caught me in its magic.

The audience must have enjoyed the concert as much as I did. When it was over, they stood and applauded enthusiastically. I held my breath for a tense moment before Ethan and Dongmei were to appear on stage, but they emerged from the wings together a second later, much to my relief. The last thing we needed was to lose another finalist. Although I could tell that Dongmei was a bit nervous about being on stage in front of such a large audience, she still seemed to enjoy the moment, beaming as the audience once again applauded for her and Ethan.

Once we'd all left the stage and had returned to the musicians' lounge, I gave Dongmei a big hug.

"I hope you win," I whispered so only she would hear.

She smiled at me. "Thank you, Midori. It's been nice having you here. I'm less anxious when there's a friendly face nearby."

I gave her another hug and she headed off to meet her family in the theater's lobby. After a few minutes spent chatting with my colleagues, I pulled on my coat and gloves and left the theater. Out in the parking lot, JT was loading the last of the recording equipment—all accounted for this time—into his truck. I said a quick goodbye to him and set off for home.

During the drive my thoughts slowly shifted from the successful concert to the mystery of Pavlina's murder. More than ever I
believed that Ethan's character left plenty to be desired and that he
was fully capable of devious behavior, including murder. Even so,
I couldn't forget the frightening glimpse I'd caught of Jeb's dark
side when he'd confronted me in the judges' lounge. The mere
memory caused a shudder to run through my body, and my grip
tightened on the steering wheel. His fierce reaction to finding me
with his phone could have stemmed from nothing more than the
fact that he was desperate to keep his relationship with Pavlina
a secret. But knowing that a much darker part of his personality lurked beneath his phony accent and self-assured attitude only
made the phone conversation I'd overheard seem more sinister.

He'd said that something was all taken care of and that no one
suspected a thing. Of course, if he'd referred to killing Pavlina,
that meant someone else knew he'd done the terrible deed. Who
would he share that information with? Another lover? One who'd
known about Pavlina and wanted her permanently out of the picture?

The photos on Jeb's phone hadn't indicated that there was another woman in his life, but perhaps I simply hadn't scrolled back
far enough. I silently cursed the fact that I hadn't had a chance to
delve into his text messages. They could have held valuable clues.

Stopping at a red light, I gave my head a shake. Jeb and Ethan
both seemed so sinister and guilty, but I still couldn't prove that
either of them had killed Pavlina. And I didn't know enough to
discount any of my other suspects. Olivia, Sasha, Cameron, and
Elena's cousin Igor all needed more investigating.

That reminded me of the fact that I hadn't yet achieved what
Hans had hoped I would. As long as Igor was still a suspect, and as

long as nothing came to light to prove that Elena wasn't in cahoots with him, the PGP was at risk of suffering from bad publicity and perhaps even the loss—temporarily or permanently—of our concertmaster.

As I parked my car in the lot beneath my apartment building, I decided to come up with a plan in the morning, a plan that would help me make more sense of all the clues I'd gathered, that would allow me to uncover more information so I could finally put some pieces of the puzzle together and get at least a glimpse of the picture that would emerge.

WHILE I WOULD have liked to laze around in bed the next morning, a dozen different thoughts chimed in my head as soon as I was awake, making relaxation impossible. With a sigh, I threw back the covers and hurried through my chilly apartment to the shower. While I shampooed my hair, I decided I'd check in with JT. The day before we'd only talked about Cameron and his potential involvement in the crimes, and I still wanted to share my thoughts on the other suspects with my friend. Hopefully he wouldn't be too busy for me to hang out with him, but I'd find out soon enough.

As I rinsed the shampoo out of my hair, I hummed a few bars of music. It was only as I shut off the water and wrapped myself in a towel that I realized I was humming the melody of JT's latest composition. I couldn't wait to hear him play the song on the piano again, and I didn't doubt that it would take my breath away just as it had the first time I'd heard it. I loved all of JT's music, but that song really was the most amazing one I'd ever heard him play.

Whenever I thought of JT's successes I practically beamed with pride. He was such a talented musician and composer, and I was so happy that he was doing well in his career. *Absolute Zero*, the science fiction television show he composed music for, had been on the air for over two months now, and the ratings so far had been strong. If the show got renewed for a second season, that would be great for JT. As the show gained more popularity, more of its fans would become aware of JT's music and remember his name. That could only bode well for his future.

As soon as I was dressed, I sent him a quick text message to see if I could hang out at his place that morning. While I waited for a reply, I dried my hair and put on some makeup. I was in the midst of applying eye shadow when my thoughts took a familiar turn. Several weeks ago I'd realized I was in love with my best friend, and had been for a while. Since then I'd fought a near-constant battle with my feelings. As much as I wanted to keep my love for him a secret in order to protect our friendship, that had become more and more difficult as the weeks passed.

At times I thought I would burst from the intensity of my emotions, and more than once I'd come close to telling him how I felt. But each time fear silenced my voice. In the beginning I'd convinced myself that keeping quiet was for the best, but now I wasn't quite so sure. Despite my uncertainty, I continued to hide behind my fear. How long I could keep doing that, I didn't know, but as I finished applying my makeup, I forced myself to focus on something else.

I mulled over my list of murder suspects as I ate a quick breakfast, but my thoughts seemed to go around in circles and I didn't make any progress. No brilliant insights popped into my head while I brushed my teeth either. I did, however, receive a reply to the text message I'd sent JT, and that helped to temper my burgeoning frustration.

Of course you can come over, his message read. *The guys and I have one last band practice this afternoon, but I'm free this morning.*

I'm on my way, I wrote back. *See you soon.*

Once I'd pulled on my coat, hat, and gloves, I grabbed my purse and was on my way. In less than ten minutes I'd arrived at JT's place. Locking up my car, I hurried through the chilly, gray morning and up to the front porch. The warmth of the house enveloped me as soon as I stepped into the foyer, and I gladly shut the door against the cold outside air. Finnegan had heard my entry and came barreling down the hall toward me. Smiling, I crouched down and gave him a big hug.

"Morning, Finnie boy. Did you miss me?"

He answered by giving me a sloppy kiss on the cheek.

"I'll take that as a yes," I said as I stood up.

JT came down the hallway toward me. "We always miss you when you're not here."

My heart did a giddy, flip-flopping dance at JT's words. He helped me out of my coat and then tucked a strand of hair behind my ear. His hand lingered at the side of my face and his eyes met mine. My heart flip-flopped again. I couldn't breathe. His fingers brushed against my cheek, but then he dropped his hand, breaking the spell.

"Come on," he said as he hung my coat in the foyer closet. "You look like you could use a hot drink and I just brewed some fresh coffee."

He headed for the kitchen, Finnegan trotting after him, but I remained frozen to the spot. My heart had settled back into its normal rhythm, but I was distracted by a hum of electric energy running through me. Drawing in a sharp breath, I shook myself out of my daze.

Had I imagine what had passed between us? Was I seeing what I wanted to see rather than what was really there?

I gave myself another mental shake as I kicked off my boots. I didn't know the answer to my questions and I wasn't entirely sure that I wanted to.

Doing my best to push all thoughts of what had happened—or hadn't happened—out of my mind, I followed my best friend and his dog to the kitchen. JT had already poured hot coffee into mugs and he handed one to me, nudging the sugar bowl across the granite countertop toward me.

"Thanks," I said, finally getting my tongue to work.

I added sugar to my coffee and followed it up with some milk from the fridge, keeping my eyes on my drink as I stirred it.

"The concert seemed to go well last night," JT said once he'd taken a sip of his own coffee.

"It did," I agreed.

"Especially since there weren't any more dead bodies," he added.

"You can say that again."

I wandered toward the large kitchen window, gazing out into the backyard where everything was encrusted with sparkling white frost. Although JT had given me the perfect opening to talk about everyone I suspected of killing Pavlina, my current thoughts were out of tune with my intended focus. As much as I tried to shake it off, the look we'd shared minutes earlier still had me distracted. It was like I was standing at the edge of a cliff, trying to decide if I should throw caution to the wind and leap into the unknown. A sense of reckless courage washed over me and I gripped my coffee mug with both hands, ready to turn around and confess to JT how I felt about him.

"What's on your mind?"

At the sound of his voice I turned around as planned, but I couldn't coax out the words I needed for my confession. I took a sip of coffee to buy myself some time. It nearly burned my tongue, and that small shock was enough to jolt me back to my senses.

I couldn't tell him. Not yet. It wasn't the right time.

It will never be the right time, a voice said in my head. *That's just an excuse.*

That was true, but I chose to ignore the voice anyway.

"Pavlina's murder," I said in response to JT's question. It wasn't all that far from the truth.

"The police haven't arrested anyone yet?"

"I don't think so." I left the window to lean against the counter. "I'm pretty sure I would have heard about it if they had."

"Aside from Cameron, who do you suspect?"

With my mug halfway to my mouth, I paused. "You really want to know?"

"Sure. Why wouldn't I?"

"Because you usually want me to leave these things to the police."

"That would be best, but I know by now that you're as likely to do that as I am to win the lotto."

"You never buy lotto tickets," I pointed out.

"Exactly." He grinned. "Come one, let's go to the living room and you can tell me all about your suspicions."

Pleased that he was willing to listen, I carried my mug to the front of the house and set it on the coffee table before getting comfortable on the couch. When JT was sitting next to me and Finnegan was curled up in front of the unlit fireplace, I explained who was on my suspect list—aside from Cameron—and why. It took several minutes to go through everything, but JT didn't seem the least bit bored. On the contrary, he listened carefully to everything I said.

I wrapped up by telling him about what had occurred in the judges' lounge the night before. When I finished, JT's forehead was creased with concern.

"I don't like the sound of this Jeb Hartson," he said. "Which judge is he?"

"The one who thinks he's a cowboy."

"Ah." He didn't seem impressed. "Yeah, I've seen him around the theater."

"The thing is, Ethan still seems like a better suspect to me. But I don't trust Jeb."

"I think you're right not to. I don't think you should trust either of them. Please tell me you'll stay away from them from now on."

"That might be difficult on Tuesday since we'll all be at the theater, but after that I probably won't see them again, at least not anytime soon."

"Tuesday's the night when they announce the winner?"

"Yes, after a concert that will include highlights from each of the finalists' pieces."

I wondered briefly if we'd still play the excerpt from Pavlina's composition. I hoped so. It would be a good tribute to her.

"Still, try not to find yourself alone with either of those guys, okay?"

His request was serious, and his concern for my well-being triggered a welling of happiness inside of me, as it always did.

I gave his hand a squeeze. "Believe me, I'll do my best. I have no desire for any one-on-one time with Jeb or Ethan." After releasing JT's hand, I took a sip of my coffee, thinking. "I feel like I'm getting nowhere. I need to find out more about Igor, Elena's cousin."

"If Clausen wants Elena's name cleared, why doesn't he do something about it himself?"

"Maybe he knows I'm good at sleuthing."

"Maybe he just wants an excuse to spend time with you."

I rolled my eyes. "Hardly."

"Are you sure about that?"

"If that's his motive—which I highly doubt—he hasn't exactly been successful, has he? I spoke to him alone in his office for about five seconds." I hurried on before JT could voice any further suspicion. "Nope. For him this is about Elena and the orchestra. Definitely not me." The doubt hadn't left JT's face so I nudged his arm with my elbow. "Forget about Hans. There are so many other things to focus on."

"Like donuts."

"Donuts?" I echoed, confused by the sudden change of topic.

"Chocolate-covered donuts filled with whipped cream, to be exact." JT got up from the couch and held out a hand to me. When I took it, he pulled me to my feet and explained, "You can't solve a crime on an empty stomach."

"I did have breakfast this morning."

"So you're saying you don't want a donut?"

"Would I ever say that I don't want a donut?"

"That's what I thought."

He retrieved my coat from the foyer closet and helped me into it while Finnegan bounced around us in excitement. When we were all bundled up and Finnegan's leash was clipped to his collar, we set off for the nearest bakery. As we walked along the sidewalk, JT asked a few questions about my suspects. Tucking my arm through his, I provided him with further details, pleased to have his company and happy that he was interested in the mystery that occupied so much of my mind of late.

Chapter Fourteen

"WHO DO YOU think killed Pavlina?" I asked once we'd had our fill of chocolate-covered donuts and had left the bakery.

"It sounds like it could have been any one of a number of people," JT said as we walked in the direction of his house, Finnegan trotting along next to us.

"That's the problem."

"I think you need to find out more about the competition's co-ordinator and her assistant," JT said.

"Olivia and Sasha. Yes, they both had an opportunity to commit the murder." I thought things over for a minute as we walked on. "I can probably do some more digging into those two the next time I'm at the theater. Somebody must know something about them."

"But you'll be careful about getting that information, right?" JT checked.

"Aren't I always careful?"

He shot me a sidelong look. "Do you really want me to answer that question?"

"Maybe not," I said, recalling some of my past sleuthing adventures—or misadventures, as some might call them. "But yes, I'll be careful."

"Good."

We were momentarily distracted when Finnegan attempted to take off after a squirrel, prevented from doing so by his leash, much to his dismay. Once the squirrel had disappeared up a tree and Finnegan had given up on the possibility of making a tasty snack out of the critter, we crossed the street and passed a few more houses before arriving at JT's place.

Only minutes after getting back to the house, JT's bandmates showed up for their final practice before their gig that night. I decided to stick around for a while and listen in on their practice, giving feedback whenever the guys asked me for some. Cameron didn't seem thrilled to see me when he first arrived, but when I didn't try to interrogate him, he relaxed and got caught up in the rehearsal.

As I listened to the guys practicing, I realized I hadn't been to one of their performances in recent months. Maybe it was time to change that.

Lounging in a beanbag chair with Finnegan curled up at my feet, I sent a text message to Mikayla, asking if she and her boyfriend, bassoonist Dave Cyders, were interested in going to the pub where JT and his band would be playing that night. Before the practice ended, Mikayla wrote back in the affirmative, and we arranged to meet at the downtown pub at eight o'clock that night.

When the guys had finished playing their last song, I filled JT in on my plans.

"Do you want to catch a ride with me?" he offered. "That would be one less parking space needed."

"Good point," I said, knowing how difficult it could be to find a place to park in that part of the city. "Sure, thanks. I'm going to run a few errands now, but I can meet you back here later."

"Or I could pick you up at your place on the way. Whatever works."

In the end we decided that JT would stop at my apartment on his way to the pub and pick me up there. With that settled, I followed Cameron, Hamish, and Rafael out the door, intending to stop at the bank and the library before heading home.

As I climbed into my car and shut the door, my eyes drifted across the street to where Cameron stood outside his beat-up gray van. He was talking to someone on his phone, gesturing as he did so. Judging by his body language and what I could see of his face, he wasn't pleased by the conversation. Seconds later he said one last terse word and ended the call. Shoving the phone into his pocket, he jumped in his van and slammed the door. He revved the engine and pulled away from the curb, almost squealing the tires in his haste.

What had him so worked up?

Maybe I could find out.

Starting up my car, I set off after Cameron.

Okay, so following him didn't mean I'd necessarily find out what he was worked up about, but I wanted to know more about him anyway. His behavior on the night of the equipment theft had been suspicious and jumpy, and now he was agitated. There was a chance there was a connection—albeit a slim chance—and I wanted to know where he was in such a hurry to go.

JT probably would have thought I was nuts for following his bandmate—even though he too was suspicious of Cameron—but he didn't need to know what I was up to.

Tossing aside my plan of running errands, I turned right onto Dunbar Street a few seconds after Cameron did. I let one car get between us so he wouldn't be so likely to notice me behind him. By the time we'd both turned left onto Forty-first Avenue, two more cars had come between us.

Although I didn't want Cameron to take notice of my blue MINI Cooper, I also didn't want to lose sight of him. I tried my best to not let any more vehicles sneak between us, always keeping an eye on Cameron's gray van while I watched the traffic around me. Two streets later the car directly in front of me turned right and I shortened the gap between me and my quarry. From there on we traveled at a relatively steady pace, still with two cars between us.

After twenty minutes of driving I began to question the wisdom of my plan. I didn't know where Cameron lived and it was possible that his home was outside of the city, maybe in a suburb like Burnaby or Surrey. If that was the case, and all he was doing was heading home, I was in all likelihood going to waste my entire Saturday afternoon by tailing him without result.

As those thoughts passed through my head, Cameron turned left onto a quieter street. I had to wait for three cars to pass through the intersection before I could safely follow him, and when I turned onto the side street I thought I'd lost him. The only cars in sight were parked at the curb, and none of them were Cameron's van. But when I paused at a four-way stop, I caught sight of his car off to my right. Turning in that direction, I drove slowly, hanging back, worried that he would recognize my car right away if he saw it in his rearview mirror.

The neighborhood we were in now was home to low-rise apartment buildings, most of which were several decades old and not in the best condition. After driving another two blocks, Cameron came to a stop in front of a four-story building that was more gray than white thanks to a buildup of grime on the exterior. As he parked, I pulled up to the curb well back from his car, leaving several vehicles parked between us.

I shut off my car's engine and sat waiting, watching to see what Cameron would do next. Seconds later he got out of his car and approached the graying building. He opened the front door without the use of a key or requesting someone to buzz him in, and he quickly disappeared inside. Grabbing my purse from the passenger seat, I hurried out of my car and jogged over to the apartment building. I approached the front door cautiously, in case Cameron had lingered in the lobby. When I reached the door and peered through the window to the left of it, I saw nobody inside. Moving quietly, I opened the door and slipped through it.

Pausing in the lobby, I listened for any voices or footsteps on the stairway. Hearing nothing, I wondered what I should do next. If this was where Cameron lived, he might not reappear until it was time for him to head for the pub for the band's gig that night. The same could be true if he'd come here to visit someone. I realized then how silly it was for me to have expected to learn something by following him. Most likely the best idea was to go straight back to my car and run my errands as originally planned.

Despite what the practical part of my brain was telling me, I wasn't quite ready to give up. Fishing my phone out of my purse, I took off my gloves so I could tap out a text message.

Where does Cameron live?

I sent the message to JT and then shifted my weight from foot to foot, impatient. After a minute or two had ticked by, I had almost resigned myself to the fact that JT was too busy to respond.

But as I was about to return my phone to my purse, it buzzed in my hand.

Why? JT had texted back.

I'm just curious, I replied.

Yeah, right. Seriously, why?

I bit down on my lower lip, wondering how to answer that.

Long story, I wrote. *But it could be important. Please tell me.*

After sending that message, I waited, staring at the screen of my phone. A creaking sound startled me, and my eyes jumped from my phone to dart around the lobby.

Was Cameron about to return?

I strained my ears, ready to make a hasty retreat if someone was indeed approaching, but I heard no further sounds. My phone buzzed again, distracting me.

Somewhere on East Eighth Avenue, JT's message read. *I'm not sure where exactly.*

Despite the lack of detail, his answer told me what I needed to know. I wasn't anywhere near Eighth Avenue, so this definitely wasn't Cameron's apartment building. If a friend or acquaintance of his lived here, was his agitated phone call related to his visit?

I'd probably never know, but since I'd come all this way I decided to take a quick look around the building. If Cameron reappeared sometime in the near future, maybe I could follow him to another destination, or maybe he'd be in interesting company, giving me some insight into his life that I currently lacked.

I left the lobby for the main-floor hallway, peering along it in both directions. The place seemed deserted, no voices or other sounds emanating from behind the closed doors of the units. My phone continued to buzz in my hand and with a sigh I stopped and read JT's latest message.

What are you up to? And don't tell me nothing because I know that's not true!

Just trying to find out a bit more about Cameron, I wrote back.

By doing what, exactly? Lurking around his apartment building?

Of course not!

Technically that was true since this wasn't where Cameron lived. There was no need to add that I was lurking inside a different building.

Tucking my phone back in my purse so I wouldn't hear the notifications for any further messages from JT—and so I could ignore him without feeling too guilty—I decided to head up the stairs and take a peek at each floor. If I hadn't spotted Cameron by the time I'd checked each level, I'd give up and head back to my neighborhood.

On my way back to the lobby I heard another creaking sound, this time from behind me. I spun around, just in time to see Cameron disappear down the right-hand branch of the hallway I'd checked out mere seconds earlier. Trying my best to not make any noise, I rushed back in that direction and peeked around the corner. Once again the hallway was deserted, but when I listened carefully, I heard footfalls close by, each one growing fainter. Darting around the corner, I found myself at the top of a stairway leading down to the basement. When I glanced over the railing, I caught another fleeting glimpse of Cameron on his way down the stairs.

Still moving as stealthily as I could in my high-heeled boots, I hurried down the stairs after him. Why he was going down to the basement, I didn't know, but I intended to find out. If this were his building, it would have been possible that he was on his way to fetch a load of laundry, but this wasn't his building.

I paused on the landing to make sure I was maintaining enough distance between us. The way was clear so I continued on down the remaining stairs, slowing my pace, not knowing what waited below. As I descended the last three stairs, a sudden sense of apprehension almost made me pause. Maybe this wasn't the best idea I'd ever had. While I doubted that Cameron was involved in Pavlina's murder, I still believed he could be a criminal. So did I really want to follow him into the basement of some old building?

It was too late for second thoughts, I decided. I'd come this far so I figured I might as well keep going. After stepping off the last stair, I stood in a dimly lit hallway that stretched off to my left and my right. There was no sign of Cameron, but in each direction one door stood open, no lights shining beyond them, leaving the doorways as dark rectangles. Not hearing any voices or other sounds, I tiptoed to my left, approaching the door cautiously. When I reached it, I stopped and peered into the darkened room.

My eyes hadn't yet had a chance to adjust to the darkness when someone grabbed me from behind. I yelped, but a hand clapped over my mouth, cutting off the sound.

"You shouldn't have followed me," Cameron said into my ear.

I couldn't see him since he held me from behind, but there was no mistaking his voice. I tried to wriggle free of his grip, but he only tightened his hold on me.

"I don't want to do this, but you've left me no choice."

My eyes widened at those words and my heart set off at a gallop.

He shoved me forward, the force of the push sending me flying through the darkened doorway. My feet flailed beneath me, trying to find their footing, but the floor seemed to fall away. I went crashing to the ground and bounced painfully down three steps to a cold floor.

Ignoring the pain coming from various parts of my body, I scrambled to my feet and clambered my way back to the rectangle of light at the top of the short stairway. But as I reached the top step, the door slammed shut in my face, leaving me in darkness.

Grabbing the doorknob, I rattled it hard, but the door held fast. "Cameron!"

I pounded on the door and rattled the knob again, but to no avail.

He'd locked the door and gone away, leaving me trapped.

Chapter Fifteen

I HAMMERED ON the door again, releasing some of my anger into the solid wood. Again, my pounding got no response, and I broke off with a growl of frustration.

Remaining at the top of the concrete steps, I felt along the wall next to the door. My fingers found a light switch and I flipped it on. A bare light bulb hanging from the ceiling came to life, allowing me to see my prison.

Cameron had locked me in what appeared to be a storage room. Wooden shelves along one of the concrete walls held cans of paint, cleaning products, and other odds and ends, everything covered in a layer of dust and cobwebs. Although the corners of the room were shadow-filled, I could see flattened cardboard boxes, a rusty bicycle frame, a dirt bike, a paint-splattered wooden ladder, and a piece of Formica countertop.

None of those items kept my attention for long, however. I was far more interested in the small window across the room. Carefully descending the three steps so I wouldn't fall and add more bruises to my collection, I hurried over to the dirty window. The spark of hope that had ignited inside of me at the sight of the window sputtered and died when I noticed that there were bars on the outside. The window was also painted shut, which only added to my frustration. I wouldn't have been able to climb through the window with the bars there, but it would have been nice to have had a chance to open it and yell for help.

Studying my surroundings again, I wondered if I could find something to cut through the paint so I could open the window rather than break it. Of course, first I'd have to be able to reach the window, which I couldn't do very easily at the moment. The ledge sat just above my eye level so I couldn't see what was on the other side of the dirty glass.

Approaching the wooden ladder, I shoved aside some cobwebs and flattened cardboard boxes and dragged it out into the open. Fortunately it wasn't heavy and I was able to haul it over to the window without much trouble. It wasn't the sturdiest ladder in the world, but I wasn't about to complain in the circumstances.

Sneezing from the dust that tickled my nose, I tested the first rung with my weight. It held fast so I continued up the ladder, moving cautiously and fervently hoping that it wouldn't break. On the second rung, I stopped. Wrinkling my nose at the grime covering the glass, I leaned closer and tried to see through it.

The window looked out on a small parking lot, giving me a view from near the ground. Two figures strode into sight and I reached up to bang on the windowpane, hoping to get their attention.

My fist froze an inch from the glass.

Cameron walked into view from the other direction, coming to a stop when he met up with the other two men. I leaned closer to the glass again, my nose almost—but not quite—pressing up against the dirty pane. Cameron was speaking rapidly to the other men, but they didn't seem impressed. They both shook their heads, and then one of them jabbed a finger at Cameron's chest, getting up in his face.

I had no idea what any of the men were saying—only that it wasn't anything pleasant—but I was more interested in who they were. I didn't recognize the burlier of the two men talking to Cameron, but the other one looked awfully familiar. I shifted on the ladder so I could peer through a somewhat cleaner part of the window. The better view only confirmed my suspicions.

The man up in Cameron's face was Elena's cousin Igor.

What the heck was going on?

Cameron removed a handful of cash from his pocket, and Igor's companion snatched it away from him. The burly man counted the money and said something to Igor, shaking his head. Igor got back up in Cameron's face and jabbed a finger at his chest again. Then he and his companion turned and walked away, leaving Cameron standing in the middle of the parking lot. He remained in the same spot for a few more seconds, and then he too walked off, disappearing from sight.

Despite my interest in what had just transpired, I was more concerned about getting the heck out of the storage room. I hoped Cameron was planning to set me free before taking off in his van. Maybe that wasn't too likely, but at the moment it was my only hope.

I climbed down the ladder and returned to the door. Pressing my ear against it, I listened for approaching footsteps, but heard nothing.

I pounded the door with my fist.

"Cameron? Cameron, let me out of here!"

When that elicited no response, I rattled the knob and threw myself shoulder-first into the door. It rattled in its frame but gave no indication that it was going to give way under my assault. I drove my shoulder into the door again, but with the same unsatisfactory result.

Rubbing my aching shoulder, I forced myself to accept the fact that Cameron wasn't coming back for me. Most likely he'd already driven off, leaving me to . . . What? What had been his intention? Did he simply want me out of the way temporarily or did he have something more sinister in mind?

Surely he didn't think he was leaving me to die. It might take a while, but somebody would eventually hear my cries for help.

Wouldn't they?

Remembering the silence of the building, I wondered if it was occupied. My spirits sank toward the floor. If it was an empty building I could be in here for days, maybe even weeks, before somebody discovered me.

I wasn't about to let that be a possibility. I'd simply have to call for help, no matter how embarrassing that might be. After digging my phone out of my purse, I checked the screen. My spirits sank down through the floor this time.

There was no reception. I wandered around the storage room, holding my phone up, willing bars to appear on the screen, but with no luck.

This can't be happening, I thought as I held my phone up higher in the air, still with no change.

My frustration was rising to a crescendo. Since I didn't know for sure if the building was unoccupied, I took out some of my anger on the door again. I drummed an insistent, heavy beat against the thick wood, shouting for somebody—*anybody*—to help me.

My voice was starting to grow hoarse by the time I gave up and slumped down on the top step. What a disaster. I couldn't believe I'd managed to get myself into this situation. I had to get out of this place.

JT would notice I was missing when he went by my apartment to pick me up that evening, but that wouldn't do me much good. He had no idea where I was. Even if he figured out that I'd been following Cameron, would the drummer admit to what he'd done?

Probably not. More likely he'd deny that he had any idea where I was.

No, I definitely couldn't rely on JT coming to my rescue.

Maybe if I could get the window open, or perhaps break the glass, I could direct my shouts for help to the outdoors. With that in mind, I returned to the ladder and climbed up two rungs for another look out the window. I couldn't see anyone out there, but that didn't mean there was no one around to hear me.

I was about to climb back down to search for something to use to break the glass when I decided to check my phone one last time. When I activated the screen there was still no reception, but as I moved the phone right up to the window, three beautiful bars appeared in the corner of the screen.

The sight made me so happy that I wanted to sing the Hallelujah Chorus from Handel's *Messiah*, but instead I directed all my attention on selecting JT's name from my list of contacts. I had to lean close to the window to maintain reception, but within seconds I heard ringing on the line.

Please answer the phone, JT.

It rang once, then twice.

Just as I was losing hope, JT picked up.

"Hey, Dori," he said.

His voice was like beautiful music to my ears.

"Hi. Um . . . I have a bit of a problem," I said.

A short pause followed, and I swore it rang with suspicion and exasperation.

"Does this have anything to do with asking me where Cameron lives?" JT asked eventually.

"Sort of."

He said something, but the connection cut in and out so all I heard was garbled sounds rather than words. I leaned closer to the window.

"Sorry, I lost you there for a second. I've barely got reception here."

"Where's here?"

"A basement storage room in some apartment building."

Silence met my words and for a moment I thought the reception had cut out again. But then JT spoke.

"Do I even want to know why you're there?"

My neck ached from holding my awkward position, but I didn't dare move. "I'm not here by choice. Cameron shoved me in here and locked the door. Now he's taken off to who-knows-where."

"*Cameron* locked you in a storage room?"

"Yes."

"Dori, what the hell is going on?"

"I'd prefer to explain later. I just want to get out of here. Can you please come and help me?"

He sighed but said, "I'm already on my way out the door. Where is this place?"

Relieved, I told him which street I was on and gave him a de-scription of the apartment building. I hadn't had enough fore-thought to note the exact address before I'd entered the building, but luckily it was the only white—or whitish—one on the block.

"All right, hang tight," JT said. "I'll be there as soon as I can."

I thanked him, and he cut off the call. Carefully, I climbed down the ladder and sat on the concrete steps leading to the door. Although I wasn't thrilled to have to spend more time in the storage room, I knew I was lucky that help was on the way. JT wouldn't be impressed when he heard the details of how I'd ended up in this predicament, but that was the least of my problems. He could be as annoyed with me as he wanted. I'd still be thrilled to see his face when he arrived.

As I WAITED, the cold from the cement steps seeped through my clothes, little by little until I couldn't ignore it any longer. I got up and paced back and forth across the storage room, but I still got colder as time passed. The room was clearly not heated and although I could see that the sun was shining brightly outside the window, the air still had a definite frostiness to it, especially in my basement prison.

After rubbing my gloved hands together, I checked the time on my phone, even though I'd done so only moments earlier. I was beginning to wonder if JT was having trouble finding the right building when I heard footsteps out in the corridor.

I rushed up the steps to the door.

"Midori, are you in there?" JT's muffled voice asked.

"Yes!" I said with immense relief. "Thank goodness you found me! Can you break the door down?"

"I shouldn't have to. Hold on a minute."

I did my best to wait patiently, one ear pressed against the door, listening to what was happening on the other side. All I heard were a few quiet clicking sounds and a slight rattling of the door.

"What are you doing?" I asked, wishing I could see through to the other side.

"Almost there," JT said without answering my question.

I heard more rattling. A second later, the knob turned and the door opened. A big smile spread across my face when I saw JT standing there in front of me.

"Am I ever glad to see you!" I gave him a hug. "How did you get the door open?"

After returning my hug, JT held up a credit card for me to see. "I jimmied the lock." He shut the door and tucked the credit card into his wallet.

"You know how to do that?" I said, surprised.

"Thanks to a childhood obsession with private eye stories and an uncle with some less-than-aboveboard talents."

"I had no idea. What other hidden talents do you have?"

JT grinned. "You'll find out one day. I have to keep a few surprises up my sleeve."

I wondered what those surprises might be, but he clearly wasn't going to enlighten me.

"Well, thank you," I said. "Thank you times a million."

"You're welcome. Now how about we get out of here?"

"Sounds good to me."

We headed up the stairs to the main floor.

"So, spill," JT said when we reached the top of the stairway. "Why did Cameron lock you in that room?"

We paused as an elderly woman using a walker ambled slowly past us down the hall. We both said hello to her, but she ignored us. Or maybe she was hard of hearing. She stopped at the door to one of the units and put a key in the lock. Obviously the building wasn't abandoned after all, but I still didn't like my chances of someone finding me in the storage room if I hadn't been able to get phone reception. The basement didn't seem to get many visitors.

As we continued on to the lobby, I gave JT a preliminary explanation. "I decided to follow Cameron from your place earlier."

"Why?" The word practically reverberated with exasperation.

"He was on the phone and seemed agitated. And I was suspicious of him. For good reason, as it turns out."

"Locking you in a basement does seem suspicious," JT said as he held the front door open for me.

I stuffed my gloved hands in my pockets and stepped out into the bright but cool afternoon. "Not just that. There's a window in the storage room that looks out on a small parking lot behind the building. I saw Cameron meet up with two other guys, one of whom was Elena's cousin Igor."

"The guy who was at the theater the other night? The one who's a suspect in Pavlina's murder?"

"The one and the same."

"Huh."

"Interesting, right? Anyway," I continued on without waiting for a response, "Cameron gave them some cash, but the guys still didn't seem happy with him."

"So then what happened?"

"Nothing, really. They went their separate ways." I noted the empty space by the curb where Cameron had parked earlier. "And Cameron took off in his van."

"Leaving you locked in that room," JT said, an edge to his voice.

I stopped next to my MINI Cooper, noting that JT's truck was parked two cars behind it. "Yes." Now that I was free, my annoyance with Cameron took center stage in my mind. "I can't wait until I see him again. I've got a bone to pick with him. A whole skeleton of bones, actually."

"You're not the only one."

There was an unusual storminess to JT's brown eyes and his jaw was set. "I say we track him down right now."

"But what about your gig?"

"Forget the gig. We'll have to cancel. I can't play in a band with that guy after what he did to you. And it looks more likely than ever that he was involved in stealing my equipment. I can't pretend like nothing happened."

"No, of course you can't. But couldn't you wait to confront him until after the gig? I don't want to be responsible for messing things up for your band."

"You're not responsible," JT assured me. "This is all on Cameron."

"But canceling would be bad for your band, and it would be unfair to the other guys. Please, JT. Just leave it for a few more hours."

The muscles in his jaw worked as he considered the idea. "All right," he said after a moment, although not without a good dose of reluctance. "But as soon as our set is done, he's going to have to start explaining."

"To both of us," I said. "Until then, I should let you go. Thanks again for coming all the way out here to help me."

"Anytime. You know that."

I gave him a grateful smile. "I do."

"Although I'm not sure all this qualifies as being careful."

"It's not that I wasn't being careful," I said. "I'm just not as good at tailing someone as I thought."

"But if you hadn't followed him into the building in the first place . . ."

"Okay, true. But how could I not? I wanted to know what he was up to."

JT shook his head like he thought there was no hope for me. "Don't you remember what they say about curiosity and the cat?"

"I'm not a cat," I pointed out.

"All the more reason to keep your curiosity in check. You don't have nine lives to play with. Just one, and I'd like you to live it for as long as possible."

"So would I," I said. "I'll do my best to stay out of trouble."

"Mm-hm." He was clearly dubious about how effective my best efforts would be.

Raising myself up on my tiptoes, I kissed him on the cheek. "Thank you, JT. You really are the best."

His expression relaxed and he almost smiled. "See you later?"

"Absolutely."

We parted ways and I drove straight home, determined to prove to JT that I could stay out of trouble, at least for the rest of the day.

Chapter Sixteen

After arriving home I set off on foot to take care of a few errands in my neighborhood. Later on, as I walked home from the bank, I tried to make sense of what I'd witnessed earlier that day while locked in the basement storage room. I didn't believe it was a coincidence that Cameron and Igor were both present at the theater on the night of Pavlina's death, not now that I knew they were acquainted. There were still plenty of questions I didn't have answers to, though.

I'd seen Cameron hand money over to Igor and his friend, so I figured it was safe to assume that Cameron either owed them money or was the victim of extortion. I had a hard time picturing him as a victim, especially since he'd locked me up and abandoned me, but that might have been my personal feelings coloring my judgment.

Regardless, I believed Igor and his burly pal expected more money from Cameron. Judging by the way they'd reacted when he handed them the cash, they weren't satisfied with the amount. Could a debt owed to Igor have driven Cameron to steal JT's equipment? I hoped that was one of many questions Cameron would answer that night.

When I arrived home, I checked the time and decided I had more than an hour to spare before I needed to get ready to go out that evening. I fixed myself a light supper and ate it while watching a rerun of *Castle* on the TV. Once I'd finished eating, I booted up my laptop, the television still on in the background. Even though I hoped Cameron would give us answers that night, there was always a chance that he'd clam up and refuse to say anything. Or he might lie to us. Since I couldn't guarantee that he'd provide me with any information about Igor Malakhov, I decided to see what I could find out on my own.

I typed Igor's full name into the search bar on the computer screen and scanned the results that popped up a split second later. With a sigh of disappointment, I realized I was most likely wasting my time. There were too many people with the name Igor Malakhov, and although I clicked on a few of the search results, none of them pertained to Elena's cousin.

Giving up on that avenue of investigation, I decided to try a few other names. Starting with my prime murder suspect, I typed Ethan Rogerson's name into the search bar and went through the same process again. While there were several people by that name with information online, I was able to pinpoint social media profiles and a couple of articles relating to the right Ethan. Unfortunately, however, they weren't the least bit enlightening. Ethan's social media profiles didn't tell me anything of interest and the news articles related strictly to his musical achievements.

Next I conducted a search on Jeb Hartson. I found a fair bit of information about the judge, but again none of it was helpful. All of it related to his career, and none of the Web pages revealed any dirt that might have tarnished the phony cowboy's reputation.

The same was true of Olivia Hutchcraft. The information I found online related strictly to her professional activities, and none of it seemed suspicious, or even particularly interesting. I wanted to know more about her assistant as well, but I didn't know his last name so that would have to wait for the moment.

Frustrated, I gave up and shut down my laptop. Although I would have liked to continue my research, perhaps delving deeper into Pavlina's past, that would have to wait as well. JT would be by to pick me up soon, and I wanted to change my clothes and touch up my makeup before going out.

Soon after I'd switched my jeans for a black wrap dress and had replaced my stud earrings with delicate, dangly ones, the buzzer alerted me to JT's arrival. A minute later I was bundled up and climbing into the passenger seat of his truck. As JT drove us downtown, I hoped we'd soon get some answers out of Cameron.

When we arrived at the pub where the band would be playing, I hung around in the back with JT and Rafael for a few minutes, but then left them for the front of the house. I didn't want to be there when Cameron arrived. Although I would have loved to see his face when he walked in to find me there, I really didn't want to mess things up for the band. If he was distracted, he might fall apart during the performance, and I didn't want that to happen. I'd have my chance to face him soon enough. I just needed to be patient.

The pub was filling up with patrons by the time I made my way to the front of the house, so I claimed a table and ordered a Bellini. Mikayla and Dave arrived a short time later, and their company distracted me from my thoughts of what would transpire later that night. Right away I noticed that something seemed off about Mikayla. She was more subdued than usual, her typical bubbliness more of a sputter here and there. But I could also tell she was trying to hide it, so I didn't raise the subject while Dave was there with us.

We ordered a platter of nachos to go with our drinks and soon we were chatting about the recent events that had transpired at the theater.

"I heard the police questioned Elena," Dave said before chomping down on a nacho laden with cheese and salsa.

"Really?" Mikayla said. "Elena is cold, but I can't imagine her getting her hands dirty by killing someone." She looked to me for confirmation. "Is she really a suspect?"

I shrugged as I took a sip of my drink. "I don't know if they consider her a suspect, but the detectives definitely wanted to talk to her. Her cousin was there on the night of the murder and he apparently had a history with Pavlina. Plus he has a criminal record."

"Whoa," Mikayla said with a shake of her head. "So maybe he killed Pavlina and the police think Elena might know something about it?"

"Something like that, I guess." I hoped that was all there was to it. After munching on a nacho, I continued. "I have a hard time picturing Elena killing someone too. She's more the type that would get someone to do it for her."

"So maybe she got her cousin to kill Pavlina," Dave said.

Mikayla frowned. "But why? I mean, I heard that Elena wasn't happy about losing the front cover of *Classical Spotlight* to Pavlina, but she'd have to be seriously crazy to want her dead because of that. Elena's a snob, but I don't think she's insane."

"No," I agreed, "I don't think she is either. But there's definitely something fishy about her cousin."

I didn't bother to fill them in on Igor's link to Cameron or the suspicious transaction I'd witnessed earlier that day. JT and his bandmates had arrived on the stage at the far end of the pub, distracting all of us from our conversation. I watched as Cameron settled in behind his drums, the sight of him igniting a spark of anger inside of me. I still couldn't believe he'd had the gall to lock me up in the basement and leave me there. If I hadn't been able to make a phone call, I'd likely still be there while he went about his life, apparently without a care in the world.

A few seconds later, he raised his gaze and looked my way. His eyes widened and he froze, one drumstick raised in front of him. I kept my expression impassive as I stared him down, although I was secretly pleased by the shock on his face. Hamish said something to him and he shook himself out of his daze. From then on, he avoided looking my way, his gaze rarely ever straying beyond the stage.

Despite the initial shock of seeing me there in the pub, he managed to gather himself and perform with the band as if nothing had happened. I was glad of that. The last thing I wanted was for him to embarrass JT and the others by ruining the concert.

Mikayla, Dave, and I ate our nachos and sipped our drinks as the band played through several songs, some of which JT had composed. I beamed with pride when their set ended and the patrons broke into enthusiastic applause. I clapped along with everyone else, and my heart danced a happy jig when JT caught my eye from across the pub and grinned at me.

"I need to use the ladies' room," Mikayla said as she pushed back her chair, diverting my attention from JT.

I glanced back toward the stage. The guys were still there, but they were getting ready to move their instruments into the back room. I didn't want to miss out on the opportunity to confront Cameron, but I was also worried about my friend.

"I'll come with you," I said, coming to a quick decision.

After making use of the facilities, Mikayla stood in front of the restroom mirror, applying a fresh coat of lipstick.

"What's going on?" I asked as I touched up my own lip gloss.

"Going on?"

"You haven't been yourself tonight."

She sighed as she returned her tube of lipstick to her purse. "Dave and I had an argument earlier."

"I'm sorry," I said sincerely. "But the two of you will be all right, won't you?"

She met my eyes in the mirror and I read her answer there before she replied. "I'm not sure." She let out another sigh. "We've been arguing a lot lately. Things were going so well before, but now . . ."

"Is there anything in particular that you argue about?"

"Not really. It's just . . . He's so rigid about everything. Set in his ways. I don't know if he was hiding that part of him before, or if I was just blind to it in the beginning because I was so into him."

I gave her a hug. "I'm sorry, Mikayla."

"Thanks, hon. Maybe we can still make things work."

She didn't seem too optimistic, and the sadness in her eyes cut at my heart. I hated to see her unhappy and I felt terrible for her. I knew how hopeful she'd been about her relationship with Dave in the beginning, and it was hard to see that slipping away from her.

We left the restroom and returned to the table where Dave was finishing off the last of the nachos. JT and his bandmates had disappeared so I didn't bother to sit down again.

"I'm catching a ride home with JT, so I'm going to go see what he's up to," I said.

I traded goodbyes with Mikayla and Dave, and collected my coat. Hoping things would get better between the two of them, I made my way around the tables and into the back of the pub. As I entered the room where the guys had stored their gear, Rafael and Hamish passed me on their way to the front of the house to get a drink.

After exchanging a few words with them, I continued on into the room. Cameron must have heard my voice when I was talking to the other guys, but he didn't acknowledge my presence. He kept his back to me as he grabbed his jacket and shrugged into it.

I shared a weighty glance with JT and then we both turned our eyes to the drummer.

"Cameron," JT said, "we need to talk."

He turned around slowly, his entire demeanor uneasy. He shifted his eyes my way, but then they skittered in JT's direction.

"Yeah?" He feigned ignorance.

"Don't pretend you don't know what this is about," I said, annoyed that he'd considered doing so.

"Look, I have to go. There's somewhere I need to be." He took a step back from us.

"Too bad," JT said. "You're not going anywhere until you answer some questions. What the hell were you thinking, locking Midori in that basement and leaving her there?"

"She was following me!"

"Of course I was following you," I shot at him. "You've been acting suspicious."

"Suspicious? I don't know what you're talking about." The fear in his eyes told a different story.

"I don't care that she was following you," JT said. "That doesn't make it okay to lock her up and abandon her. What if she hadn't been able to get help? Would you have left her there for days? Did you even care what would happen to her?"

Cameron shook his head, as if trying to deny that any of this was unfolding. "I knew she'd be okay. I knew someone would let her out eventually."

"Eventually?" I echoed. "Like when I was dead?"

"You wouldn't have died."

"How do you know?" I challenged. "I barely got a call through to JT. There was hardly any reception down there."

His face paled. "I didn't think about that. I figured you'd have no problem using your cell phone." He took another step back and raised his hands as if in surrender. "Listen, guys, I'm sorry about that, okay? I didn't mean any harm."

"Didn't mean any harm?" JT said, incredulous.

Cameron's eyes shifted to me. "I just wanted you out of the way. There was something I needed to do, and I didn't want you interfering. If you had, something worse might have happened to you."

"You mean if I'd interrupted your little meeting?"

More color drained from his face.

"There was a window in the basement, you know," I went on. "I saw you meeting with Igor and that other guy."

Cameron had the look of a cornered, frightened animal now.

"What was that about?" JT asked him.

"Nothing." The word came out weak, unconvincing.

"You gave them money," I pressed. "And they didn't seem very happy with you."

"So what? Look, I'm sorry about locking you up, but none of that other stuff is any of your business."

"You made it our business when you put Midori in danger," JT said, his expression colder than I'd ever seen it.

"I was keeping her *out* of danger."

"Please," I said, not buying that explanation. "You didn't want me finding out what you were up to, plain and simple. You didn't want me to know you stole JT's equipment."

"What? That's crazy." His denial rang with the discordance of a lie.

"You stole his equipment with the help of Igor, and maybe his friend too," I continued.

"No. No, I didn't." His voice wavered.

"Give it up, Cameron," JT said with annoyance. "We know you did. Quit lying to us."

Cameron's shoulders dropped and he seemed to shrink, his remaining defiance leaking away. "I didn't want to. I swear I didn't."

"Then why did you?" I asked.

"I owe Igor money. A lot of money. Even before I lost my job I couldn't make my rent. I've maxed out my credit cards and I needed cash. Igor has a poker game every week and I thought if I could win some money, my troubles would be over."

I rolled my eyes at that. As if gambling was a great solution to money problems.

"Except you lost, right?" JT guessed.

Cameron nodded, miserable. "On the night of the concert, he texted me, wanting to meet. I told him I was busy, working at the theater. The next thing I knew, he was there, demanding money from me. I didn't have any to give him, but when he realized what I was doing there, he told me to get him access to your equipment so he could steal it. He said he'd deduct the value of the equipment from my debt. So I left the truck unlocked after we'd loaded up most of the gear." He met JT's eyes for the first time. "I'm sorry, man. I'm really sorry."

I glared at him, fiercely angry on behalf of my best friend. "What else did Igor do?"

His eyes turned to me, surprised. "What do you mean?"

"There was a murder that night," I reminded him. "Maybe Pavlina overheard you and Igor planning to steal JT's equipment. Maybe she threatened to tell someone."

"What?" His eyes widened with fear. "You think I know something about that girl's death?"

"Do you?" JT asked.

"No!"

"Are you sure?" I said. "Igor had a history with the victim. Maybe he ran into her while he was at the theater and things turned sour."

Cameron raised his hands. "Hey, if Igor had anything to do with that girl's death, I know nothing about it. I helped him steal the equipment, I admit to that. But I know nothing about the murder. I swear."

I stared at him for several seconds, weighing his words, his body language. I shifted my gaze to meet JT's. Although we said nothing, plenty passed between us. After a moment, JT nodded at me, the anger gone from his face, though he still wasn't happy. He believed what Cameron had said about the murder, and— although I wasn't eager to admit it—so did I.

The drummer was guilty of theft, guilty of betraying his friend and bandmate, but he didn't know anything about Pavlina's murder.

Chapter Seventeen

"ARE YOU GOING to turn me in?" Cameron asked, the question laden with fear.

We both looked to JT for an answer. He scrubbed a hand down his face as he thought it over.

"I'm not sure," he said. "I'm guessing there's not much chance of recovering my equipment."

Cameron shook his head, his face miserable. "Igor has his fences. He probably got rid of the stuff within the first few days. I'm sorry, man. Really."

JT didn't acknowledge Cameron's apology. Instead he looked my way, and I saw turmoil in his eyes. I wished I knew the right decision so I could share it with him. Cameron deserved to be turned in to the police, but what good would that do? Maybe it would deter him from future misdeeds, but maybe it wouldn't. And if what Cameron had said was true, turning him in wouldn't get JT's equipment back. Still, letting Cameron go scot-free didn't seem right either.

"I need time to think," JT said after a moment.

"What if I paid you back?" Cameron said, a note of desperation creeping into his voice.

"With what?" I asked. "You have no money. That's what got you into this mess in the first place."

"If I could get a decent job . . ."

"Let's talk about it another time," JT said, shutting the conversation down. "But whatever I decide to do, you can't be in the band anymore, not after what you've done."

Cameron's shoulders sagged. "I get that."

He remained standing there, his eyes going back and forth between me and JT. When neither of us said anything more, he took the hint and gathered up his gear. JT, being the good guy that he was, gave him a hand loading his drum kit into his van. I stood out in the alley behind the pub, shivering in the cold night air, watching as they got everything loaded away.

Before climbing into the driver's seat of his van, Cameron looked at JT once more. "I really am sorry."

JT didn't respond, and Cameron didn't seem to expect him to. He got into his van and shut the door, starting the engine a second later. We watched him drive away and then went back inside without a word. JT retrieved his jacket and guitar, and we left the pub for a final time. We didn't say much as we walked out to his truck, or even once JT had merged with the nighttime traffic and had set a course for my neighborhood.

Although Cameron had confessed and had confirmed my suspicions about his involvement in the theft, I felt no satisfaction, no sense of triumph. I hated that JT's bandmate had betrayed him, and I hated that my best friend would now have to decide what to do or not do about it. The whole situation left me feeling as though a heavy weight sat across my shoulders.

At least I knew now that Cameron didn't know anything about Pavlina's death. Yes, I only had Cameron's word to go on in that respect, and he wasn't the most honest person in the world. However, he also wasn't great at hiding his feelings, judging by the agitation he'd displayed on several occasions over the past week. Igor was still on my suspect list, though. According to Cameron's story, Igor had shown up at the theater only after finding out that Cameron was there. So, more likely than not, Igor hadn't known Pavlina would be at the theater that night, but that didn't mean he hadn't killed her.

Had he run into Pavlina in the back hallways? Had seeing her brought his festering grudge to the surface, flooding him with anger and the need for revenge?

Possibly.

Sitting there in the passenger seat of JT's truck, I tugged on my left earlobe as I thought things over. There was still something bothering me, something I couldn't quite pin down. Maybe it was nothing important, but I sensed that it was. But no matter how much I sifted through my memories, I couldn't find that elusive piece of information.

"You okay?" JT asked as he stopped the truck at a red light.

"Yes," I said. "Just thinking. Are *you* okay?"

He nodded as the light turned green and he eased the truck into motion again. "Disappointed, but okay."

I reached over and gave his arm a squeeze. "I'm sorry you had to find out about Cameron's betrayal."

He flashed me a sad smile. "Better to know than to go on thinking he was someone I could trust."

That was true.

"You're not going to turn him in to the police, are you?" I knew him well enough to guess that was the case.

"I don't think so, but I don't mind letting him squirm for a day or two."

"He deserves that, at the very least," I said with approval.

JT turned the truck onto my street and stopped in front of my building.

"Thanks for the ride," I said. "And I really enjoyed the concert."

"I'm glad." JT put the truck into park. "You look great tonight, by the way."

Butterflies fluttered in my stomach and my cheeks grew warm. "Thanks."

I wanted to say more, but I couldn't come up with any words. My phone buzzed in my purse, and I dug it out, hoping JT wouldn't notice the color in my cheeks.

"Oh no," I said, my butterflies dying mid-flight as I read the text from Mikayla.

"What is it?"

"Mikayla and Dave had an argument. Another one. They already argued earlier in the day."

"Things aren't going too well for them?"

"Unfortunately." I felt so bad for Mikayla. It was terrible knowing she was upset. "Why do relationships have to be so difficult?" I said out of frustration.

"I don't know," JT said. "They all take work, but maybe the ones that are really difficult aren't meant to be."

"Maybe you're right."

I stared out the windshield, thinking. Knowing that Mikayla and Dave's relationship had started out so well and now seemed to be going downhill fast only stoked the fears I had about being in love with JT. Even if my feelings were reciprocated, if our relationship ever fell apart, I'd be devastated.

Was it worth the risk?

My phone buzzed in my hand, nudging me out of my thoughts. Mikayla had sent another text message.

"I should probably get back to her," I said, more to myself than to JT.

"All right. I'll see you on Monday."

"Monday," I agreed.

I hesitated, but then opened the door and slid out of the truck. After saying good night to JT, I hurried through the chilly night air to my apartment building, for some reason feeling upset for myself as well as for Mikayla.

AFTER TAKING OFF my coat and gloves, I texted Mikayla to see if she wanted to talk. She thanked me but said she was going to try and get some sleep. I decided to do the same and changed into my pajamas.

I thought I might lie awake for hours, my mind spinning around like a carousel, centered around thoughts of Cameron's confession and all the remaining suspects in the murder case. Fortunately, that didn't happen. Within minutes of resting my head on the pillow, sleep pulled me into its depths and I didn't stir until after eight in the morning.

Since it was Sunday and I didn't have to be anywhere, I took my time getting out of bed. Once I'd showered and dressed, I enjoyed a leisurely breakfast while reading a couple of chapters from a historical mystery novel I'd recently checked out of the library. Taking a sip of tea, I set down the book and considered the real-life mystery I had yet to solve. I wondered if the police had made any more progress with their investigation than I had with mine. As far as I knew they still hadn't made any arrests, but that didn't mean they weren't closing in on someone.

I wished I knew how much information the police had, which people were on their suspect list aside from Elena and Igor. Detectives Van den Broek and Chowdhury wouldn't share that information with me though, of that I was certain.

While I was sitting there pondering the mystery, I heard a quiet buzzing sound. My phone. I tried to remember where I'd left it the night before and located it seconds later on my coffee table. As I picked up the device, I was surprised to see I had a text message from Hans. He hadn't sent me a private message since our relationship had ended months ago.

Have you had any luck clearing Elena's name? his message read.

"And good morning to you too," I grumbled.

Before I had a chance to tap out a real response, he sent me another text.

She says the police are harassing her. We really need to get this cleared up.

I rolled my eyes. "Harassing" in Elena's case probably meant the detectives had dared to ask her a few questions, but I wasn't about to quibble about her likely exaggerations. The truth was that I could use some inside information on Igor Malakhov, and Elena was likely the best source for it.

Do you think she'd talk to me? I wrote. *I need to ask her some questions about her cousin.*

Good idea, he wrote back seconds later, not directly answering my question. *I talked to her a few minutes ago. She's at Café Marciano on Fourth Avenue. You could meet her there.*

"Great," I said aloud. "Just how I wanted to spend my Sunday morning."

Despite my grumbling, I wrote back to Hans, agreeing to the suggestion. After all, I did want to find out more about Igor.

I'll let her know you're on the way, Hans's final text message read.

With a sigh that might have been described as overly dramatic if anyone had heard it, I finished off my tea and rinsed my breakfast dishes, leaving them in the sink to be washed later. After brushing my teeth and getting bundled up, I set off for Café Marciano, less than thrilled about who I'd be meeting there.

Chapter Eighteen

WHEN I ARRIVED at Café Marciano, I wasn't surprised to find it bustling with activity, filled mostly with hipsters enjoying fancy caffeinated concoctions, their conversations creating a rumble of sound around me. Despite the number of patrons present, I spotted Elena within seconds. She sat on her own at a table halfway along one wall, flipping through a magazine while sipping at a cappuccino. She didn't look up until I'd pulled out the chair across from her.

"Good morning," I greeted cheerily, knowing I wouldn't receive the same type of reception.

I was right.

Elena flicked her eyes up at me for a fraction of a second before returning them to her magazine. "Melody, isn't it?" she said with a slight sigh, as if my mere presence was putting her out.

I gritted my teeth and forced myself to smile as I sat down at the table. "Midori," I corrected, knowing she wouldn't care. It wasn't the first time she'd called me by the wrong name and I suspected she'd done so on purpose.

"I hope this isn't about Hans," she said as she turned a page of the magazine, still not bothering to look at me.

"Um, no," I said, confused. "Didn't he tell you why I wanted to talk to you?"

She let out a quiet huff and finally tore her attention away from her riveting magazine. "He told me you wanted to ask about my cousin, but how was I to know if that was the truth? For all I know, you want my advice on how to get back together with Hans."

If I'd been eating or drinking I probably would have choked. "I have no interest in getting back together with Hans," I said once I'd recovered enough to speak.

And even if I did, I most certainly wouldn't come to you for advice, I added silently.

"If you say so." She sipped at her cappuccino, her eyes straying beyond me to wander around the café.

I knew her actions were meant to tell me that my interests—and my presence, for that matter—were of zero importance to her. Her act of superiority grated at my nerves, but I forced myself to remain polite.

"I understand the police think you and your cousin could have been involved in Pavlina's murder," I said as I shrugged out of my coat and let it drape over the back of my chair.

I pulled my knitted hat from my head and smoothed my hand over my hair, hoping I didn't look as though I'd been electrocuted. Elena's hair, of course, was absolutely perfect, every shining blond strand in place.

"Utterly ridiculous," she said with contempt, setting her cappuccino cup on the table. "They think I got Igor to kill her on my behalf. They also believe he might have killed her for his own purposes. They can't even choose between those theories." She shook her head, as if she'd never encountered stupidity as great as that she attributed to Detectives Van den Broek and Chowdhury.

"But you didn't get him to kill her, right?" I asked, deciding it would be best to check.

She directed her contemptuous blue eyes at me. "Of course not. Why would I waste my time on someone like Pavlina?"

Her response took me aback for a second, although it shouldn't have. It was typical of her to suggest that the idea of arranging Pavlina's death was ridiculous because the composer wasn't of sufficient importance to warrant her attention.

"Okay," I said, unable to help drawing the word out. "Do you think it's possible that Igor killed her for his own reasons? He has a criminal record and it wouldn't be surprising if he'd had a grudge against Pavlina after what happened when they were in high school."

Elena regarded me with her icy eyes for a long moment. I didn't know if she was trying to intimidate me, or if she was simply taking time to choose her next words. Although I was tempted to squirm beneath the chill of her gaze, I forced myself to remain still and keep my face politely impassive.

Eventually she stopped her study of me and took another sip of her cappuccino. "Igor is a stupid boy," she said. "He always has been. Stealing, lying. He's a disgrace to our family."

"So you think he could be capable of killing someone?"

"It's possible. He doesn't think. He just acts."

"So if he'd run into Pavlina at the theater that night, maybe all his anger came bubbling up to the surface and he lost control."

Elena shrugged, somehow making the ordinary gesture elegant and haughty. "It could have happened."

"Did you tell that to the police?"

Her eyes narrowed. "Of course not."

"But if Igor killed Pavlina, he should be in jail."

"That would break my aunt's heart."

"That's unfortunate, but if he's killed once, he could kill again."

That didn't seem to concern her. I tried a different tactic.

"As long as this case remains unsolved, the police will keep bothering you," I pointed out. "And that could damage the orchestra's reputation, not to mention your own."

I knew my last words were the most likely ones to have an effect, and they did. It was subtle, but a hint of her disinterest fell away.

"Fine." She reached into her designer purse and pulled out her phone. "I've had enough of this. We'll put an end to it once and for all."

"How?" I asked as she tapped out a message on her phone.

"I've always been able to tell when Igor's lying," she said, still typing. "I'll tell him to meet us here and I'll ask him if he killed her. No matter how he answers, I'll know if it's the truth."

"You mean you haven't asked him that already?"

She set her phone down on the table, and for the first time I caught a brief glimpse of a crack in her armor of superiority. In that tiny rift I saw uncertainty, maybe even a hint of fear.

"I didn't want to know the answer." She cleared her throat and let her gaze wander around the café again, her haughtiness shifting firmly back into place.

I wanted to shake my head at her state of denial. Wouldn't it be better to know the answer than to go on wondering if her cousin was a killer?

To me the answer to that question was easy. My curiosity would have driven me to ask him right away, if he were my relative. But maybe Elena wasn't quite as cold and untouched by the world around her as she appeared. Maybe she couldn't bear the thought of her younger cousin doing something so terrible.

I didn't follow that thought too far, however. I had no desire to start sympathizing with Elena in any way.

Her phone buzzed on the tabletop and she snatched it up. "He's on his way," she said after she'd checked the new message.

Setting her phone down again, she returned her focus to the magazine, acting as if I were no longer there. After half a minute of being ignored, I decided I might as well enjoy what the café had to offer since the company left plenty to be desired.

Leaving my coat on my chair, I got up and made my way around two tables until I was near the counter. I got in line behind the patrons ahead of me, studying the food and drink choices on the menu on the wall. When it was my turn to be served, I ordered a vanilla latte and a sandwich—smoked salmon and veggies on a croissant. It hadn't been all that long since I'd eaten breakfast, but I figured I'd need the fuel to help me survive more time spent with Elena.

On my way back to the table with my purchases, I snagged a newspaper from a rack of free copies. If Elena was going to ignore me in favor of her magazine, it would be nice to have something to do aside from stare across the table at her. She didn't acknowledge my presence when I returned, and that was as I expected. It didn't bother me, and I settled in to enjoy my food.

I'd read a few articles and had consumed half my croissant sandwich when Igor Malakhov appeared next to our table, looming over us. Frowning, he fixed his steely gray eyes on me before turning his attention to his cousin.

"I'm here."

"I can see that," Elena said, with no more warmth than she'd shown me. "Sit down."

It was an order rather than a request, and Igor obeyed. He pulled out a chair and slouched down into it, not bothering to remove his coat. Most likely he wasn't planning on staying long.

"Who's she?" Igor asked his cousin, with barely a nod in my direction.

"She's . . ." Elena glanced my way. "A colleague." She closed her magazine and fixed her gaze on Igor again. "We're going to ask you some questions, and you'd better answer truthfully."

"Fine. Whatever," he said with a shrug, slouching so far down into his chair that I was afraid he'd slip under the table.

"Did you see Pavlina when you were at the theater last week?" I asked, not wasting any time getting straight to the questions.

Igor's sullen gaze shifted in my direction. "Who?"

Elena let out an angry exclamation in Russian. I didn't know what exactly she'd said, but it seemed effective.

"Fine," Igor said. "I saw her. So?"

I decided to go for the most important question next. "Did you kill her?"

He turned sharply to his cousin and spoke rapidly in Russian. He didn't seem pleased, but Elena was even less so.

"Answer the question," she said in a tone that left no room for argument.

Igor's jaw set with annoyance, but he did as told. "No, I didn't kill her." He glared at me. "Who are you to ask me that, anyway?"

Elena spoke up before I had a chance. "That doesn't matter. I'm sick of the police bothering me, all because of you. We want to get this mess cleared up."

"I told the police I didn't kill her," Igor said. "But of course it did no good. Once they decide who they want to pin a crime on, they don't care about the truth."

Even though the detectives on the case weren't my favorite people in the world, I thought Igor's assessment was a tad harsh. I had no intention of pointing that out to him, though. Instead I looked Elena's way, waiting for her judgment.

"He's telling the truth," she said to me. "He didn't kill her."

I knew she expected me to accept her word as a solid fact, but could I be certain *she* was telling the truth? Was she willing to lie along with Igor to keep her cousin out of trouble?

I wasn't sure. Based on the way she'd talked about him before his arrival, I suspected that she wouldn't be too hesitant to throw him to the wolves if he were guilty. But what if she was a good actress? That was something I'd have to consider. For the moment, however, I didn't say anything, knowing that showing any doubt as to the veracity of Elena's statement would cause discord and shut down the conversation.

Igor pushed back his chair. "I answered your questions. So we're done here, right?"

"Hold on," I said quickly, stopping him before he stood up. "When you saw Pavlina, what did the two of you talk about?"

He scowled at me for a second or two, but when Elena snapped his name, he replied. "At first she didn't talk to me at all. She walked right past me in the hallway. So I asked her if she was going to pretend she didn't recognize me."

"What did she say?" Elena asked.

"She took a good look at me and then acted all surprised, like she hadn't recognized me at first."

"Maybe she didn't," Elena said. "It's been almost ten years since you last saw each other."

Igor's scowl deepened. "Maybe it was easy for her to forget. For me, it wasn't so easy. I went to jail because of her."

His words had grown heated with anger and I realized that it was no wonder he was a suspect. He clearly had a deep grudge against Pavlina and if she'd failed to recognize him right away—or had at least pretended she didn't know who he was—that could have stoked the flames of his fury, causing a deadly explosion.

"But she did recognize you eventually," Elena prodded.

Igor nodded. "She said she hoped I'd turned my life around, but she was too busy to talk with me." He glowered at the memory. "Then she walked away."

"Did you follow her?" I asked, before I could stop myself.

"No. Are you still trying to pin her death on me? I told you, I didn't kill her!" His voice had risen in volume, drawing startled glances from other patrons.

"Keep your voice down," Elena ordered. She glared at me. "Of course he didn't follow her. Didn't you hear me before? I told you he wasn't lying."

I stifled a sigh. "I wasn't suggesting that he'd killed her," I said, although I still hadn't ruled out that possibility completely. "I was simply wondering how much he knew about her movements that night." Not waiting to give the others a chance to speak, I forged ahead with another question for Igor. "When exactly did you talk to her? Was it before the concert or after it started?"

He directed his answer at Elena. "A few minutes after I talked to you. I was on my way out of the theater when I saw her."

"So just before the concert started," Elena said to me.

I nodded, a bit disappointed. I was hoping Igor might have had some valuable information about others Pavlina had interacted with backstage after she'd left her seat in the audience.

"Did you see anyone else talking to Pavlina that night?" I asked.

"No," Igor replied. "After she walked off, I left."

"To wait for Cameron to do his part in your plan to steal the recording equipment," I said, unable to keep myself from bringing up that point.

"What?" Elena's eyes went from me to her cousin.

Igor sent a death glare my way.

"You stole that equipment?" Elena said in a low, but icy voice. "I knew you were up to no good that night!"

"You can't prove anything," Igor said to me instead of responding to his cousin.

Elena sat back in her chair and threw up her hands, letting out an exclamation in Russian.

Igor ignored her. "And if Cameron talks, he won't like what happens next."

Elena looked like she was ready to slap him. Perhaps he clued in to that fact as well because he stood up and stepped away from her. "I'm done here."

Before either of us could protest, he made a beeline for the door and disappeared out of the café.

Elena muttered something under her breath. "You see what I mean?" she said more audibly. "A disgrace to our family."

"But you still believe he didn't kill Pavlina."

Elena took a second to compose herself. "No, he didn't kill her. But how do we make the police believe that?"

By "we" I assumed she meant me, because I couldn't imagine her pleading with the detectives to believe in her cousin's innocence. She might coolly set out the facts to them, but if they didn't believe her she would no doubt attribute that to their incredible stupidity and walk away in a huff. And I doubted that the detectives would take her word at face value. Igor had a strong motive to kill Pavlina and he easily could have returned to the theater—or never left—to kill her after the concert was under way. The police would no doubt think Elena was trying to protect her family. Heck, I still wasn't completely convinced that she wasn't. Although, as much as I disliked the concertmaster, I had to admit I was leaning toward believing her.

"The police will require proof," I said in answer to her question. "Either proof that Igor didn't kill her or proof that somebody else committed the murder."

"He has no alibi. At least not a good one," Elena said. "He told me before that he was with a friend after he left the theater, but that friend is a criminal too. The police won't believe them."

I figured Igor's friend was the same one I'd seen with him while watching Cameron's meeting from my storage room prison. Silently, I agreed that he wasn't the type of person the police were likely to believe.

Elena slipped her magazine into her designer purse. "You'd better get busy. I'm sick of the police poking their noses into everything. Get this sorted out so we can move on."

Without further parting words, she stood up, snatched her jacket from the back of her chair, and headed for the door. I stared at the spot she'd vacated, stunned by her exiting words, although perhaps I shouldn't have been. She seemed to think I was her servant, someone she could boss around. While that irked me to no end, I planned on doing as she suggested. I'd continue to work on the puzzle, to figure out who the guilty party was. I wouldn't do it for Elena, or to make her life easier, but I'd do it for Pavlina, the orchestra, and all the innocent people who were at risk with a murderer on the loose.

Chapter Nineteen

BEFORE TAKING ANY steps to further my investigation, I decided to enjoy the rest of my sandwich and latte. I took my time, flipping through the newspaper as I ate, and savoring every delicious bite. Without Elena and Igor at the table with me, the atmosphere in the café was far more pleasant and relaxing. The conversation I'd had with them never strayed too far from the forefront of my mind, however.

After finishing my scrumptious lunch, I returned to my car, thinking over everything they'd told me. Although I was leaning toward believing Elena's endorsement of her cousin, I wasn't completely convinced and decided it wouldn't hurt to get a second opinion. While still parked by the curb, I sent a text message to Hans, telling him that Igor had denied killing Pavlina and that Elena insisted he was telling the truth.

Should I believe her or is she likely to lie to cover for him? I asked to finish up the series of messages.

By the time I'd sent the last text, a car had stopped behind my parking place, clearly hoping I was about to leave so they could snag the precious space by the curb. Returning my cell phone to my purse, I freed up the parking spot for the waiting hatchback and set a course for home.

While riding the elevator up to my third-floor apartment, I checked my phone to see if Hans had replied to my messages. He had.

Elena doesn't think much of Igor and wouldn't lie for him. I'm sure of it. If she says he's innocent, he is.

"Innocent" wasn't quite the word I'd have used to describe Igor, since he was a thief, but I knew what Hans meant. And if anyone knew Elena well, it was Hans. The two of them had been in an on-again off-again relationship for years. Knowing that led me to go with my inclination to believe Elena, and if I'd had a physical list of suspects, I would have scratched out Igor's name.

Another message from Hans arrived on my phone. *Does this mean Elena's in the clear now?*

I disembarked from the elevator and tapped out a response as I slowly made my way down the hall to my apartment.

Not yet. I can't prove Igor didn't kill Pavlina or that Elena knows nothing about her death.

After sending that message, I let myself into my apartment and shed my outerwear. By the time I'd hung up my coat, I had another message from Hans.

As long as she's under suspicion, that's bad news for the orchestra.

With a heavy sigh, I typed out a response. *I know. I'm doing my best.*

If that wasn't good enough for him, he'd have to get into sleuthing mode himself.

Fortunately, he sent back a simple thank-you and we left it at that.

I wandered around my apartment for the next several minutes, doing a bit of tidying here and there, my mind elsewhere. What I hadn't mentioned to Hans was that I wasn't sure what step to take next. There were still several suspects on my list, but I wasn't sure what I needed to do to find more clues.

Maybe it would be best to give my mind a short rest, to focus on something else for a while and come back to the problem refreshed in the morning. With that strategy in mind, I called Sharon, a friend from my university days, and arranged to meet up with her for a couple of hours that afternoon. I drove to her place and we took her five-year-old son to a nearby park to play while she and I chatted. As I'd hoped, it was refreshing to do something completely unrelated to the murder case, and I returned home that evening ready to tackle the murder mystery anew during the coming week. I still wasn't sure how to proceed, but I knew I'd figure that out eventually.

While heating up some soup for my dinner, I shuffled through the small stack of magazines I kept on a shelf in my living room. I was looking for the latest issue of *Classical Spotlight*, the one featuring Pavlina on the cover. I found it easily and took it to the kitchen table so I could flip through it while I ate. The magazine might not prove helpful at all, but I wanted to read up on Pavlina in case there was some tidbit about her that would give me insight into her life, that would help me figure out who might have wanted her dead and why.

I'd read the magazine when it first came out—or had skimmed through it, at least—but that was nearly a month ago now, and at the time I hadn't had anything more than a passing interest in the story about the young, upcoming composer.

Once settled in at the table with a steaming bowl of vegetable soup in front of me, I studied the cover of the magazine. In the picture, as in life, Pavlina had a certain spunky style. Her hair was stylishly blown about by the power of an unseen fan and she wore several necklaces of different lengths and a collection of bangles on her left wrist. On her right wrist was the charm bracelet I'd seen her wearing at the theater.

The charm bracelet!

With my spoon halfway to my mouth, I stopped, my thoughts kicking into motion, racing through my head.

That was it. That was what my subconscious had been trying to draw my attention to over the past several days. Every time I'd seen Pavlina alive at the theater, she'd had that pretty charm bracelet on her wrist, including on the night of her death. But when Mikayla and I found her body in the washroom, her right wrist was bare of any jewelry. There'd been a smear of blood on her lower arm, drawing my attention to it. At the time, I hadn't noticed the absence of the bracelet, but now the fact that it had been missing screamed at me with possible significance.

But what exactly was the significance?

If it had come off during a struggle with her attacker, it should have been on the floor of the washroom. It was possible that it had been hidden beneath Pavlina's body and that the police had found it once they'd moved her. However, I suspected that the killer had taken Pavlina by surprise. The only visible wounds were to the back of her head. There was no injury to her arm that I had noticed, so the smear of blood on her wrist—and the smear I'd noticed on the counter—could have been the result of splattered blood or contact between those two spots with the wound on her head as she'd collapsed to the floor.

So, if the bracelet hadn't been lost during a struggle, what had happened to it?

My best guess was that the killer had removed it.

But why?

A hum of excitement ran through my body, starting out low and then growing in volume. I didn't know the answer to that question, but it was likely important. If I knew why someone would want to remove Pavlina's charm bracelet from her body, that might help me identify the killer.

Judging by the magazine photos and the two nights I'd seen Pavlina at the theater, she made a habit of wearing lots of jewelry. Yet while her necklaces and bangles changed with her outfits, the one constant seemed to be her charm bracelet. What significance had it held for her? Was it a gift from someone special?

I didn't think the answer would lie within the pages of the magazine, but I returned my attention to it anyway. As I resumed eating my soup, I read through every word in the article about Pavlina before studying the picture on the cover as well as the smaller photos on the inner pages. By the time my bowl was empty and I'd finished reading, I unfortunately had no further insight into the importance of the bracelet or the identity of the murderer.

If the magazine didn't hold the answers I needed, I'd have to look elsewhere. With a decided lack of enthusiasm, I realized I needed to pay a visit to the police. They were about as likely to tell me if they'd found Pavlina's bracelet at the scene of the crime as they were to give me a million-dollar check just for the heck of it. But if they hadn't found the bracelet and they didn't know it was missing from Pavlina's wrist, I needed to inform them of that fact. They'd probably dismiss the information as unimportant, but that wasn't my problem. I felt it was my duty to tell them what I'd discovered. As usual, what they did with the information was up to them.

Deciding to pay a visit to the police station before my teaching hours started the next day, I spent the rest of the evening reading and watching television, thoughts of Pavlina and her bracelet hovering at the edge of my focus, like background music that I was always peripherally aware of.

Even in my sleep that night, the bracelet didn't stray far from my thoughts. I had a strange dream about it, one where the charms were scattered on the floor. I was trying desperately to gather them up, only to have each one slip through my fingers as soon as I'd picked it up.

In the morning I shook off the dream as well as my residual sleepiness, wasting no time getting ready for the day, despite the fact that I wasn't looking forward to speaking with Detectives Chowdhury and Van den Broek. It was best to get it over with, I told myself, and—if I were extremely lucky—maybe I'd be able to get a feel for how the police investigation was going.

That was unlikely, but my interminable curiosity pushed me to be hopeful.

MY MEETING WITH the police didn't get off to a good start. They kept me waiting for nearly an hour in the reception area, where I had little choice but to sit in one of the hard chairs, playing games on my phone to pass the time. I knew the detectives were busy and there was no guarantee they'd be able to see me when I arrived, but I couldn't help but suspect they were making me wait on purpose.

Perhaps I didn't really suspect that of Detective Chowdhury, but I certainly wouldn't have put it past Detective Van den Broek. The guy wasn't my biggest fan by a long shot, although I doubted he was anyone's biggest fan. I decided to give him the benefit of the doubt, though, and made no comment when he finally appeared to accompany me to the back of the building.

"Is Detective Salnikova in?" I asked out of curiosity, my gaze falling on her unoccupied desk.

"Not at the moment." Van den Broek gestured to a chair by his desk. "She's not working the Nicolova case."

"I know," I said.

I didn't bother to add that I was interested in simply saying hello. No doubt he would view that as frivolous and a desire on my part to waste police time.

"Cute kid," I said when I noticed a framed photo of a young girl on the detective's desk. She had dark curly hair and a big smile with dimples. "Is she your daughter?"

A shadow passed across Van den Broek's face. "Yes."

The way he said that one word told me the subject was off bounds. Maybe he was divorced and didn't get to see his daughter anymore. Whatever the case was, he clearly didn't want to talk about it. I glanced around for Detective Chowdhury, but it seemed he wouldn't be joining us, and I counted that as a stroke of bad luck. Spending time alone with Van den Broek wouldn't be a barrel of laughs.

Deciding it would be best to get our conversation going so it could end as soon as possible, I sat down and jumped right into what I had to tell him.

"There's something that's been bothering me lately. Something about Pavlina's body," I explained. "I couldn't figure out what it was until last night. You see, she wore a charm bracelet on her right wrist. She was wearing it on the evening she was killed, but when Mikayla Deinhardt and I found her body, it was missing."

The detective's face revealed nothing, no interest or lack thereof, no indication of whether this information was new to him or not.

Undeterred, I continued. "I don't know if the bracelet was found at the scene of the crime or not. But if it wasn't, that could mean the killer removed it. And if that's what happened, there must be some significance to it."

Van den Broek tapped his fingers against the desktop in a slow, steady beat. "As I recall," he said after several seconds, "you'd never meant Ms. Nicolova before the composing competition started."

"That's right," I confirmed. "I'd heard about her, of course, but I'd never seen her in person before."

Van den Broek nodded, his fingers still maintaining their steady rhythm. "And yet you feel certain she was wearing a specific bracelet on the night of her death."

"Because I saw it on her wrist earlier that evening," I said, barely muted impatience hovering beneath my words.

"And that was something you took enough notice of to realize that it was missing later that night."

I didn't miss the skepticism in his voice.

"Yes. Eventually."

I wanted to say more. I wanted to clench my teeth in frustration, but I refrained from doing either.

Van den Broek finally ceased the drumming of his fingers, but his face remained devoid of expression and he said nothing, studying me silently from across his desk.

I refused to squirm beneath his gaze, meeting it head-on instead. "It may or may not be important," I said, although I definitely believed that it was significant. "I simply thought I should share with you what I'd noticed."

"I appreciate that."

His tone of voice didn't match his words, and I fought the urge to roll my eyes.

Pushing my chair back, I got to my feet. "I won't take up any more of your time."

Walking with me toward the reception area, Van den Broek said, "We're working hard to solve this case, Ms. Bishop, despite what you might think."

I stopped short in the hallway and faced him. "I never suggested otherwise, Detective. I would have thought you'd want people to share any information they might have, no matter how significant or insignificant it turns out to be."

"We do."

"Hmph" was the only sound I could come up with in response.

One corner of Van den Broek's mouth twitched. I didn't know if it was a sign of growing anger or if he was fighting a smile, but I highly suspected it was the former.

"I simply don't want civilians getting in the way of our official investigation," he said.

"All I've done is share my observations."

"And as I said, I appreciate that." He sounded no more sincere than the first time he'd said those words. "I hope you'll continue to do no more than observe."

Not bothering to respond, I pushed through the door to the reception area and left the station without looking back. Once I was safely closed away in my car, I let out a growl of frustration. That man was infuriating. What he had against me, I didn't know, although I suspected it was something he had against people in general rather than just me.

Whatever his problem was, I'd told him what I knew, and that left me with a clear conscience. If I found myself in possession of any further information that needed to be shared with the authorities, I'd do my best to share it with Detective Chowdhury, because I had no desire to speak with Detective Van den Broek ever again.

Chapter Twenty

ALTHOUGH I LEFT the police station with an imaginary gray cloud hovering over my head, courtesy of Detective Van den Broek, my mood had improved by the time I reached JT's house. I was looking forward to my afternoon of teaching. Working with my students—both children and adults—was enjoyable and rewarding for me, at least most of the time. Whether I was teaching, playing with the orchestra, or practicing on my own, music had a way of calming and relaxing me, and I was glad to have something to take my mind off my conversation with the less-than-agreeable detective.

I had some time to spare before my first student would arrive and I was pleased to find that JT was at home. He appeared along with Finnegan when I let myself into the house.

"Hey, guys," I said as I gave Finnegan a pat on the head.

"How's your day going so far?" JT asked as I shed my coat and hat, storing them in the closet.

"I stopped by the police station," I replied. "That wasn't exactly thrilling, but otherwise things are fine. How about you?"

"I'm fine, but why were you at the police station?"

I didn't miss the suspicion in his eyes. "Just sharing some information."

Before he could become any more suspicious, I filled him in on what I'd remembered about Pavlina's charm bracelet.

"Why would the killer want to take her bracelet?" JT asked once I'd finished.

"I don't know. But if I did know, I bet I'd be a lot further ahead with this investigation."

"I'm sure you'll figure it out before too long."

Although I detected a hint of good-natured exasperation in his words, I was pleased by his belief in me. Maybe it was confidence in my nosiness more than anything, but I chose to see it as a compliment.

Digging around in my tote bag, I pulled out a container holding the sandwich I'd packed that morning before leaving home. "Are you going to be around for a bit?" I asked, hoping I'd have his company while I ate.

"Actually, I have to go out in a few minutes. I've got a meeting with the *Absolute Zero* team. But first," he continued before I had a chance to comment, "I was wondering if you could do me a favor."

"Of course."

"I'm thinking of putting together an album of some of my music."

My face lit up. "That's great, JT."

I'd been telling him for years that he should get his music out in the world. Yes, his score for *Absolute Zero* was on television for the world to hear, but he had dozens of compositions unrelated to the sci-fi show that deserved to be heard by the public as well.

JT dug a flash drive out of the pocket of his jeans. "I picked out the songs I think I want to use, but I was wondering if you could give me your opinion on the song choices and the order."

"I'd love to." I meant it sincerely. I always enjoyed listening to his music, no matter the occasion.

"Great. Thanks." He handed me the flash drive. "No rush. I don't have a real timeline or anything."

"I'm so glad you're doing this. Really." Something occurred to me then. I held up the flash drive. "What about your new song? Is it on here?"

"It is." JT grabbed his coat from the foyer closet and pulled it on. He suddenly seemed in more of a hurry to leave. "I'd better get going. I'll catch you later."

"Have a good meeting!" I called after him as he disappeared out the door.

When he was gone, I addressed Finnegan. "I guess it's just you and me for the moment."

Sitting in the middle of the foyer, Finnegan wagged his tail, a big doggie grin on his face.

"You'll keep me company while I eat, right?"

He gave an enthusiastic bark and raced ahead of me to the kitchen, never one to miss out on the chance to catch any crumbs or other scraps of food that might end up down at his level.

I tucked JT's flash drive into my pocket and perched on a stool at the breakfast bar to eat my lunch. I was eager to check out the songs JT had chosen for his album, but that would have to wait until I got home and had access to my laptop. Besides, I wanted to give the selection of songs my full attention, and I couldn't do that when my first student was due to arrive in less than twenty minutes.

As I ate my sandwich—giving the occasional tidbit to an appreciative Finnegan—I thought over the puzzle of Pavlina's missing charm bracelet. The magazine hadn't held any clues as to the significance of the bracelet, and I doubted I'd find the information I needed online. More likely than not, the only way to figure out who would want to steal the bracelet was to talk with people who knew Pavlina well.

The easiest person to approach would be Dongmei, but Pavlina had been no more than an acquaintance to her. Still, their paths had crossed more than once over the past few years and Dongmei seemed to know some of the gossip within their circle of young composers. Maybe it was a bit of a stretch to expect her to know anything about a specific piece of Pavlina's jewelry, but I decided to start with her anyway.

If she couldn't help me, I'd move on to someone else. Jeb was the person I figured was most likely to know personal details about Pavlina, but I wasn't particularly looking forward to that conversation. Recalling how angry he was when he'd found me with his phone, tiny patters of dread waltzed up my spine. If I did approach him with questions about Pavlina, I'd have to make sure I did so at a time when other people were well within shouting distance. I didn't want him lashing out at me with anything more than words if I managed to trigger his temper again. I needed to remember that he was on my suspect list, and that it was entirely possible he'd killed Pavlina. The killer wouldn't think too kindly about me poking my nose into the matter, and that was definitely something to keep in mind.

If JT had known I was considering a chat with Jeb, he would have warned me that it was risky, and I wouldn't have been able to argue with him. I planned to do my very best to keep myself out of danger, but I was still determined to ferret out the information I needed.

I tucked those thoughts aside as I finished off my lunch and let Finnegan out in the backyard for a few minutes. When we returned indoors, my first student of the day was letting herself in through the unlocked front door.

I spent the next several hours focused on my students, and the time passed fairly quickly. By the time I said goodbye to my final student of the day, darkness had fallen. I bundled up and let Finnegan outside again before giving him a goodbye pat and heading out to my car. The evening wasn't quite as cold as I'd thought it might be, probably because a bank of clouds had moved in, the moon only peeking out occasionally. Still, it definitely wasn't warm out and I was glad of my cozy coat and my car's heater.

Before pulling away from the curb, I sent Dongmei a text message, asking if she knew anything about Pavlina's charm bracelet. Then I returned my phone to my purse and set off into the night. Although it was my initial intention to head home, I turned left instead of right when I reached Dunbar Street.

It was Monday evening and I had no concert or rehearsal to attend. On Tuesday night there would be a finale concert, and all the remaining finalists and the judges would be in attendance. The orchestra would play excerpts from each of the top compositions, after which the winner would be announced. Since Jeb would be there that night, I'd originally intended to question him then, if Dongmei's response to my text message didn't provide me with the information I was after. But when I was alone with my thoughts again, I realized it made me uneasy to wait that long.

I knew there was a judges' meeting scheduled to begin in less than an hour, and that it would take place at the theater. It would give the judges a final chance to confer and decide on the winner. Jeb would be there, and with any luck I'd have a chance to speak with him.

As I arrived at the theater and pulled into a parking spot behind the building, I had second thoughts. Maybe it would be smarter to go home and wait for a response from Dongmei. Still sitting in my car, I pulled my phone out of my bag. I hadn't received a reply to my message.

Tapping my fingers against the steering wheel, I considered my options. I was about to back out of the parking space and head home when my phone buzzed. Shutting off my car's engine, I checked the device.

Sorry, I don't know anything about it, Dongmei had replied. *Is it important?*

I'm not sure, I wrote back. *I'm hoping to find out.*

Climbing out of my car and locking it up behind me, I hurried across the parking lot and entered the theater through the stage door. The corridors were deserted and almost eerily silent. I made a quick circuit of the backstage hallways on the main floor, but found no one. If the judges were already at the theater, perhaps they were upstairs.

I made my way up to the second floor, where it was just as quiet as down below. The door to the judges' lounge stood open, however, and the light was on inside the room. I poked my head around the door frame, but the lounge was empty. Frowning, I checked the time on my phone. The meeting wasn't scheduled to begin for another twenty minutes or so.

I took a few steps farther along the hallway to see if Hans was in his office, but the door was shut and locked, and there was no response to my knock. Deciding to wait downstairs for Jeb's arrival, I turned around and headed for the stairway. As I made my way down toward the main floor, heated voices floated up from below. I slowed my steps, making as little noise as possible, not keen on walking straight into the middle of an argument.

Although I couldn't make out any specific words, I could tell that two men were in the midst of a disagreement. They spoke in lowered voices, but I thought one belonged to Ethan and the other perhaps to Jeb, minus his phony accent.

As I made my way down the last few stairs, I thought I heard the words "threaten me" and "mistake," spoken by Jeb. Ethan said something fiercely in return, but I couldn't make out any specifics.

I stepped off the last stair and almost collided with Jeb. Fury practically radiated off of him and it wouldn't have surprised me to see steam pouring out of his ears. Ethan had disappeared from sight, and despite the judge's dark mood, I decided to take advantage of the fact that I'd almost literally run into Jeb.

He stepped around me, his features still shadowed by anger. Perhaps that should have frightened me, but I didn't give myself a chance to think about it.

"Mr. Hartson," I said, stopping him before he could continue on to the second floor. "I was hoping to ask you something."

He stopped on the first step and turned back, towering over me. "Is that right?" His drawl was back in place, but there was a steeliness to his eyes that told me he hadn't forgotten our previous encounter.

A shrill note of unease whistled away in the back of my mind, but I ignored it and pressed on. "I was wondering if you knew anything about Pavlina's charm bracelet."

Something shifted in his eyes. The steeliness remained, but now wariness and calculation accompanied it. "Why would you think I'd know anything about some bracelet of hers?" He set the words out carefully, his eyes fixed on my face.

"Because you were close to her."

"Was I now?" He stepped down off the stair and I fought the temptation to move back to maintain the same distance between us. "What gave you that idea?"

I swallowed, but did my best to remain outwardly calm. I didn't want him to know that he was intimidating me, that my heart was dancing a wild tarantella in my chest. For a split second I considered lying and telling him I'd simply heard rumors, but I discarded that idea. If he was certain he'd kept his relationship with Pavlina a secret from everyone except Olivia, he might know I was lying. In that case, I might get more out of him if I went with the truth.

"I accidentally overheard you speaking with Olivia Hutchcraft last week. You and Pavlina were in a relationship."

Jeb stood very still. A twitch from a muscle in his jaw was the only detectable movement from his entire body. His eyes drilled into me, and I suddenly realized I hadn't made sure that there were people within shouting distance before starting this conversation. Hopefully there was someone nearby, since the judges' meeting was set to begin soon, but I couldn't guarantee that. After all, I hadn't seen or heard anyone other than Jeb and Ethan since I'd arrived.

Several seconds passed before Jeb spoke. "You know, eavesdropping on private conversations isn't something I'd recommend."

I did my best to maintain my unruffled demeanor. "Like I said, it was accidental." That was only a slight stretch of the truth. I hadn't purposely stumbled upon their conversation, although I could have stopped listening early on.

"Be that as it may, I suggest you forget about what you heard. I don't take kindly to threats."

"I'm not threatening you," I said. "And I have no intention of doing so."

I wondered if he was so quick to jump to that conclusion because of the argument he'd just had with Ethan. My guess was that the photos Ethan had taken of Jeb's phone had factored into the conversation.

"Then what exactly is your intention?" he asked.

"I'm trying to find out about Pavlina's bracelet," I reminded him.

"And why's that?"

This time I decided it would be safer to lie than to tell the truth. If he was the killer, I didn't want him to know I'd realized that the bracelet had gone missing.

"It was beautiful," I said. "I was hoping to get one like it, so I was wondering if you knew where she'd bought it."

Jeb seemed to relax a fraction. "She didn't buy it. It was a gift from her best friend."

He turned around, ready to head back up the stairs again.

"Her best friend, Tiffany Alphonse?" I asked. "The girl who died a few years back?"

Jeb faced me again. Steely suspicion had returned to his eyes. "That's right. That's why she never took it off. It was important to her."

"I see."

"Why are you really asking these questions?" he demanded.

"Like I said—"

He cut me off before I could say more. "Don't give me that crap. You're not looking to buy a bracelet. You're sticking your nose where it doesn't belong. First I find you snooping through my phone and now you're asking strange questions. I don't like people who don't mind their own business."

He took a step toward me and the warning whistle in my head shot up an octave and cranked up the volume. This time I took a step back, suddenly all too aware of how easily he could grab me.

"Everything all right here?"

I jumped at the sound of the voice behind me, and then nearly stumbled back as a wave of relief hit me. Harold Dempsey had come along the corridor without me or Jeb noticing. He waited for a response, his eyes going from me to his fellow judge.

"Everything's just fine," Jeb drawled. He flashed a smile at me, but didn't bother trying to infuse it with any sincerity. "Now, if you'll excuse me, I have things to attend to." He nodded at Harold. "Dempsey. I'll see you upstairs."

Without another word, he took the stairs at an unhurried pace, disappearing seconds later into the second-floor hallway.

"Are you really all right?" Harold asked me.

"Yes, fine," I said quickly. "Thank you."

My heart still dancing frantically in my chest, I hurried down the corridor, sensing Harold's eyes on me until I was able to escape around the corner and out of his line of sight.

Chapter Twenty-One

I DECIDED I needed a few minutes to calm down before leaving the theater and getting mixed up in the evening traffic. The last thing I needed was to get in a car accident because of my swirling thoughts and frazzled nerves. Digging a key out of my shoulder bag, I unlocked the door to the musicians' lounge and flicked on the overhead lights. Once I had the door shut behind me, I dropped my bag onto the nearest couch and flopped down next to it.

My encounter with Jeb had left me so flustered and uneasy that I couldn't seem to collect my thoughts. They'd scattered like sheets of music caught by a gust of wind, and it took me several minutes of sitting quietly on the couch to gather them up and shift them into order.

For the second time, I was lucky Harold had appeared to defuse the situation. If he hadn't arrived on the scene, I no doubt would have discovered just how violent Jeb's temper could be. I was more convinced than ever that Jeb belonged at the top of my suspect list along with Ethan. Behind his fake accent and cowboy façade, he was a frightening man.

Once my heart had given up its wild dance and had slowed to a more sedate pace, I considered the information I'd gleaned from the judge. Pavlina had received the bracelet from her late best friend and had worn it constantly. But if the bracelet was a gift from Tiffany Alphonse, what had the killer wanted with it?

I reminded myself that I didn't know for certain that the killer had taken the charm bracelet. It wasn't as if Detective Van den Broek had confirmed my theory. Still, I had an inkling that the police hadn't found the bracelet under Pavlina's body or anywhere else near the scene of the crime. So unless it had fallen off her wrist earlier that evening—after staying in place for at least three years since it was given to her—someone had removed it from her body.

While it wasn't outside the realm of possibility that somebody had stumbled upon Pavlina before me and Mikayla and had decided to steal the bracelet, I highly doubted that was how things had played out. Some of Pavlina's rings and necklaces had appeared far more expensive than the bracelet, so why take the one item and leave the others?

No, I decided. The killer was the most likely person to have taken the piece of jewelry.

The problem was that I still had no idea why.

I let out a sigh and shook my head. I wasn't sure my conversation with Jeb had been worth it. The information he'd given me didn't seem to have moved me forward with my investigation, and I knew for a fact that I'd made an enemy of the judge. At any rate, I decided I'd calmed down enough to drive home. I got up from the couch and opened the lounge door carefully, desperately hoping that Jeb was still upstairs. Running into him again was the last thing I wanted to do.

When I poked my head out the door, my heart nearly broke into an encore performance of its earlier wild dance. There was someone out in the hallway. Almost as soon as I'd realized that, relief replaced my burgeoning panic. The person I'd spotted was Sasha rather than Jeb.

He was heading my way, a file folder stuffed with papers in one hand and his phone in the other. A plan popping into my head, I grabbed my phone and quickly snapped a picture of him. Fortunately, he didn't notice, his attention focused on his own device. As I switched off the light and locked the door to the musicians' lounge, Sasha disappeared up the stairs to the second floor, never giving a sign that he'd noticed me.

The sight of Olivia's assistant had reminded me of the fact that he and his boss were still murder suspects. Jeb and Ethan were likelier suspects in my mind, but that didn't mean I could ignore the other possibilities. Sasha had claimed that he'd been away from the theater during the time when Pavlina was killed. That meant he couldn't provide Olivia with an alibi for that time period, but did it really provide *him* with an alibi?

At the moment I only had his word that he'd been delayed at Starbucks by a long line of caffeine-craving customers. It was possible that he'd gone to the coffee shop and quickly fetched coffee for Olivia, leaving time for him to kill Pavlina either before he left or when he returned. I still couldn't come up with a reason for him to want Pavlina dead, especially since he'd claimed he didn't know her prior to the competition, but that didn't mean no motive existed.

I checked the time on my phone. It was only seven in the evening. My stomach was rumbling, demanding dinner, but that wasn't a problem. With the plan I'd recently formed, I could assuage my hunger while checking out Sasha's alibi at the same time.

Glancing over my shoulder to make sure Jeb was still nowhere in sight, I left the theater and stepped out into the night. Instead of heading for my car, I turned the opposite way and struck out on foot for the Starbucks located half a block away from the theater.

The trip only took a minute or two and warm air greeted me when I stepped inside the coffee shop. Letting the door fall shut behind me, I pulled off my gloves and tucked them in my coat pockets while surveying my surroundings. Fortunately, the place wasn't crowded and there was only one person at the counter ahead of me. I hoped that meant the two baristas on duty would be willing to chat with me.

When it was my turn to order, I asked for a tall vanilla steamed milk and a chocolate chip cookie. Not exactly the healthiest dinner, but I told myself I'd eat some fruit when I got home to balance it out at least a little bit.

"Were you here on Friday night two weeks ago?" I asked as I handed a ten-dollar bill to the twenty-something woman behind the counter.

"Sure," she said as she counted out my change. "I'm usually here on Friday evenings."

Once I'd accepted my change from her, I pulled up the picture of Sasha on my phone and showed it to her. "Do you remember if this guy came in?"

She squinted at the photo. "No, sorry. I don't recognize him."

Disappointment weighed down my shoulders.

"What about you, Kelsey?" she asked her coworker, who was on her way by. "Do you recognize this guy?"

Kelsey leaned over her coworker's shoulder for a closer look at the photo. "Sure, I remember him. He's been coming in a lot lately."

A spark of optimism replaced my disappointment. "Was he here two weeks ago, on Friday night?" I asked, hoping Kelsey had been working at that time.

She thought for a second. "Yes, he was here that night. I remember because we chatted about the hockey game that was on at the time."

"So he stayed for a while?" I asked.

"Nah. We only talked for a minute, if that."

"But was it busy that night? Did he have to wait in line?"

"No, it was pretty quiet. I don't think there was a line at all when he came in."

"Lying boyfriend?" Kelsey's coworker guessed as she slid my drink and cookie across the counter toward me.

"Something like that," I said, slipping my phone into my bag. I picked up my order. "Thanks."

When I turned around, I nearly froze. Sasha had just entered the coffee shop. Flashing him a quick smile, I hurried out onto the sidewalk, hoping the baristas wouldn't mention that I'd been asking questions about him.

Walking briskly, I nibbled on my cookie as I headed back toward the theater. Kelsey's memory of Sasha seemed quite clear, and her account of his visit to the coffee shop on the night of Pavlina's death didn't match his. If he'd been in and out of Starbucks within a few minutes, he would have had plenty of time to kill Pavlina either before or after his coffee run.

I frowned as I continued along the street. I couldn't think of any reason why Sasha would have lied to me if not to cover up his involvement in Pavlina's death. But although he'd apparently had an opportunity to commit the crime, I still couldn't figure out his motive.

Maybe he'd also lied to me when he'd said he didn't know Pavlina before the competition. That was a possibility, but at the moment it was purely speculative. I'd have to ask around to find out if that really was the case. But even if it wasn't, and they did have history of some sort, would anyone else know about it?

Not necessarily.

Reaching the theater, I turned down the side alley that would take me to the back parking lot. Once settled in my car, I finished off my cookie, too hungry to drive home without something in my stomach. After I'd polished off the last crumb, I took a long sip of my steamed milk, thinking. Maybe I wasn't ready to leave the theater after all. If I went back into the building, there was a chance that I might be able to talk to Olivia Hutchcraft. She was the most likely person to know some details about Sasha. Perhaps she'd heard or witnessed something that would expose his claim of not knowing Pavlina as a lie. A long shot, yes, but that was all I had to go on at the moment.

I couldn't seem to find any definitive evidence to point to one single person as the culprit, and that frustrated me to no end. While there was a chance that Olivia wouldn't want to talk to me, I'd give it a go and see what happened. Of course, the trick would be to catch her alone, without Sasha hovering nearby, since it was likely he'd returned from Starbucks while I was enjoying my makeshift supper. If he was the killer, I didn't want him to know I'd disproved his alibi. That might tempt him to silence me, which wasn't a pleasant thought. It was bad enough that I'd already angered one of my top suspects. I didn't need to be in Sasha's bad books too.

Hoping desperately that I wouldn't run into Jeb—at least not without anyone else present—I got out of my car, taking my steamed milk along with me. Once inside the theater, I made my way along the corridor toward the staircase. I paused at the bottom of the steps, my attention caught by a low murmur of voices.

"You really thought I wouldn't recognize you?"

The voice belonged to Ethan. I was certain of that.

A quieter voice said something in return, but I couldn't make out the words. I couldn't even tell if it was a man or a woman talking.

Ethan laughed scornfully. The voices were coming from farther down the hall and out of sight, perhaps near the washrooms.

I decided to tiptoe closer to see if I could hear more of the conversation. As suspicious as I was of Sasha and his lies, Ethan was still one of my top suspects and I didn't want to pass up the chance to gather potential clues.

I turned away from the stairs, but movement flickered in my peripheral vision and a thud pulled my attention back to the stairway.

"Oh no!" Olivia exclaimed.

She was one stair from the top, on her way down, but she'd dropped her phone and a sheaf of papers. Her phone had hit the carpeted stair below her and remained there, but the papers were still floating down the stairway, landing all over the place. As she stooped down to grab her phone and the nearest papers, I hurried up the steps to lend a hand.

"Here, let me help," I said as I gathered up several papers.

"Thank you," she said as I handed the papers over. "I can't believe I was so clumsy."

"How's your phone?" I asked.

She activated the screen and it came to life without a problem.

"It looks all right, thank goodness." She shook her head. "Sorry about that."

"Not a problem," I assured her.

She continued past me down the stairs and I followed her.

"Ms. Hutchcraft?"

"Yes?" She paused at the bottom of the stairs, but her attention was directed more toward her phone than to me as she tapped out a text message.

"Your assistant, Sasha, was friends with Pavlina, right?" I asked.

She glanced up briefly, a crease between her eyebrows. "No, I don't believe so. I don't think they knew each other at all before Sasha started this job."

"Oh," I said. "My mistake."

She nodded, distracted by her text messaging again, and set off down the corridor.

So Sasha hadn't lied about not knowing Pavlina?

I took a sip of my cooling steamed milk, continuing to think things over. Why Sasha would want to kill someone he'd only known for a couple of weeks, I didn't know. But I also didn't know why he would have lied about his trip to the coffee shop if he wasn't trying to cover something up.

Maybe I could find Olivia's assistant and ask him a few more questions. Although if he knew I'd been asking about him at the coffee shop, he might not be too receptive to chatting with me. It was unusual that he wasn't following Olivia around, but maybe he'd lingered at Starbucks or was up in the meeting room. I decided to go upstairs and take a look, but I didn't get farther than the first step before a shrill scream shattered the quiet of the theater's main floor.

Startled, I glanced down the hallway in the direction Olivia had taken. A split second later she stumbled into view from around a corner, her eyes wide and her face pale.

"Help!" she cried before bursting into tears.

I rushed her way and she pointed around the corner with a trembling finger.

Apprehension plucking at my taut nerves, I took another step so I could see what had upset her.

Ethan was lying on the floor, unmoving, the front of his shirt soaked with blood.

The killer had struck again.

Chapter Twenty-Two

I STOOD FROZEN for a second or two until another sob from Olivia jolted me into action. Dropping my bag on the floor and setting down my cup of steamed milk, I crept closer to Ethan's body and crouched down, pressing two fingers to his throat.

"No pulse," I said as I stood up, my legs trembling beneath me.

Olivia cried harder. I backed away from Ethan's body, not wanting to be so close to it and not wanting to contaminate the crime scene any further. I was about to retrieve my bag so I could find my phone and call for help when Harold Dempsey jogged along the corridor toward us.

"What's going on?" he asked with concern, his eyes on Olivia.

Her screams must have alerted him to the fact that there was a problem.

"It's Ethan," I said, pointing around the corner.

As I had done moments earlier, he stepped forward so he could see the body. His mouth set into a grim line.

"He doesn't have a pulse," I said.

Harold removed his cell phone from the pocket of his pants.

Olivia continued to sob, her papers clutched to her chest and one hand covering her eyes so she couldn't see Ethan's body.

"I'll call for help," Harold said to me. "Could you take Ms. Hutchcraft elsewhere?"

"Of course. I'll take her to the musicians' lounge."

I tucked an arm through Olivia's. "Let's go, Ms. Hutchcraft."

I hesitated, remembering my bag, but Harold had already picked it up. "Are these yours?" he asked, holding out the bag and my steamed milk.

"Yes. Thank you."

I hooked my arm through the straps of the bag and took the drink, using my other arm to guide Olivia down the hallway. When we reached the locked door to the musicians' lounge, I glanced over my shoulder. Jeb Hartson, Yvonne Charbonneau, and Sasha had appeared on the scene, likely drawn by Olivia's screams as well. They were all crowded at the end of the corridor near Ethan's body, conferring with Harold.

As soon as I had the door unlocked, I flipped on the lights and put an arm around Olivia's shoulders to guide her into the room. I left the door open so we'd be easy to find once the police arrived. No doubt we'd all have to be questioned again like we were on the night of Pavlina's death.

I got Olivia settled on one of the couches and retrieved a small packet of tissues I kept in my locker. She accepted them with tremulous thanks and pulled one from the package to dab at her tears. I set my bag on one of the tables, my steamed milk next to it. What remained of the drink had gone cold, but I didn't care. At the moment the mere thought of eating or drinking anything sent my stomach into a sickening twist.

Sitting down on the couch across from Olivia, I stared blankly at the crying woman for a minute or two before the worst of the shock of seeing Ethan dead wore off.

Another victim. Another murder.

I could hardly believe it, but I'd seen the evidence right there in front of me.

Pavlina's murderer had killed again. I didn't doubt that for a second. The chance that the two murders could be unrelated was infinitesimally small in my opinion. The deaths were most likely connected, caused by the same hand.

But who was the killer?

Ethan had been one of my top suspects, but I could now strike his name off my list. That left Jeb at the top of my list, followed by Sasha. I also hadn't ruled out Olivia's involvement. As the first person on the scene of Ethan's death, she easily could have killed him and then started screaming, pretending she'd stumbled across his body. She'd also had an opportunity to kill Pavlina.

Studying the woman across from me, I thought she looked genuinely distressed, but I couldn't discount the possibility that she was a great actress. I didn't spot any signs of blood on her skin or clothing, but Ethan's wound was more of a seeping one, with no splattering at the scene, and Olivia could have easily washed her hands after stabbing him since the murder took place right outside the washrooms.

But why would Olivia kill Ethan?

I recalled Ethan's recent behavior. He'd snapped photos of pictures on Jeb's phone and he'd had a heated conversation with the judge earlier that evening. My guess was that Ethan had threatened Jeb with exposure, hoping to force the judge to vote for him in the competition. If Ethan was willing to blackmail a judge, maybe he was also willing to threaten a murderer.

Had he known who the killer was? Had he tried to use that to his advantage in some way?

If so, that would be strong motivation for the killer to get rid of him.

That could have been Olivia's motive, but it also could have been Sasha's. And if Ethan really had threatened to expose Jeb's relationship with Pavlina, that could have been enough for the judge to kill him, if Jeb had worried that his professional reputation and career would be at risk. So, basically, Ethan was the only suspect I could rule out.

My heart skittered about in my chest as I realized I could be sitting mere feet away from the murderer. I was glad I'd left the lounge door open, and I was also relieved when I saw two police officers pass by the room, heading toward the crime scene.

Minutes later, Harold, Jeb, Yvonne, and Sasha entered the lounge, accompanied by a uniformed officer.

"We'd appreciate no talking amongst yourselves until all your statements have been taken," the officer said.

"And when will that happen?" Yvonne Charbonneau asked.

"Soon, ma'am" was as specific as the officer got.

As the new arrivals scattered about the lounge to claim seats, I observed each of them in turn. Jeb's eyes passed over me, pausing and filling with dark anger before moving on. He took a seat on the other side of the room, and for that I was glad. Yvonne sat primly on the couch next to Olivia, her hands folded in her lap. She was the one person in the room—aside from the police officer and myself—whom I didn't suspect of killing Pavlina and Ethan. Perhaps she'd had an opportunity to commit the second murder, but she'd remained in the audience for the entire concert on the night of Pavlina's death and hadn't had a chance to commit that crime.

Sasha perched on the table where I'd left my belongings, prodding the screen of his smart phone. From his actions, I guessed he was playing a game to help pass the time. He didn't seem too disturbed by what had happened to Ethan, but maybe he was just good at hiding his emotions. Harold and Jeb both had grim expressions, but beyond that I couldn't read anything from their faces or body language.

It seemed like forever before Detectives Van den Broek and Chowdhury made an appearance in the lounge. Several people had gone back and forth along the corridor before their arrival—other police officers, crime scene technicians, and the coroner. When the detectives asked who had found the body, Olivia stood up, her lips still quivering, although her tears had stopped flowing.

Detective Chowdhury asked her to accompany him out of the lounge and Van den Broek's eyes settled on me.

My stomach dropped.

"Ms. Bishop, would you come with me, please?"

Of course he had to be the one to question me. I would have much preferred to speak with his partner, but I doubted a request of that nature would be well received.

"Excuse me," I said to Sasha as I retrieved my bag from the spot next to him on the table.

He barely looked up from his game.

Dropping my cold steamed milk into the garbage can by the door, I followed Detective Van den Broek around a corner and down the hallway before he led the way through a door and into the large room used for the Point Grey Philharmonic's receptions and other gatherings.

Someone had already turned on the lights and set out two folding chairs. Aside from four busts of famous composers decorating the red-carpeted room, it was otherwise empty. I suppressed a shiver as I remembered how one of the symphony's benefactors had dropped dead of poisoning in that very room a few months earlier. Once again, murder had found its way into the theater, contaminating the otherwise pleasant building.

Detective Van den Broek directed me to take a seat, and I did so, placing my bag on the floor at my feet. I wondered if he'd make a snarky comment about me being at the scene of the crime again, but fortunately he didn't, instead going straight to his questions.

"What brought you to the theater this evening, Ms. Bishop?"

Most likely he knew by now that there was no rehearsal or concert scheduled that night, and I realized he probably wouldn't be too impressed by my answer.

"I came by to gather information."

As usual, the detective's face revealed no emotion. "Information."

I told him about my conversation with Jeb and how the judge had said Pavlina's charm bracelet was a gift from her best friend who died a few years ago. When I'd finished recounting that exchange, we sat in silence for a moment. Judging by the shifting of his jaw, I suspected the detective was grinding his teeth.

"Ms. Bishop," he said eventually, "we discussed this earlier today. You said you were simply making observations and wouldn't get in the way of the official investigation."

"The information I shared this morning did consist of observations," I defended myself. "And I wasn't getting in the way of the official investigation. All I did was ask some questions. I didn't obstruct the police in any way."

He was less than pleased by my answer, and I got the sense he was struggling to keep his temper in check.

"Do you realize," he said, his words measured, "that if you ask the wrong questions of the wrong person, you could be putting yourself in danger?"

"I had thought of that, yes. And, I'll admit, Jeb Hartson isn't pleased with me."

"Then you'll agree that the sensible thing to do would be to back off and leave the investigating to the professionals."

I'd heard this so many times before from JT, Detective Salnikova, and her partner. As much as their lectures had exasperated me in the past, I much preferred hearing those things from JT and Salnikova than from Detective Van den Broek. Still, as much as it irked me to have Van den Broek scold me, I couldn't argue with him.

"I do agree," I said. "And I'm the first to admit that my curiosity sometimes gets the better of me."

"So you'll stop asking questions?"

That was almost like asking me not to breathe, but the detective's unflinching gaze told me he wasn't going to back down on the subject and, as I'd just admitted, he was right. I'd already ruffled feathers by asking questions and as much as I wanted the murderer caught, I didn't want to put myself in any more danger than I already had.

"I'll stop asking questions." I had to pull the words out of myself like sore teeth, but I managed to say them.

Van den Broek's eyes weren't completely without suspicion, but he didn't voice his doubt.

"There's something else you should know," I said.

The detective let out a breath, and I had a sneaking suspicion he was counting to ten in his head, once again trying to keep his temper reined in. "And what's that?"

"I overheard Ethan talking to someone shortly before he was killed." When a muscle in his jaw twitched, I hurried to add, "It was purely accidental."

He didn't believe that. It was clear on his face, but I forged on.

"I don't know who he was talking to, but he said something about recognizing the person, like 'Did you think I wouldn't recognize you?' I don't know if that's significant or not."

"And you have no idea who that person was?"

"No. I couldn't even tell if it was a man or woman. Whoever they were, they were talking too quietly."

Van den Broek let out a heavy sigh and wrote something in his notebook. "I'll need you to start from the beginning, from the moment you entered the theater. Tell me where you went, who you saw, what you heard. As best as you can remember."

I did as requested, and as I recounted how I'd met Olivia on the stairway and helped to clean up her papers, I realized that she most likely hadn't killed Ethan. Even if she'd had the murder weapon—a knife, probably—secreted beneath her clothing, she would have had mere seconds to stab Ethan and dispose of it. Knowing that didn't make me confident enough to eliminate her from my pool of suspects, but it did bump her down to the bottom of the list.

Once I'd finished telling Van den Broek everything I could remember and had filled out a witness statement form, he reminded me about my agreement to stop asking questions and I assured him that I'd stick to it. After that, he allowed me to escape from his presence. I left the reception room and headed down the hall. Several official personnel still lingered near the crime scene, but I spared them no more than a glance. I wanted to get out of the theater, to go home.

Exiting through the stage door, I made my way along the side alley toward the parking lot. As I reached the edge of the building and was about to turn the corner to enter the lot, I heard a voice and stopped in my tracks.

It was Jeb's voice, and he was the last person I wanted to meet alone in the dark. I waited out of sight from the parking lot, hoping he'd get in his car and leave without seeing me. It sounded like he was on the phone, and the next words I overheard sent an icy chill along my spine.

"They still don't suspect anything." A short pause followed before he said, "I'll take care of it first thing tomorrow morning."

My heart thudded in my chest. What did nobody suspect? That he was the killer? And what would he take care of tomorrow? Was he planning to kill someone else?

My mouth had gone dry and I found it hard to swallow. I leaned against the rough exterior of the building, my legs suddenly shaking beneath my weight. I listened as Jeb said goodbye to whomever he was speaking with, and seconds later I heard a car door slam. An engine roared to life and I peered around the corner in time to see Jeb drive toward the lot's exit.

I hurried toward my own car and climbed inside, shutting and locking the door as quickly as possible. Jeb's words had left me spooked, on edge. I considered returning to the theater to tell Van den Broek what I'd heard, but I was worried that might be the final straw. If he lost his temper with me, would he slap me in handcuffs and haul me down to the police station? I didn't think he could actually charge me with obstructing justice or anything else, but I wasn't sure that would stop him from using his authority to give me a good scare.

Starting my car, I decided to go home as originally planned.

When I pulled out of the parking lot and into the alley, the tail-lights of Jeb's car shone through the darkness ahead of me and then disappeared as he turned out onto the street.

You promised Van den Broek you wouldn't ask any more questions, I reminded myself as I considered abandoning my plan to return home.

I have no intention of asking questions, I argued with myself.

That was true. By following Jeb I wouldn't be going against my word to the detective. Although I'd told him I wouldn't ask questions, I never said I'd stop investigating completely.

And this time I'd do a better job of tailing my suspect than I had with Cameron.

My mind made up, I turned out onto the street and set off in the same direction as Jeb's vehicle.

I didn't expect to gather any significant clues by following the judge. What I had in mind was to find out where he lived. Once I knew that, I could return in the morning and follow him again. Hopefully I could then find out what he was planning to do. If he did anything suspicious, if I felt I was in the slightest danger, I would call the police. But for now I simply wanted to know where I could find him in the morning.

It didn't take too long to tail him to his home. It turned out that he lived in a townhouse not far from the University of British Columbia. I was a bit disappointed that I wouldn't be able to pinpoint his particular unit because he turned into the gated underground parking lot and I couldn't follow him any farther. Pulling up to the curb, I shut off my car and sat there in the dark, tugging at my left earlobe. Should I wait and see if any lights came on in one of the nearby units, or give up and go home? I decided to wait for a while, but when no interior lights flashed on nearby, I resigned myself to the fact that I wouldn't be able to identify his unit.

Perhaps that wasn't a total loss, though. Since he'd parked his car in the underground lot, he'd have to come out that way in the morning too. If I returned to this same spot in the morning and waited, I could still catch him leaving to do whatever suspicious deed he had planned.

Deciding that was the best course of action, I finally set off for home and what I hoped would be a good night's sleep.

Chapter Twenty-Three

I ARRIVED AT my apartment a short time later, but sleep eluded me when I went to bed. Images of Ethan lying dead kept appearing every time I closed my eyes, and snippets of all the conversations I'd had or overheard that night went around and around in my head.

Eventually I drifted off, but still the events of the night didn't leave me alone. I had uneasy dreams of shadowy threats lurking out of sight. At one point I awoke with a start, and it took me several panicked seconds to remember I was safe at home rather than trapped in the derelict building of my dreams, a killer haunting the hallways.

When morning arrived, I gladly left my bed behind, hoping my next night's sleep would be far more peaceful. I was up earlier than usual, but that suited my plans well. I didn't know if Jeb was an early riser or not, and I didn't want to miss his departure from his townhouse.

After a quick shower, I dressed in jeans and a black sweater, pausing only to eat a piece of toast before brushing my teeth and donning my coat. Pulling on my slouchy knitted hat, I grabbed my bag and violin and set off down to the underground parking lot.

Less than twenty minutes later I pulled my MINI Cooper up against the curb, parking it across the street from the entrance to the underground lot at Jeb's townhouse complex. I knew there was always a chance that Jeb had already left, but it wasn't yet eight o'clock, and I figured my chances were even better that he was still at home.

Over the next half hour I watched three cars leave the underground lot, but none were driven by Jeb. Rubbing my gloved hands against my cold legs, I wished I'd thought to bring a travel mug full of hot tea or coffee. The frosty, cloudy morning was proving less than ideal for my stakeout.

To help pass the time, I decided to text JT. As I dug through my bag, searching for my phone, I came across a folded piece of white paper. Puzzled, I pulled it out. I didn't remember putting it in my bag. As soon as I unfolded the sheet, my movements stilled and I felt the blood drain from my face. Someone had written a note with a black Sharpie, a note that wasn't the least bit friendly.

Leave the past in the past, or else, it read.

I dropped the note onto my lap, appalled by it. My hands trembled ever so slightly as I picked up the paper again. I stared at it, but the words became no less frightening. I folded the sheet and tucked it back in my bag, out of sight, but the words had firmly imprinted on my mind.

Leave the past in the past, or else.

Or else what? Nothing good, that was certain. Most likely it meant I'd be the next victim.

Snatching up my phone, I pulled off my gloves. More than ever

I wanted to get in touch with my best friend. Although my fingers shook, I managed to type out a message to JT.

Someone left me a threatening note, I wrote. *I'm a little freaked out.*

As soon as I'd sent the message, I realized JT had no idea what had transpired at the theater the night before.

Ethan was killed last night, I typed. *At the theater.*

Once again I wished I'd brought a drink with me. Even a cold one would have sufficed at the moment. My mouth had gone dry and my pulse was skipping along faster than normal. I checked to make sure the car doors were locked and returned my eyes to the driveway across the street. Jeb still hadn't emerged.

Had he written the note?

I thought back, searching my memories for any possible opportunity that he might have had to slip the note into my bag. The only time he'd been close to me since I'd last rummaged through my tote was when I questioned him about Pavlina's charm bracelet. Unless he was highly skilled in the art of misdirection, I didn't think he would have been able to put something in my bag without me noticing.

I recalled something else. I'd left my bag sitting on the table in the musicians' lounge. It was there when Jeb and the others entered the room with the police officer. Jeb would have passed by my bag and could have surreptitiously slipped the note into its depths as he did so. That would have been risky though, with the police officer not far behind him and with Yvonne, Harold, and Sasha entering the room at the same time.

Still, it wasn't impossible that the note had come from Jeb. Considering the content of the threat, the judge was a good suspect.

Leave the past in the past.

When we'd spoken about Pavlina's charm bracelet, the death

of her best friend had come up. Was that the part of the past the note referred to? If so, why was Jeb so determined to leave those past events undisturbed?

Could the death of Tiffany Alphonse have something to do with the more recent deaths of Pavlina and Ethan?

Possibly, but I didn't see how.

The mechanical gate blocking the entrance to the parking lot rose. I peered across the street as a car drove up the short driveway to the road, but as soon as it came fully into view I lost interest. The car was blue, unlike Jeb's dark green truck, and a woman was in the driver's seat.

My phone vibrated in my cold hands and I glanced down to read the message JT had sent me.

This is getting out of hand, his message read. *Give the note to the police and stay away from the theater.*

I have to go to the theater tonight, I reminded him. *I'll give the note to the police, but I'm busy at the moment.*

Doing what??? he wrote back seconds later.

I could almost feel his suspicion radiating out of my phone. For a brief moment I considered evading the question, but the note had left me rattled, and I decided I'd feel better if JT knew where I was and what I was doing.

As succinctly as possible, I told him I was parked outside Jeb's townhouse complex. I added what I'd overheard him say the night before, and then I mentioned that it was possible Jeb was the author of the note.

If he wrote the note, you shouldn't be anywhere near him.

If he wrote the note, he's most likely the killer, and somebody needs to keep an eye on him, I countered.

Ten seconds ticked by before my phone vibrated again.

Send me the address. I'm coming over there.

I considered arguing, but not for long. The truth was that I'd feel safer with his company, as well as less bored. This whole stake-out thing was turning out to be pretty dull.

I sent JT the address of the townhouse complex and he told me not to go anywhere until he arrived. I didn't make any promises. If Jeb emerged before JT appeared, I couldn't just let him go off and fulfill his sinister plans, whatever they involved.

Returning my attention to the underground parking lot, I pulled my gloves back on over my chilled hands and drummed my fingers against the steering wheel. Time moved along at a le-thargic pace, or at least that's how it seemed. Another four cars left the complex and one entered the parking lot, but there was still no sign of Jeb. I shifted in my seat, growing tired of sitting there in the cold. I hoped JT would arrive soon, and that Jeb would appear shortly after. As determined as I'd been that morning to follow the judge, my patience had worn thin.

Luckily JT's truck turned onto the street a minute later and pulled up to the curb a short distance away from my own car. I watched through my rearview mirror as JT approached, and I popped the lock when he reached my car. He opened the passen-ger side door and ducked down to look into the vehicle.

"Any sign of him?"

"Not yet." I shivered as cold air wafted in through the open door. "Get in. It's freezing with the door open."

"There's no way I'm hanging out in this toy of a car."

"It's not a toy!"

"To someone my size, it might as well be."

Okay, so that was true. The MINI Cooper was just the right size for me, but JT was over six feet tall and would no doubt feel cramped within seconds.

I grabbed my bag from the passenger seat. "All right, we'll move to your truck."

Always keeping an eye on the complex across the street, I retrieved my violin from behind the seat and left my car for JT's. I was happy to find that the cab of his truck was warmer than my MINI Cooper since he'd had the engine and heat on more recently than I had.

"Can I see the note?" JT asked as soon as he was settled in the driver's seat.

I withdrew the sheet of paper from my bag and passed it to him.

He frowned as he read the short message. "You really need to give that to the police."

"I will," I assured him as I returned the paper to my bag. "But not until I know what Jeb's up to."

"Do you really think he's the one who wrote that note?"

"It would make sense if he's the killer, but he didn't exactly have ample opportunity to put the note in my bag. It could have been one of several people."

"Maybe I should come to the theater with you tonight."

Since the final concert was a recap of the two previous ones, JT hadn't been hired to record it.

"I'm sure that's not necessary. There'll be lots of people there."

"Including the killer, most likely."

"True, but I'll make sure I'm always with someone I trust."

"I hope that's a promise."

I reached over to give JT's arm a reassuring pat. "It is."

He surprised me by placing his hand over mine and giving it a

squeeze. I met his eyes—the gorgeous color of sunlit root beer—
and my heart flip-flopped when he held my gaze.

Hopeful butterflies took flight in my stomach. "JT . . ."

A dark truck drove out of the underground parking lot.

JT let go of my hand as I leaned closer to the windshield.

"Is that him?" he asked.

After a second I sat back, disappointed. "No."

I opened my mouth to say more, but the moment between us
had passed. My disappointment intensified.

JT rubbed his hands together. "You could have picked a warmer
day for a stakeout."

I brushed my nagging feeling of regret aside.

"It's not like I can choose when a potential killer is going to act
extra suspicious," I said. "Besides, now that you're here, this could
be fun. It's like we're Castle and Beckett waiting for a villain to
make a move."

"In the cold."

"In the cold," I conceded. "And I should have brought snacks.
Or at least coffee."

"I won't argue with you there."

"Live and learn."

I settled back in my seat, my eyes still fixed on the driveway
across the street.

"Did you have a chance to listen to the tracks I gave you?" JT
asked a moment later.

"Not yet," I said. "But I'm looking forward to it. I want to listen
at a time when I can give the songs my full attention."

"No worries. Like I said before, there's no rush."

"I'll listen before the end of the week," I assured him.

A dark truck emerged from the underground parking lot.

I sat up straighter and swatted JT's arm. "That's him! Quick!"

JT started the engine and put the truck into gear. I pulled on my seat belt and snapped it into place.

"Don't lose him," I cautioned, leaning forward, as if that could keep me closer to our quarry.

"I won't," JT said. "Relax."

I tried to, but the best I could manage was to sit back in my seat. My heart continued to beat faster than normal and I gripped the armrest with my gloved fingers.

"If he does anything illegal or puts anyone in danger, we're calling the police, right?" JT checked.

"Of course."

I held my breath as Jeb drove through an intersection, but JT managed to follow him through before the light changed. The tense pursuit continued and after a couple of minutes I wondered if Jeb was heading for the Abrams Center. He was taking us in that direction, at least. But a moment later he drove right past the theater.

"You know, he could be going to get groceries or something innocent like that," JT said as he continued to travel behind the dark truck, leaving some space between the two vehicles.

"We just passed a grocery store," I pointed out.

"Maybe he likes shopping at a different one."

"There's nothing secretive about buying groceries, and he's definitely up to something secretive. Why else would he be worried about someone suspecting what he's up to?"

JT didn't argue with me on that point.

"He's pulling over!" I said a few seconds later.

"I can see that."

I ignored his dry tone, searching frantically for a free parking space at the side of the road.

"There's a spot up there." I pointed to the space by the curb.

JT drove past Jeb's truck, now parked, and claimed the spot I'd indicated. As soon as we stopped moving, I unclipped my seat belt and twisted around so I could look out the rear window. Jeb had climbed out of his truck and was circling around the front of it to reach the sidewalk. As soon as he was off the street, he headed in our direction.

I slid down the seat to hide. "Get down!" I said to JT.

He didn't move. "Why?"

"He'll see you!"

"So?"

"He might recognize you."

"Not too likely," JT said, not the least bit concerned. "Even if he saw me at the theater I doubt he'd remember me, especially out of context."

I let out a huff of frustration, still scrunched as low as I could get.

"Besides, he's already passed us."

I shot back up, my eyes going straight to the window. I caught sight of Jeb as he disappeared through the front door of a store. My gaze shifted up to the awning above the entrance.

"Suzie's Party Supplies?" I read, surprised.

"Yeah, he's definitely up to no good," JT said, unsuccessfully fighting to keep the amusement out of his voice. "He's probably planning to throw a killer surprise party."

I narrowed my eyes at him. "Very funny."

He struggled to keep the grin off his face but couldn't manage it. "This is what we sat in the cold waiting for? To watch him buy party supplies?"

"This might be a stop on the way to another place," I said.

"Like a bakery so he can pick up a cake?" JT was still grinning.

I glared at him again. "It's not only innocent people who throw parties. Killers can too."

"Okay, sure. But you have to admit the words 'They don't suspect a thing' has more than one connotation now."

I frowned as I stared through the window at the party supply store. "Fine," I admitted reluctantly, knowing he was right. "Maybe he was talking about a surprise party. But," I added quickly, "we don't know that for sure. His phone conversations aren't the only things that put him on my suspect list."

"Are you saying you still want to follow him when he gets out of there?"

"Yes."

JT sighed, no longer grinning. "Can I at least go get a coffee?" He nodded at the coffee shop across the street.

"There's no time," I said. "Here he comes."

I didn't miss the rolling of JT's eyes as I slid back down out of sight. He might have thought I was being silly, but I didn't want to know how Jeb would react if he found out I'd been following him. Getting better acquainted with his nasty temper was something I'd rather avoid.

"What do the balloons say?" I asked, having caught a brief glimpse of several helium ones as Jeb exited the shop.

JT leaned closer to the passenger side window. "Happy fiftieth anniversary. The party's probably for his parents."

"Probably," I agreed.

When JT turned the key in the ignition a moment later, I carefully rose up from my hiding spot. A quick glance over my shoulder showed me that Jeb was in his own truck again, signaling to pull out into traffic. Two cars got between us before JT was able to follow, but he was still well within sight.

At the end of the street, Jeb made a right turn onto a side street and JT did the same several seconds later. After another right turn a minute or so later, my hopes of catching the judge in the act of something sinister faded away like the last note of a song, a decrescendo into nothing.

"Looks like he's heading home," JT said.

It didn't take long to get confirmation of that theory. We soon followed Jeb onto the street where he lived, my shoulders sagging with disappointment. The dark truck disappeared into the underground parking lot and JT pulled to a stop outside the townhouse complex, across the street from my MINI Cooper.

"Don't look so dejected, Dori," JT said as I unclipped my seat belt.

"I really thought he was up to something bad."

"Like you said, he could still be the killer. His phone calls just weren't as incriminating as you thought."

I made a vague sound of acknowledgment, staring out the window toward the entrance to the underground parking lot. A few raindrops hit the windshield, drizzling down the glass and obscuring my view.

"I have to get home," JT said. "The studio's booked for eleven."

"Okay." I did my best to appear less dispirited. "Thanks for hanging out with me."

"You're not going to stay here for the rest of the morning, are you?"

"No, that would probably be a waste of time." I took a second to consider my options. "Is it all right if I hang out at your place and get some practice in?"

"Of course."

"All right." I reached for the door. "See you soon then."

With my tote bag over my shoulder and my violin case in hand, I crossed the street to my car, getting pelted by the raindrops that now fell steadily from the sky. Soon after, I pulled my car out into the street behind JT's truck and trailed him to his house. Once in my studio, I immersed myself in some Paganini, allowing the music to file the edge off the disappointment that came from failing to identify Pavlina and Ethan's killer.

Chapter Twenty-Four

BY THE TIME I'd finished teaching for the day, I'd recovered from my disappointment over not catching Jeb in the act of something incriminating. One fruitless stakeout didn't mean all was lost. The killer could still be caught, whether that person was Jeb or somebody else. I simply needed to continue searching for clues.

As I prepared to leave JT's house, I remembered the threatening note still tucked away in my bag. I needed to deliver it to the police, but I didn't have time to do so that day. It would have to wait until the next morning. Detective Van den Broek would no doubt be less than thrilled to see me again, but the feeling would be mutual.

Despite heavy traffic made worse by the pouring rain, I arrived at the theater early that evening. The musicians' lounge was empty upon my arrival, and once I'd secured my belongings in my locker, I wondered what I should do next. I'd promised JT that I'd stick close to someone I trusted while at the theater, but until Mikayla or my other fellow musicians arrived, I was on my own.

Recalling the discovery of Ethan's body the other night—a

short distance down the hallway—my skin prickled. I didn't feel comfortable hanging out in the lounge on my own. The silence was creeping me out.

Although I knew it meant I'd have to pass by the judges' lounge, I decided to go upstairs and see if Hans was in his office. He wasn't my first choice for company, and while he wasn't the most honest person—as I'd learned from experience—I knew he wasn't a killer. I might not have the time of my life while hanging out with him, but I'd be safe.

I quietly climbed the carpeted stairs to the second floor and peered into the hallway. I let out a breath of relief when I saw that the door to the judges' lounge was shut. I continued to move quietly, not wanting to draw attention to myself from any corner, and my relief intensified when I realized that the door to Hans's office was open and the room was illuminated by the overhead light.

When I reached the door, I tapped on the frame. Hans looked up from his seat behind his desk.

"Midori," he greeted. He glanced over my shoulder at the hallway and lowered his voice. "Any news?"

I pushed his office door shut all but a crack and sank down into the chair in front of his desk. "No, not really. Ethan was my prime suspect, but now that he's dead . . ."

Hans nodded. "I guess that strikes him off the list, assuming that the two deaths are related, which seems most likely."

"It does," I said, agreeing to everything he'd said.

Hans glanced at his watch and got to his feet. "I need to have a quick word with the judges before everything gets under way."

I was about to protest, to tell him that I didn't want to be alone, but I quickly changed my mind. I didn't want to sound helpless or needy, especially not in front of him. Eyeing the laptop on his desk, I got an idea.

"Is it all right if I hang out here for a bit and borrow your laptop?" I asked. "I want to do a little research into something to do with Pavlina."

Hans paused by the door. "Go ahead. Will this research help you find out who killed her and Ethan?"

"I don't know, but I don't want to leave any stone unturned."

He glanced at his watch again. "Let me know if you find anything of interest. And please shut the door when you leave. It'll lock automatically."

I assured him that I would honor both requests and he headed off down the hall, leaving the door standing open. Being alone in the office wasn't ideal, but it beat hanging out in the musicians' lounge all by myself. At least up here on the second floor I knew that Hans was likely within shouting distance, probably meeting with the judges two doors down. Until more people arrived at the theater, there was a good chance that no one would hear me call for help if I were downstairs.

Pulling the laptop across the desk, I turned it around so I could see the screen. Hans had left the computer turned on, so I was able to access the Internet within seconds. I didn't know for sure if the death of Tiffany Alphonse at the music retreat three years earlier had anything to do with the recent murders, but I figured it warranted some consideration. So many people involved in the composing competition had been at that retreat, and both murder victims had been close friends with Tiffany. Maybe that wasn't significant in any way, but until I dug deeper into the past, I wouldn't know if that was the case or not.

My first search turned up nothing of interest. All the results that popped up on the screen related to an upcoming version of the retreat, scheduled to take place in Banff, Alberta, in the spring. Trying again, I added Tiffany Alphonse's name to the search terms, and this time the results appeared far more promising. I clicked the top search result and read through an article about Tiffany's death. As I'd already known, she'd drowned in a lake near the hotel where the retreat attendees were staying. According to the article, the theory was that she had wandered out into the night alone while drunk, and had either fallen into the water or had decided to go for a swim. Either way, she hadn't made it out of the water alive.

What I hadn't already known was that her body was found just after dawn the next day by a man out for an early morning jog. My eyes widened when I read the name of the man who'd discovered Tiffany's body.

Harold Dempsey.

So Pavlina, Ethan, and Dongmei weren't the only people associated with the composing competition who'd been at the retreat. According to the article, Harold was one of the instructors. When speaking with the author of the article, he'd expressed shock and sadness at finding the young woman floating lifelessly in the water.

"It's a terrible loss," he was quoted as saying. "Not just for her friends and family but for the music community as well. Ms. Alphonse had a promising career ahead of her and, unfortunately, she has been taken from us far too soon."

I sat back, considering what I'd read. Harold, now a judge for the composing competition, had been present at the retreat when Tiffany had died. He was also the first person—aside from me—to arrive on the scene after Olivia found Ethan's body. Were either of those facts significant?

Maybe, and maybe not. After all, three of the competition's finalists were at the retreat as well. But the only one still alive was Dongmei, and I didn't suspect her of killing anyone.

I tapped my fingers against the desk, but further thought didn't bring me any brilliant insights so I went back to reading. I found another article with similar information to the first, but it included quotes from some of Tiffany's friends who were at the retreat with her.

"I'm devastated," Pavlina had told the reporter. "She was my best friend. I don't know what I'll do without her."

The reporter went on to note that no one had admitted to being with Tiffany that night, to drinking with her, or to seeing her drunk. That was attributed to either fear or guilt, or a combination of the two. However, the police investigation had revealed that Tiffany was most definitely intoxicated at the time of her death, and the drowning was officially ruled accidental.

But was it really an accident? After all that had happened recently, I couldn't help but wonder if the official ruling was wrong.

I tugged on my left earlobe as I stared at the computer screen without really seeing it. I needed more information, but I wasn't sure that the Internet would be able to provide it. In case I was wrong, I spent a few more minutes sorting through the search results. After that didn't turn up anything, I returned to the original article and read it through once more. Still, I didn't find what I needed.

The floor creaked to my left and I jerked my head around. Harold Dempsey stood in the doorway. His eyes shifted from the computer screen to me.

"I'm looking for Maestro Clausen," he said.

"Um." I struggled to recover from my surprise at his presence. "I'm not sure where he is. Sorry."

Harold nodded and disappeared down the hall. Once he was gone, I realized that my heart was booming out a loud beat in my chest. I'd seen something in Harold's eyes in that moment when he'd shifted his gaze from the computer screen to me.

Was it fear? No, more like anger. Dark, smoldering anger. It had only been there for a second or two, but I knew I hadn't imagined it.

Wondering how much he'd seen, I checked the screen. Even if he had perfect vision, he wouldn't have been able to read the body of the article from the doorway, but the headline was much larger and easy to see.

"Music Retreat Ends on Sour Note with Drowning Death," it read.

Had the headline simply brought back unpleasant memories from that time? Harold was, after all, the one who'd found Tiffany's lifeless body.

No, I decided. That didn't explain his anger. There had to be more to it.

Ill at ease, I shut the Web browser and closed the laptop. I crept quietly toward the door, apprehension skipping along my spine like a series of urgent, staccato notes. When I peered out into the hallway, the coast was clear, although I could hear a low murmur of voices coming from nearby.

Pulling the office door shut as Hans had asked me to do, I hurried down the hall. As I passed the judges' lounge, I cast a quick glance through the now-open door, spotting only Yvonne Charbonneau, Olivia, and Sasha. They didn't notice me, and I continued on along the corridor and down the stairway.

I nearly jumped out of my skin when I turned the corner at the bottom of the stairway and came face-to-face with Hans. With my hand over my heart, I took a step back and closed my eyes briefly, relieved he wasn't someone from my list of murder suspects.

"Everything all right?" he asked.

"Yes," I said, now recovered. "You startled me. That's all."

"What did your research turn up?"

I glanced up and down the corridor to check if we were alone. We were.

"I'm thinking there could be a connection between the two murders and the death of a girl named Tiffany Alphonse at a music retreat a few years ago."

"What kind of connection?"

"Tiffany's death was ruled an accident, but I'm wondering if it was actually murder."

"And if it was?" Hans asked. "What does that have to do with Pavlina's and Ethan's deaths?"

"I'm not entirely sure yet," I admitted. "Maybe Tiffany's killer felt threatened by Pavlina and Ethan and decided to get them out of the way."

"But you said the death at the music retreat happened years ago. If Pavlina and Ethan knew something that made Tiffany's killer feel threatened, why wait until now to get rid of them?"

"I don't know, but it's something I can't dismiss yet." I recalled Harold's appearance in the office doorway. "Did Harold find you? He was looking for you a few minutes ago."

"I just talked to him." Hans stepped around me so he could reach the stairway. "You'd better go get ready. It's almost time to head for the stage."

I put a hand on his arm to stop him from ascending the stairs. "How much do you know about Harold?"

"Professionally or otherwise?"

"Otherwise."

Hans thought for a moment. "Not much. He's a wealthy man, only in part because of his successful career. He married into money."

"Have you heard of any rumors about him over the years? Any hint of behavior that might not be aboveboard?"

"No." Hans looked at me more closely. "Do you suspect him of murder? Because I don't see how he could possibly be the killer. He was sitting in the audience when Pavlina was killed."

"True," I conceded. "And I'm not sure what I suspect him of, if anything."

"Make sure you don't go around making any accusations without evidence to back them up," he said. "None of the judges would take kindly to having their reputations tarnished."

"I have no intention of making public accusations against anyone without evidence," I said, slightly miffed that he'd thought I might.

He seemed oblivious to my reaction. "Good. I'll see you later."

I shot a glare at his retreating back as he disappeared up the stairway, but then I pushed him out of my thoughts. The concert was set to start soon and I had something I wanted to do before taking my place on the stage.

When I hurried into the musicians' lounge seconds later, a buzz of conversation and activity greeted me. Most of the orchestra had arrived in my absence, and several clusters of musicians were chatting with each other while other individuals warmed up on their instruments. Spotting Dongmei in the crowd, I made my way to her side and drew her into a relatively private—if not quiet—corner of the room.

"How are you doing?" I asked, although I could tell by the worried expression on her face that she was nervous.

"Okay," she replied, "but my heart is going about a thousand miles a minute."

"You'll be fine," I assured her. "No matter what the results are."

She drew in a deep breath and nodded. "Of course I want to win, but however things turn out, I'll be glad when I know. Waiting to hear the results is the hardest part."

I could imagine.

Out of the corner of my eye, I noticed Olivia enter the musicians' lounge. Knowing she would likely direct Sherwin and Dongmei to take their places in the audience at any moment, I hurried to address the questions weighing on my mind.

"Dongmei, when Tiffany Alphonse died at the retreat in Banff, were there any rumors going around about her death?"

Her forehead furrowed. "What kind of rumors?"

"She was drunk when she died, but I read in a news article that no one admitted to drinking with her that night or seeing her drunk. Surely someone must have, though. Don't you think?"

"It was a bit odd," Dongmei said, "especially considering that her closest friends were at the retreat. But both of them swore they weren't with Tiffany that night, and I'm pretty sure they had people to back them up on that." She thought for a moment. "There was a rumor, but I don't know that it was anything more than that."

"What rumor?" I pressed.

Dongmei looked uncomfortable. "I don't like to gossip about someone who's dead . . ."

"I understand that, but this could be important. It could have something to do with the recent murders."

"Really?" She sounded both surprised and slightly dubious.

"Possibly."

"There was talk that Tiffany was seeing someone."

"Someone who was at the retreat?"

Dongmei nodded. "I got the feeling that's who her friends thought she was with on the night she died."

"Who was this person?" I asked, anxious to know.

She shrugged. "I don't know. I don't think anyone knew for certain. It might not even be true."

"Dongmei!" Olivia's voice rang out over the chatter in the room.

"I have to go," Dongmei said, suddenly looking terrified.

"Good luck," I called to her as she hurried across the room to Olivia.

Mikayla waved to me from the bank of lockers along the wall and I wound my way around several woodwind players to meet her. Minutes later, instruments and music in hand, we made our way toward the stage. But although I should only have been thinking about the music we were about to play for the audience, everything Dongmei had told me swirled around and around, a constant source of background noise in my head.

Chapter Twenty-Five

DESPITE THE DISTRACTION my thoughts created, I managed to get through the concert without making any mistakes. Before the music started, everyone had observed a minute of silence for Pavlina and Ethan. Although their deaths had narrowed the field of finalists down to only two candidates, we played excerpts from all four compositions as originally planned. I thought it was a nice way to honor the memories of the two late competitors.

Once we'd finished our performance and the audience had stopped applauding, it was time to reveal the winner of the competition. I glanced toward the wings of the stage and spotted Dongmei standing with Olivia and Sasha. Even from a distance I could tell that Dongmei was terrified. She had her hands clasped tightly in front of her and was taking deep breaths. I hoped she wouldn't pass out. The competition had already had enough drama.

Hans stood facing the audience, an envelope in hand. A hush fell over the audience and the stage as everyone in the theater waited to hear who would be named the winner.

"Ladies and gentlemen," Hans began, "thank you all for joining us here this evening. This competition has highlighted the work of supremely talented young composers, and the Point Grey Philharmonic is honored to have been a part of showcasing their work." He paused for a second to lift the flap of the envelope. "And now, without further ado, I'm pleased to announce that the winner of this year's competition, and the recipient of a five-thousand-dollar scholarship, is . . ."

I held my breath, hoping to hear Dongmei's name. It seemed to take forever for Hans to slide the small card from the envelope, although in reality it only took seconds.

He glanced at what was written on the card and then raised his head to address the audience. "Dongmei Pan."

Applause erupted throughout the theater, and I smiled as I joined in as best I could while holding my violin. Dongmei emerged from the wings, her eyes wide and dazed as she made her way toward Hans. When she glanced toward the orchestra, I caught her eye and gave her a thumbs-up. Finally, a smile replaced her shocked expression, growing wider as she shook hands with Hans.

Sasha hurried on stage and passed a giant bouquet of flowers to Hans, and he presented them to Dongmei with another handshake. The audience was still clapping, and she bowed and waved before retreating to the wings. Aside from the celebration to follow, the competition was finally over.

Twenty minutes later I'd stashed my instrument in my locker and had made my way with Mikayla and my other fellow musicians to the theater's reception room, where a celebratory gathering was under way. Dongmei was, of course, the center of attention, everyone wanting a chance to personally congratulate her.

While I waited for my opportunity to speak with her, I chatted with friends and helped myself to a plate full of catered food. After finishing up the last morsel on my plate, I made my way through the crowd toward Dongmei and her family. After giving her a hug and telling her how happy I was for her, I moved on so other people could have their turn with her. I spent a few minutes chatting with her sister, but then excused myself when I saw Mikayla leaving the reception room.

Hurrying down the hallway, I caught up to her as she returned to the musicians' lounge. Only a handful of other orchestra members were present in the lounge, and I was glad of that. I wanted a chance to speak with Mikayla privately. Although we'd sat next to each other throughout the whole concert, we hadn't had a real opportunity to chat that evening.

"Hey," I said as I leaned against the bank of lockers while she opened her combination lock. "How are you doing?"

"All right," she said as she retrieved her coat from her locker.

"Really?" I asked, noting that she lacked her usual vivacious energy.

"Well, maybe not." Tears welled in her eyes and she blinked them away.

It was the closest I'd ever seen her come to crying.

"What's wrong?" I asked, worried. "Is it Dave?"

She nodded. "We talked before the concert."

"Did you argue again?"

"No, not exactly. But we broke up."

My heart grew heavy. "Mikayla, I'm so sorry."

She blinked away more tears as she pulled on her coat. "It's for the best, really. We weren't happy together anymore."

"But still . . ." I said, knowing that didn't make their breakup easy.

"Yeah, I'm not exactly in a celebratory mood."

I gave her a hug. "I'm sorry. Do you want company? We could go to the pub down the street."

She smiled sadly. "Thanks, but I think I'll just head home."

"Okay, but call me if you want to talk."

"Thanks, Midori. I will."

My spirits dampened by Mikayla's unhappiness, we exchanged subdued goodbyes and she left the lounge. More musicians had trickled into the room by then, the party down the hall likely winding down. I decided to head home, but before I could reach my locker I got caught up in a conversation with some of my fellow musicians. Another twenty minutes had passed before I pulled on my coat and retrieved my instrument and tote bag from my locker.

Mindful of my promise to JT and my own desire to stay safe, I walked out of the theater with Bronwyn, a first violinist. When we reached the parking lot out back, we said good night and headed to our respective vehicles. My MINI Cooper was farther across the lot than Bronwyn's car and she was already pulling out of her parking space by the time I'd stashed my violin behind the driver's seat of my own vehicle.

I climbed into the car and shut the door, shivering from the cold. The rain had stopped at some point during the evening and the temperature had plummeted. As soon as I had the engine running, I cranked up the heat, hoping to ward off the worst of the chill as soon as possible.

After backing out of my parking spot, I steered my car toward the end of the line of vehicles. As I turned a corner, my headlights flashed across the back of the theater, briefly illuminating a figure standing next to the building. My breath caught in my throat, and a frostiness that had nothing to do with the outside temperature spread through my veins.

I'd recognized the figure as Harold Dempsey, and he'd been staring right at me.

Alarmed, I quickly turned my car toward the exit. Although I'd only caught a brief glimpse of Harold in the beam of lights from my car, that had been enough to see the dark expression on his face, and I didn't like it one bit. The mere memory of it sent another chill through me.

All I wanted to do was to get home, to lock myself safely away in my apartment. Before that evening, Jeb had been the judge I'd focused on the most as a suspect, but now I sensed that Harold deserved more of my attention. He hadn't had an opportunity to kill Pavlina, but there was still something very frightening and dangerous about him. I suspected more than ever that Tiffany's death was tied to the recent ones, and there was a good chance that Harold was involved in all of them. How, exactly, I didn't know, and I wasn't in a state to figure it out right then. I was too shaken. If I hadn't walked out with Bronwyn, would Harold have approached me? Harmed me?

I didn't want to know.

Glad to leave the theater and Harold behind me, I turned onto Tenth Avenue. I relaxed slightly, comforted by the distance I was putting between myself and Harold, but that relief was short-lived. A car had followed me from the lot and had pulled in behind me. My heart thumping away like crazy, I checked my rearview mirror, trying to get a look at the driver, but I couldn't see much more than headlights. I thought I caught a glimpse of a man's figure behind the wheel, but I couldn't be sure. That didn't seem to matter to my heart, though. The possibility that it could be Harold had sent its tempo up another notch.

My hands tightened around the steering wheel and I struggled to think clearly.

If it was Harold, was he planning to follow me home?

Spotting the bright lights of a grocery store up ahead, I flicked on my turn signal and pulled into the store's parking lot. To my immense relief, the car behind me continued on straight ahead. I pulled into a parking spot and stopped my car, realizing then that my hands were shaking.

It wasn't Harold. You're fine, I told myself.

My hands continued to tremble as I dug through my tote bag until I found my cell phone. Pulling off my gloves so I could use the touch screen, I tapped out a text message to JT.

I thought someone was following me home from the theater, I wrote. *Turns out they weren't, but I'm a bit freaked out. Can I stop by your place?*

After sending the message, I stared at my phone, as if I could will JT to respond immediately. The device remained silent and my eyes strayed to the street beyond the parking lot.

If I wasn't in any danger of being followed home, I could head for my apartment without a problem. But I didn't want to. Maybe it was silly, but I wanted the company of my best friend, if only for a few minutes before going home.

I continued to wait, my car growing colder by the minute. I'd just decided to give JT another two minutes to respond when my phone buzzed in my hand.

Definitely, he'd written. *Are you sure no one was following you?*

Yes, I wrote back. *But I'm still a bit shaky.*

I'll be watching for you. And be careful. The roads are icy tonight.

Letting out a relieved breath, I started up my car again and left the parking lot. I was lucky to have a friend like JT. He was always good to me and, looking back, it seemed inevitable that I'd fallen in love with him over time.

Something tugged at my heart as I turned onto Blanca Street. I really did need to find the nerve to tell him how I felt. Recalling the moment earlier in the day when he'd held my hand and looked right into my eyes, my heart gave a hopeful flutter. Perhaps it was dangerous for me to think there was a chance he reciprocated my feelings, but those few seconds of intense connection had given me a sliver of hope. Another flutter of my heart almost caused me to forget about my fear of Harold, but my wariness refused to disappear completely.

As I followed Sixteenth Avenue to Southwest Marine Drive, I wished I'd taken a different route to JT's house. This last stretch of road that would take me to the edge of his neighborhood was dark and lonely, bordered by woods on both sides for most of the way. I tried to tell myself that I didn't need to worry since no one was following me, but that didn't loosen my grip on the steering wheel or diminish my anxiety. I kept my speed slightly below the posted limit, worried as well about the icy conditions. Black ice could be lurking anywhere and was probably a greater threat to me than anyone on the road behind me. Somehow, though, that was still hard for me to believe, especially when a quick glance in my rearview mirror revealed a bright set of headlights in my wake.

It's nothing, I told myself. *Just another innocent driver.*

I glanced at the rearview mirror again. The car was gaining on me. Fast. Maybe the driver wasn't following me, but they were definitely speeding. Staying in the right-hand lane, I hoped the car would pass me without incident. But the headlights grew brighter and brighter.

My hands held the steering wheel in a death grip now.

You have lots of room to pass! I wanted to yell at the other driver.

The car kept coming. At the last second, I tried to move out of the way, but my MINI Cooper hit a patch of ice and I skidded onto the shoulder of the road. As I fought to regain control, the other vehicle hit me from behind, sending my car spinning.

I screamed as the world went off kilter. Bright headlights flashed in my eyes and the nose of my car dipped down. I was vaguely aware of an impact, of something smacking me in the face, and then I lost all awareness of the world around me.

Chapter Twenty-Six

THE FIRST THING I noticed was an acrid, burning smell. I wrinkled my nose, and my face ached in response. Voices murmured around me, as if I were hearing them from under water. The acrid smell needled my nose and throat. I coughed, sparking a volley of aches in my head, face, and upper body.

"Ma'am? Can you hear me? Can you open your eyes?"

Now that I could make out some words—these ones spoken by a man—I did my best to force my eyes open in response to his question. It took some effort, but my eyelids lifted. Bright lights pulsed through the darkness and a radio crackled in the distance.

"You've been in an accident," the voice said.

"Have I?" I said vaguely.

I realized then that I was still in my car, the nose of it angled downward. I took in the sight of the young paramedic leaning over me, the owner of the voice that had spoken.

"The smell," I said, wrinkling my nose again, and regretting it as much as the time before. My face ached more than ever now.

"It's from the airbag."

I undid my seat belt and made a move to climb out of the car. The paramedic put a hand on my shoulder.

"Just hold still."

"I'm all right." I tried to wave him out of the way and climbed out of the car, his hand on my arm.

As soon as I was on my feet, the world tipped precariously beneath me and my vision went dark. I was vaguely aware of strong hands lifting me, and when I became fully conscious again, I was lying on my back on a stretcher.

I groaned. "My car."

I couldn't believe I might have totaled it after only a few weeks of owning it.

"Don't worry about your car," a female paramedic said. "What's your name?"

"Midori. Midori Bishop." Through the thick fog clouding my thoughts, I remembered something. "My violin!"

After further explanation, one of the paramedics fetched my instrument from my car and assured me it would make the trip to the hospital with us. That allowed me to calm down, and I let the fog obscure my thoughts again.

The two paramedics tended to me for another minute, fitting a small tube beneath my nose and placing a blanket over me. I lay there on the stretcher, answering questions when asked, thankful to be out in the night air and free of the harsh burning smell inside my car. But as the paramedics loaded me into the back of an ambulance, I shivered, the cold air finally registering. Once I started shivering, I couldn't stop, not even when the female paramedic covered me with an additional blanket. I became aware of blood trickling along my forehead, and the paramedic told me I had a gash near my hairline that would require stitches. She bandaged up the wound temporarily and soon the ambulance was on the move.

Although I didn't lose consciousness again, my mind wasn't working quite right. I couldn't figure out what had happened to me—other than the fact that I'd been in an accident—and I couldn't be bothered to try to think beyond that at the moment. I simply let time slip past me as the ambulance delivered me to the hospital, where I was moved into a curtained cubicle.

A nurse brought me a heated blanket and finally my shivering eased. Soon after, a female physician introduced herself as Dr. Tremaine. She informed me that the soreness of my face and torso had resulted from the impact of the airbag and was nothing serious. She did, however, confirm that the gash on my head needed stitches. She also asked me a bunch of questions and checked my vision and reflexes.

I was relieved that all my fingers worked normally, without any pain. Although my arms were a bit sore, they were otherwise fine, and that meant I could still play my violin once the rest of me was feeling up to it.

A headache had taken hold inside my skull and was now throbbing away furiously. Dr. Tremaine gave me something for the pain and numbed up my forehead before stitching my gash closed. It was only as she put the last stitch in that my mind finally managed to piece together the events leading up to the accident.

"I was run off the road," I said.

"You'd better tell that to the police officer," Dr. Tremaine said as she wheeled into view on her stool. "There. You're all stitched up."

"Thank you." My sluggish brain registered her words. "Police officer?"

"He's waiting to speak with you about the accident." She stood up. "You've got a minor concussion and you'll be sore for a few days. Is there anyone at home who can look after you?"

I shook my head and regretted it. The painkillers had taken the edge off my headache but hadn't obliterated it completely yet. The room also seemed to shift around me in a dizzying way. "I live alone."

Dr. Tremaine glanced at the watch on her wrist. "It's nearly midnight. I'd like to admit you overnight, but you'll probably be good to go home in the morning."

I zeroed in on her first words. "Midnight?"

I tried to sit up, but another wave of dizziness hit me and I groaned, lying back down.

"Take it easy," Dr. Tremaine cautioned.

"I was supposed to meet my best friend," I explained. "He must be worried sick."

"You can contact him soon, or someone will do it for you. Shall I send in the police officer now?"

"Sure," I said, still focused on thoughts of JT.

I thanked the doctor and she left my cubicle. Seconds later, a uniformed police officer approached my bed. When I repeated my worries about JT to him, he produced my tote bag and cell phone along with my beloved violin. Thankfully, my phone was undamaged, having weathered the accident better than I had. I hoped the same would be true of my instrument.

As soon as I activated the screen of my phone, I saw that I'd received numerous text messages and phone calls from JT.

"I need to tell him I'm okay," I told the officer.

Slowly, I eased myself into a sitting position. After a few seconds, my dizziness wore off and I was able to focus on my phone.

Dori, I'm freaking out here. Where the heck are you? I'm coming to find you, JT's last message read.

He'd sent it several minutes ago and my stomach clenched as I pictured him coming upon my damaged vehicle by the side of the road.

I was in an accident. I'm at the hospital but I'm okay! I wrote back.

Tired from the effort of sitting up and focusing on the device, I lay back down. When the officer—Constable Darzi—asked me about the accident, I told him what I could remember.

"Whoever it was, I think they ran me off the road on purpose." I explained to him about the recent murders and the fact that I'd been doing some digging into the lives of the suspects. "And I think I know who the driver was. Harold Dempsey was watching me when I left the theater. I think he followed me and was trying to kill me."

I shivered despite the warmth from the blanket. I hoped the officer didn't think my story was the result of my head injury, but he seemed to be taking me seriously. He accepted the threatening note I dug out of my purse, and when I gave him the names of the detectives working on the homicide cases, he assured me he'd get in touch with them.

He disappeared a few minutes later and I checked my phone.

Which hospital? Are you sure you're all right???

VGH, I wrote in reply to his first question. *And yes, I'm sure. It's nothing serious.*

I'm on my way, his next message read.

Those words warmed me, easing my shivering and allowing me to relax. I closed my eyes, and the sounds of the emergency room blended together and faded away. I must have drifted off for a while because when I next opened my eyes, JT was standing by my bed.

"Thank God, Dori," he said when he realized I was awake.

I'd never seen him look so worried.

"I told you I was okay," I reminded him, although I was touched by his concern.

I raised a hand from the bed and he wrapped it in one of his.

"You scared me half to death. When you didn't show up at my place and you weren't answering your phone or my text messages . . ." He cleared his throat, unable to finish.

I squeezed his hand. "I know. I'm sorry."

He returned the pressure on my hand. "Not your fault. But you're really okay?" His eyes traveled up to my forehead where the doctor had stitched my wound.

"I promise. Just a cut, some bruises, and a minor concussion. I'm not so sure about my poor car, though."

"Cars can be replaced. You can't."

"I guess that's true." I smiled up at him. "I'm glad you're here."

"I wouldn't be anywhere else."

My heart gave a happy skip. If my smile was on the goofy side, I hoped he'd attribute it to the painkillers.

"Are they letting you go home?" he asked.

"Not until tomorrow."

The curtain swished aside and Detective Salnikova stepped into view.

"Detective," I greeted with surprise. "What are you doing here?"

Salnikova nodded a greeting at JT before turning her attention to me. "Detective Van den Broek has had to take some time off for a family emergency, so I've stepped in to investigate the murders along with Detective Chowdhury."

Hallelujah, I wanted to say, but I held my tongue.

I was glad I had when the rest of her words registered. "Family emergency? Does it have anything to do with his daughter?"

"It does, yes," Salnikova said, a shadow of sadness passing across her face.

"Oh no," I said, remembering the picture of the cute little girl. "Is she going to be okay?"

"I don't know," the detective replied. "She's been very sick for a while now and took a turn for the worse. Detective Van den Broek is a single father and wanted to be with her as much as possible."

I swallowed back a lump of emotion, feeling terrible for the little girl and her father as well. No wonder Van den Broek hadn't been a joy to spend time with. He must have been so worried about his daughter.

"You said you'll be investigating the murders now," JT said, redirecting the conversation. "What does Midori's accident have to do with those cases?" He shifted his gaze to me. "Wait—was someone following you after all?"

"I think so."

"What's this?" Salnikova asked.

I backed up and told her about my initial suspicion that Harold had followed me from the theater. "I thought I was imagining things, but I guess I wasn't. I was run off the road. Intentionally."

JT's hand tightened around mine. "You could have been killed."

"I think that was the plan."

He frowned, but Salnikova wanted to hear more so I filled her in on everything I'd learned recently, including my research into Tiffany Alphonse's death three years earlier. "I think Harold killed Tiffany," I said to wrap up, my voice growing scratchy. "I don't know how he could have killed Pavlina, but he's involved somehow. I'm sure of it."

"What about the other judge?" JT asked. "Could it have been him who ran you off the road?"

I considered that possibility. "Not unless he used someone else's vehicle," I said as I recalled the headlights behind me on the dark road. "It was a car that hit me, not a truck like Jeb's."

"Can you pick up this Harold guy?" JT asked Salnikova. "If he finds out that Midori's still alive, he might try to finish the job."

A shudder ran through my body.

JT must have felt it through my hand, still clasped in his. "Don't worry," he assured me. "He's not getting near you again."

"I certainly want to question him," Salnikova said.

"Tonight?" JT asked.

"If possible. If he is indeed guilty of murder, we don't want him making a run for it."

"Will you let me know what happens?" I requested. "I don't think I can rest peacefully until I know he's not going to come after me again."

Salnikova nodded. "I've got your number."

After we'd exchanged a few more words, Salnikova left the cubicle.

"It's late," I said to JT. "Why don't you go home and get some sleep?"

"I'm not leaving your side until the guy who did this to you is off the streets."

I smiled at him again. "You really are the best, JT." I squeezed his hand. "I love you, you know."

The words slipped out before I realized what I was saying. JT leaned over and kissed me on the forehead, well away from my stitched-up gash. He hadn't yet straightened up again when the curtain twitched aside and a man dressed in scrubs appeared.

"Time to transfer you up to the ward," he said cheerily.

I glanced toward JT as he let go of my hand.

"I'll be right behind you," he said.

If my words had alarmed him, he didn't show it. Maybe he'd interpreted the declaration as meaning that I loved him as a friend, as I had for years. That possibility both disappointed and relieved me.

I tried not to think about it, which wasn't too difficult, thanks to the painkillers flowing through my system. My thoughts became fuzzy and I closed my eyes, fading in and out as the orderly wheeled me onto an elevator and then out onto a different floor. I came more awake once I was settled on a ward with three beds, the one next to me occupied by an elderly lady. The third bed was empty, and I hoped that meant I'd have a peaceful night's rest.

A nurse bustled around me for a few minutes, but then left the ward.

As JT settled deeper into the chair at my bedside, I whispered, "Are you sure you don't want to go home and get some sleep? Now that the police are on to Harold, I'm probably safe."

"Probably isn't good enough for me," he replied in a low voice. "I'm staying."

I smiled sleepily at him. "Thanks, JT."

"Get some sleep."

I closed my eyes again, more than happy to do as suggested.

As I drifted off, something tickled at the back of my mind, trying to get my attention, but I didn't have the energy to grab hold of it and pull it to the forefront of my thoughts. Instead, I gave in to the haze of sleep surrounding me, and the world drifted away.

I DIDN'T KNOW how much time had passed when I opened my eyes again. The chair by my bed was empty and I wondered if JT had finally gone home or if he was somewhere nearby. The ward was quiet aside from the occasional incoherent mumble from my elderly neighbor, and the lighting remained dim, the main source of illumination coming from the hallway beyond the open door. I closed my eyes again, but immediately knew that sleep had left me for the time being.

My headache had dwindled to a dull pain, thankfully, but when I tried to sit up, I discovered that my dizziness hadn't abated completely. Lying back down against the pillow, I stared up at the ceiling, thinking over the events that had landed me here in the hospital.

Had Harold really meant to kill me? Or did he simply want to scare me?

I suspected it was the former, but either way he'd endangered my life. It still bothered me that he hadn't had an opportunity to kill Pavlina, but maybe he was in cahoots with someone who'd done that for him. Who though? Olivia?

I had no information to make me think that might really be the case.

Pushing the problem aside for the moment, I considered Harold's motives. If he'd killed Tiffany—as I now suspected he had—perhaps Pavlina and Ethan had known that to be the case, or had come to believe it. But if that was true, why would Harold wait three years to eliminate them? It didn't make sense.

Maybe I was wrong about everything. That wasn't a comforting thought.

Confused and frustrated, I rubbed my eyes, but quickly stopped with a sharp intake of breath. My face was still sore to the touch.

Was I certain Harold was the person who'd run me off the road?

No. It seemed the most likely possibility since he'd watched me as I left the parking lot, but I couldn't be one hundred percent sure he was to blame.

If it wasn't him, who else could it have been?

The second most likely person in my mind was Jeb, but as I'd said earlier, my MINI Cooper had been hit by a car rather than a truck. While it was possible that he'd used another vehicle, that seemed like a bit of a stretch.

Who else would have wanted me out of the way?

I thought back to the threatening note I'd received. I wasn't sure if Harold was responsible for it. I figured it was my research into Tiffany's death that had worried him, and I'd delved into that after I'd received the note. Although he could have overheard me bring up Tiffany's name when I was talking to Jeb.

My other suspects were Olivia and Sasha. They'd both had the opportunity to kill Pavlina and Ethan, but were they connected to Tiffany Alphonse in any way?

Try as I might, I couldn't connect Sasha or Olivia to Tiffany. As far as I knew, they weren't present at the music retreat.

I sighed with frustration and shut my eyes. They flew open a second later. I finally knew what had been bothering me earlier when my mind was foggy. I sat up—too quickly—and had to wait a few seconds for my dizziness to subside. Once it had, connections formed rapidly in my head.

Tiffany's brother had been adamant that his sister was murdered, blaming Pavlina and Ethan. I still thought Harold had done the deed—although I didn't know his motive—but none of that interfered with the theory I now subscribed to. As long as Tiffany's brother believed that Pavlina and Ethan had killed his sister, that was enough motive for him to want them dead.

I didn't know how I hadn't made the connection earlier. I'd never once suspected that Tiffany's brother was in our midst. But now it seemed so clear.

Ethan had recognized someone—Tiffany's brother—who'd attempted to disguise himself.

Alexander Alphonse.

There were several nicknames for Alexander. Alex, Lex, Xander . . . and Sasha.

Why Sasha had waited three years to avenge his sister's death, I didn't know, but at the moment that didn't matter to me. Whoever had murdered Tiffany, I knew now that Sasha was responsible for killing Pavlina and Ethan.

I glanced at the empty chair next to my bed, wishing I hadn't suggested that JT go home. Snatching my phone off the bedside table, I sent him a text message.

I don't think it was Harold who ran me off the road. I think it was Sasha. He's the brother of the girl who was killed at the music retreat years ago. And he's still on the loose!

I sent him another message. *I'll get in touch with Salnikova.*

Now that I'd checked my phone, I knew it wasn't quite four-thirty in the morning. Even if she'd tried to question Harold that night, the detective could be in bed by now, sleeping soundly. Still,

I needed to try to get in touch with her. Although Sasha had been questioned initially along with the rest of us, I didn't know if he was on the detectives' radar anymore, especially since I'd focused their attention on Harold.

As I scrolled through my list of contacts, searching for Salnikova's name and number, quiet footsteps came across the ward toward me. The curtain blocked my view, but a man's hand grabbed it and swept it aside.

"JT?" I said hopefully, but as soon as the name was out of my mouth, my hope shattered and my mouth went dry.

Sasha stood at the foot of my bed, a pillow in one hand.

I opened my mouth to scream as he lunged toward me. I barely managed to make a sound before he slammed the pillow into my face, knocking me down against the bed. Panic coursed through me like an electric shock and alarm bells rang in my head, shrill and frantic.

Sasha was smothering me.

I couldn't breathe.

I fought and struggled, trying to push the pillow off my face, trying to pound my fists against Sasha.

He kept the pillow firmly against my face.

My flailing limbs grew sluggish. The alarm bells in my head faded.

As consciousness slipped out of my grasp, I heard a scream.

Chapter Twenty-Seven

Shouts seeped into my limited, hazy sphere of awareness.

I drew in a deep breath and the darkness obscuring my thoughts leaked away. It took me a second or two to realize that I was breathing, that I was alive, the pillow no longer smooshed against my sore face.

"What's going on in here?" a female voice asked sharply.

"He was trying to smother Midori. Is she breathing?"

That was JT's voice, underscored by fear. I opened my eyes to find a female nurse hovering over me.

"I'm okay," I said.

I'd meant to say it loudly, but it came out as a whisper.

"She's all right," the nurse told JT as she checked me over.

Another nurse appeared and the first one called out, "Get security in here!"

The second nurse took off at a run.

Ignoring the fact that the first nurse was trying to take my pulse, I sat up. I hadn't seen JT at first, but now I spotted him on the floor, holding Sasha pinned down, face-first.

"JT?" I said, still a bit dazed. "I thought you'd gone home."

"I was just stretching my legs. When I heard a scream, I came running. You're really okay?"

"I am," I assured him.

I was about to ask who'd screamed when my elderly neighbor piped up.

"Oh, he's a naughty boy. A very naughty boy!"

The nurse at my side turned her attention to my neighbor. "Yes, Mrs. Dixon. No need to worry."

"Creeping into my bedroom in the middle of the night!" Mrs. Dixon tsk-tsked.

"You're in the hospital, remember?" the nurse said in a soothing tone.

Mrs. Dixon's voice faded into incoherent mumbling.

On the floor, Sasha struggled to free himself, but JT held him firmly in place. Moments later, two security personnel showed up. They took charge of Sasha as JT and the nurse explained the situation.

"We'll get the police here," one of the security officers said.

Sasha sent a chilling glare my way as the officers led him off out of sight.

I sagged back against my pillow and closed my eyes with relief. I was safe.

"Dori?" JT took my hand.

I opened my eyes and smiled at him. "What a night, huh?"

The concerned furrow across his forehead smoothed out and he grinned at me. "I wouldn't mind a little less drama next time."

"I'll keep that in mind."

He gave my hand a squeeze and settled into the chair by my bed. I explained about Sasha, expanding on the information I'd sent in the text message he hadn't seen, and recounting how I'd only realized that Sasha was Alexander in the seconds before he appeared at the foot of my bed. As I finished telling him everything, uniformed police officers showed up, and I had to go through the story all over again.

Salnikova also appeared eventually, but I allowed her colleagues and JT to fill her in. Now that I'd recovered from my panic and the hullabaloo that had followed Sasha's attack, exhaustion had me in a firm grip. I answered a few questions when prodded, but I soon drifted off. Aside from a groggy moment when a nurse checked on me, I didn't wake up again until after ten o'clock in the morning. The police had disappeared long ago, but JT was still by my side.

After a visit from Dr. Tremaine, I was declared fit to go home. JT drove me to my apartment and only left after I'd assured him several times over that I was fine and that all I wanted to do was rest. I canceled all my violin lessons for the next two days and watched TV for a couple of hours, but then I crawled into bed and fell asleep, not waking until the next morning.

While I nibbled at some toast, I responded to a text message JT had sent me an hour earlier, checking in to see if I was okay. I told him I was fine and still resting, and then I texted Mikayla, giving her a bare outline of what had transpired after I'd left the theater the other night. Shortly after I'd finished my breakfast, my phone rang. As soon as I saw Detective Salnikova's name on the screen, I snatched up the device and answered the call.

I spoke to the detective for close to twenty minutes, pummeling her with questions over the phone line. Once she'd patiently answered all my queries about the investigation, I changed subjects.

"Is there any word on how Detective Van den Broek's daughter is doing?" I asked.

"She had surgery yesterday," Salnikova replied. "She's not out of the woods yet, but we're all hoping she'll be okay."

"So am I." My gaze fell on the brand-new teddy bear sitting on a shelf across the room. I'd bought it from the hospital's gift shop after I was discharged. "I have a present for her. If I drop it off at the station tomorrow, would it be possible to have it passed on to Detective Van den Broek?"

"Yes, of course. That's kind of you."

"I'm afraid I judged him unfairly."

"Don't worry too much about that. You couldn't have known about his personal circumstances. And like I said before, he's not exactly Mr. Congeniality at the best of times."

That made me feel a bit better, but not a whole lot. We exchanged a few more words before ending the phone call. Minutes later, I received a text message from Mikayla.

I need details. Can I come by after work?

Sure! I wrote back.

I got dressed, but then flopped across my bed and fell asleep again. My apartment buzzer jolted me awake hours later.

Groggily, I left my bedroom and answered the buzzer. Mikayla had arrived, and a minute later she appeared at my door.

"Oh my God," she said, her eyes going straight to the stitches near my hairline. "Are you sure you're all right?"

"Positive." I stepped back to let her into my apartment.

"It was really Olivia's assistant who ran you off the road and tried to smother you at the hospital?"

"Yep."

"That's crazy."

"You can say that again."

I made us a pot of tea and we settled into armchairs in my living area.

"I had no idea he was a killer," Mikayla said, with a shake of her head. "I thought he was just a cute hipster."

"I know. But that was part of his disguise, along with using the nickname Sasha. Apparently he normally goes by Alex and doesn't wear glasses. He typically looks much scruffier too."

"But he was the brother of Pavlina's best friend. She never recognized him? I know glasses work for Superman but . . ."

I shrugged. "Maybe she did before she died, but maybe not. Ethan recognized him, though. Eventually, anyway."

"So he was avenging his sister's death?"

"That's what he thought."

"But why now? Why not years ago?"

"Apparently he was in jail for a couple of years on drug charges. I guess once he was free he decided to track down Pavlina and Ethan." I took a sip of my tea before continuing. "He was always convinced that Tiffany was murdered. She was terrified of water, and all along he insisted that she never would have gone into the lake of her own accord. But she was drunk at the time, so the police didn't take his concerns too seriously."

"But he was right."

"About the murder, yes," I said. "But not about who'd killed her."

"So it wasn't Pavlina and Ethan?" Mikayla said, surprised.

My text message hadn't covered that part of the story.

"Nope. I'm pretty sure it was Harold Dempsey, and the police think so too now. Apparently his wife went to the music retreat with him, skiing while he worked with the musicians. When the police originally looked into Tiffany's death, there was a rumor that she might have been with a mystery man that night. Harold and his wife both claimed they were together in their hotel room the entire evening, but now she's come forward to say that wasn't the case."

"Why now after all this time?"

"Apparently she recently found out that he's been having an affair. Now she believes he was also having an affair with Tiffany back then. At the time of Tiffany's death, he asked his wife to lie about his whereabouts, supposedly because he was out for a nighttime jog and wanted an alibi to avoid any bother or rumors. But now she thinks there was more to it. Tiffany tried to approach her at one point during the retreat, but Harold intercepted her. His wife believes Tiffany was going to tell her about their affair, and that's why Harold killed her. According to Detective Salnikova, his wife is filing for divorce. And the police are reopening Tiffany's case, so it sounds like he's in trouble on more than one front."

Mikayla took a moment to absorb that information. "So Sasha . . . Alex . . . whatever his name is—he didn't end up avenging his sister's murder after all."

"Nope. Pavlina and Ethan had nothing to do with it."

"Wow." Mikayla paused to take a drink of her tea. "And then he tried to kill you. Twice. Talk about scary."

"Terrifying," I agreed. "He didn't like that I was asking questions, checking out his alibi, and snooping into things."

Apparently he'd ranted to the police about my nosiness, a tirade that had lasted several minutes, but I didn't bother to mention that part.

"I thought maybe Sasha had left me a threatening note that I found in my bag, but it turns out Harold did that. He probably overheard me talking to Jeb about Tiffany and got nervous. But I kept looking into the past after I found the note, and he knew that. If Sasha hadn't tried to kill me, Harold might have given it a go."

I shuddered at that thought, glad that both men were now behind bars. It still terrified me to think about what would have happened if Mrs. Dixon hadn't screamed about a strange man on our ward, bringing JT running.

"Pavlina had a charm bracelet that Sasha took from her after he killed her," I continued. "It was a gift from Tiffany, and Sasha didn't think she deserved it, since he thought she'd betrayed Tiffany by killing her."

Mikayla shook her head as she absorbed the story, and we both sipped at our tea in silence for a moment.

"How are you doing?" I asked eventually, ready to change the subject.

"Pretty well, actually," Mikayla said. "I'm sad that things didn't work out with Dave, of course, but I also feel kind of relieved. We really weren't happy together in the end. I wish things could have worked out differently, but they didn't."

"Relationships can be so tough," I said, thinking about my own dilemma with JT.

"They can," Mikayla agreed, "but I don't regret giving it a go with Dave."

"No?"

"No. There was a chance we could have had something great and that chance was worth the risk, no matter the outcome."

I considered her words as we continued to chat, wondering if they applied as much to me as to her. I didn't come up with a firm answer.

Once Mikayla had left, I thought about watching television or reading for a while, but then I remembered the flash drive JT had given me. I searched through the items scattered across my coffee table until I found the flash drive under a library book. Then I settled into an armchair with my laptop.

When the computer had finished booting up, I plugged the flash drive into a USB port and opened the folder. It contained fifteen tracks. I scanned down the list of titles, recognizing most of them. When I came to the last track on the list, I froze, my eyes fixed on the title.

My heart fluttered and I forced myself to move, clicking on the track. Familiar music floated from my laptop's speakers. Even though the computer didn't provide the best quality of sound, the song was still beautiful, entrancing. I listened to it twice and then stared at the title again.

Snatching up my phone, I tapped out a quick text message, sending it to JT.

Are you home?

I listened to the song again as I waited for a response. When I next checked my phone, JT had replied.

Yes. You want me to come by?

Not at the moment, I wrote back.

Shoving my phone into my purse, I pulled on my boots and coat, grabbing gloves and my slouchy hat on my way out the door. My poor car had been towed from the scene of the accident to a garage, and it would have to stay there for a while. Luckily it wasn't totaled, but both bumpers needed to be replaced and some scratches repaired. I'd been without a car for many years before I'd bought the MINI Cooper off my cousin, though, and I didn't mind using public transportation.

I fidgeted on the bus, unable to sit still, and I bounced up off my seat as the bus approached my stop. Fortunately, I no longer suffered from any dizziness, so the abrupt movement didn't bother me. From the bus stop, I walked the remaining distance to JT's house at a brisk pace. I jogged up the front steps and knocked on the door, digging through my purse for my keys, so anxious to get inside that I couldn't bring myself to wait for JT to open the door. But as I was about to insert my key into the lock, the door opened.

"Dori? Did you walk here? I could have come and picked you up."

"It was nice to get some fresh air," I said, giving Finnegan's head a scratch as I stepped into the foyer. "Sorry I didn't tell you I was coming. I wanted to get here as quickly as I could."

"Why? What's wrong?"

"Nothing's wrong."

I held up the flash drive so he could see it. Understanding showed in his eyes.

"Did you really name your new song after me?" I asked.

He hesitated, but only for a second. "Yes. That song . . . It's how you make me feel."

My heart swelled with such elation that I thought it might burst. "I make you feel float-away-happy?"

His eyes didn't move from mine. "Yes."

I recalled the song's melancholy moments. My heart sank. "And sad? I make you feel sad?"

"Only when I think about being without you."

Joy bubbled through me, bringing a smile to my face. Barely aware of Finnegan bouncing around us, I threw my arms around JT and kissed him.

He kissed me back and I forgot about the world around us, my recent brushes with death, everything other than me and JT. I only pulled back when Finnegan gave a bark, vying for our attention. Giving him a distracted pat on the head, I met JT's brown eyes and smiled again, this time so brightly it probably could have been seen from outer space.

"That's the sweetest, most amazing, most perfect thing ever."

JT grinned, his arms still around me. "The song or the kiss?"

"Both," I said.

Then I kissed him again.

Acknowledgments

THANK YOU TO my agent, Jessica Faust, and my editor at HarperCollins, Rebecca Lucash, for believing in this series and helping me share it with the world. Thanks also to the art department at HarperCollins for designing such fantastic covers for the books in this series, and to the entire Witness Impulse team. I'm also immensely grateful to Sarah Blair for her friendship, support, and willingness to read early versions of my manuscripts.

About the Author

SARAH FOX was born and raised in Vancouver, British Columbia, where she developed a love for mysteries at a young age. When not writing novels or working as a legal writer, she is often reading her way through a stack of books or spending time outdoors with her English springer spaniel.

www.authorsarahfox.com

Discover great authors, exclusive offers, and more at hc.com.